Sanctuary

This book is a work of fiction. Although Best Friends is a very real place (which, by the way, is as awesome as I've described), names, characters, and incidents are the product of my imagination. Any resemblance to actual persons is entirely coincidental.

Although the authorship of the poem *Don't Weep for Me* is still disputed, credit is most often given to Mary Elizabeth Frye, who is said to have written it in 1932 for a friend who was unable to visit her mother's grave. It is her only poem.

To Gianna:

Thank you for being my constant supporter, tireless
cheerleader, and most of all…my friend

This book is also dedicated to all of those who

work to rescue animals in shelters;

especially Dave, Mary, Lisa, Whitney, and the people

who dedicate their lives to Best Friends

My deepest thanks go out to many people for their help and support in the creation of this story.

First, to my mother, who reads all my drafts and is a sounding board for my crazy ideas.

Next, to my agent, Liz, for her guidance and advice as this project came to fruition. It's a better book because of her expertise, and I can't express how much I appreciate her faith in me.

To Haven, my insider at the sanctuary, and all of those who work tirelessly to end the senseless killing of homeless pets.

My husband, Brian, who puts up with me working evenings and weekends to fulfill my dreams.

And of course, all my friends and family who read early drafts and supported me in all the ways I needed it. I couldn't keep burning the candle at both ends without you!

For Lori ~

Sanctuary

With best wishes...

Kim DeSalvo

Kim DeSalvo

Prologue

From the moment her plane landed at O'Hare, Grace Burton told herself it was silly to worry; that there was a logical explanation for why Danny hadn't left his usual welcome home message or returned her calls or texts. His phone battery died, or he left it lying around somewhere. Maybe he and Zoe had gotten busy cleaning up in anticipation of her arrival, and he'd forgotten.

But she knew it wasn't true.

She'd been busy—the post-conference banquet had run late, and she'd had to pack in a hurry before her SoHo shopping trip with Gwen. The airport was a mess and she'd barely made her flight, so it wasn't until she'd landed that it fully sunk in. The last time she'd talked to Danny was after her presentation, when she'd called to tell him about the audience's warm response to her personal story about "sparks" and healing after the loss of a loved one. Over forty-eight hours ago.

Thick rain pelted the windows, and icy fear clawed Grace's heart as the limo approached the curve in the road. Where her cozy ranch should have been ablaze to welcome her home, a gaping hole loomed amidst houses lit up against the October thunderstorm.

Grace grabbed her bags and sprinted for the door, but stopped just before she reached it, ignoring the cold rain that soaked her. Payton wasn't at the window to announce her arrival. A thick coil of dread curled in her gut—something was very wrong.

Shaking hands fumbled with the lock and she stepped inside, hoping for the warmth and comfort of her family. Instead, she stepped into air as cool and damp as outside, despite the rattle of the furnace. A sharp crack of thunder sent her fight-or-flight instincts on high alert as she tapped the light switch.

"I'm home!" she yelled. Her words echoed back, punctuated with a thunderclap.

"Hey, guys?"

Grace shed her soggy jacket and shoes, adrenaline flooding her system. Hesitantly, she made her way to the kitchen, freezing in horror when she flicked on the light.

So much blood. It splattered the counters, the cabinets--a wad of bloody towels lay in the sink and another on the floor, soaked from rain that blew in through the shredded screen door. A smeared, brown handprint marred the wall, and beyond the kitchen, rust-colored footprints led from the closed basement door.

"Oh, my God," she gasped, hand flying to her mouth as her stomach lurched. Her senses sharpened; breath wheezed in her chest. An accident...a bad one. Danny hadn't called because they were at the hospital, and he didn't want her in a panic all the way home. Wide eyes scanned the counters for a note, but a distant explosion shook the house, and she was suddenly plunged into darkness.

A guttural snarl forced its way past the lump in her throat, and she sloshed through the puddle, pulling the sliding door shut against the storm. She grabbed a flashlight from the junk drawer, searched again, but found no note.

Of course not, she reasoned. *They had to leave in a hurry...Oh God, let them be OK.*

In a daze, Grace spun, eyes darting around the room. *Run*, her brain screamed, but legs that were not her own carried her to the basement door. Everything in her rebelled against opening it, but she gritted her teeth and turned the knob.

A blast of heat hit her like a punch, heavy with the sickly-sweet stench of rot. Grace gagged as she stumbled down the stairs, flashes of lightning illuminating the room like a strobe and revealing a nightmare in macabre spurts of vision.

The overturned couch. Popcorn strewn across the floor. The glint of broken glass. And, what her eyes saw but refused to acknowledge, a dark shape in the middle of the floor.

Grace directed the beam, a cry strangling her. Her precious Payton, the gentle black Lab who'd been the spark that had helped her live again, lay horrifically still.

"Oh, Payton…no, baby, no…" she croaked, starting toward him. She took two steps, and her heart stopped. From beneath Payton's crumpled form, a tiny leotard-clad leg twisted in a dark pool of blood.

For a moment she stood paralyzed, then maternal instincts kicked in and she rushed over, dropping to her knees.

"Zoe!" Her arms slipped through a cold, coagulated mess as she tried to gather her child into her arms. Zoe was cold, her flesh unyielding; pale skin and wide, unseeing eyes over a dark gash in her throat. "OhGodohGodohGod," she wheezed as the horror pounded at her brain, demanding to be let in.

"No…no…no…" The words caught in her throat as her legs tried to scramble away from the grisly scene. Grace dropped the flashlight, and the beam landed on Danny's gnarled body; his face a ghastly green, shirt stiff with dried blood.

Grace howled like a wounded animal and scrambled away in terror. She staggered up the stairs and into the street, screaming bloody murder.

∞ ∞ ∞

Eleven days of hell, of not knowing, of not wanting to accept that everything she loved most in the world was so brutally taken. Chunks of time blurred by blue uniforms and endless questions; nauseating flowers and shocked faces as she watched her family lowered into the ground. Eleven nights haunted by their glazed eyes, imagining the terror and suffering they endured.

Mandy pushed a cup of tea into Grace's hands as she stood vigil at the window in anticipation of Detective Milton's arrival. She prayed for answers, but her hopes were dashed when he pulled in, a grim expression clouding his rugged features.

"Please," she croaked as she opened the door.

He pursed his lips, and shook his head. "Not yet," he answered, catching Grace as her knees buckled, "but we won't stop looking."

They settled in the kitchen, her sister and brother-in-law holding her hands tightly beneath the table. "I hope you have *some* good news for us, detective," Matt said.

The detective's eyes shifted to Grace, then dropped to the table. "We've completed our investigation at the house, but unfortunately, neither the fingerprints nor DNA have come back with a match."

"So, you basically have nothing," Matt snarled.

"It tells us the guy hasn't been processed before…but the same fingerprints have been found at two other break-ins in the area, which makes it much less likely that the attack was personal. That should help you rest at least a little easier."

Grace couldn't remember the last time she'd gotten any rest, and didn't anticipate any in her near future. Especially after hearing this news.

"The fact that he doesn't have a record likely means that he's a petty thief who got himself into more than he bargained for."

"No one saw anything?" Grace asked.

Detective Milton shook his head. "I'm afraid not." A neighbor reported that he heard the dog barking pretty frantically around 9:30 PM that night, which corroborates our timeline, but no one saw anything out of the ordinary."

"What about the hospitals?" Mandy asked. "All that blood…"

"Definitely the intruder's," Milton confirmed. "We believe that he picked the lock, and that the dog was outside when he encountered your family."

"Oh, Payton," Grace whispered. "He ripped through the screen to save them."

The detective nodded. "He put up a good fight."

Grace choked back a sob, and Mandy squeezed her hand.

"We know the perp had significant injuries, but there were no dog bites treated at any nearby hospitals."

"So all you have are a lot of dead ends," Grace said.

The detective tugged at his collar. "Not dead ends, just loose ones. You have my promise, Grace, that we won't stop looking for this guy."

Grace knew, even if just from television, that the first forty eight hours were critical in a police investigation. This guy'd had well over a week to go into hiding, and all the police had was useless evidence and a few theories. She choked back a sob, and stood to go.

Detective Milton rose, and took Grace's hands. "I swear we're not giving up, Grace. Neither should you."

She dropped her head and went to her room, falling onto the bed and letting the tears come.

Chapter 1

Grace squeezed the key until it cut into her flesh. She'd stared at the door of storage unit 19B from her car many times over the past six months, but today she was determined to open it and face the ghosts of her past.

She was still rattled by the nightmare; but then, she could count on one hand the number of times since the murders that she hadn't woken up with the gruesome images of her family burned into the backs of her eyelids--and most of those had been nights she hadn't slept at all. What had her even more shaken this morning was her own reflection in the bathroom mirror.

The woman looking back at her was an imposter; she had to be. Bloodshot eyes rimmed in dark circles, deep hollows beneath protruding cheekbones...how had she come to this?

What happened to the woman who hosted book clubs, holidays, and progressive dinners? The one whose Bears vs Packers parties were legendary among her neighbors? What happened to the Grace who had lived?

Gone, all of them.

She'd run the water cold, tried to scrub away the façade, but the image didn't change.

Who are you? she'd whispered. Then, the more important question, *Who do you choose to be?*

Gwen had asked her that question six years ago, when the first tragedy nearly ended her; then again, just yesterday. She hadn't an answer the first time around, either, but it had come, eventually. It had been a long, hard road, but she'd prevailed--built a rewarding new career that helped others deal with the pain and grief of loss, had another child, and forged a new life. Of course, she'd had Danny and Payton, then later, Zoe, to help guide her…this time, she'd have to make her own way. The rest of her life started on a blank page and she realized, finally, that she owed it to herself, her fans, and especially her family, to write it well.

Who do you choose to be? She'd inched closer to the mirror, nose-to-nose with her reflection. Frustration and anger boiled up and she let them come, until finally, a shred of strength sparked in her eyes. Grace Burton didn't wallow in self-pity; she found beauty and joy in the world around her, and guided others to do the same.

It was way past time she followed her own advice.

"I don't know who I am anymore," she'd said to the dull and broken woman in the mirror, "but I choose not to be you."

Behind this weathered door was her former life, packed into boxes and plastic tubs. If she was ever going to have a fresh start, she needed to make peace with her past, pick up the proverbial pieces, and find a way to move on.

Grace opened the door and stepped inside. For a moment she could actually smell them--light lingering aromas of chamomile shampoo, slobbery tennis balls, and Danny's *Cool Water* cologne. Memories crashed like a tidal wave, and she flared her nostrils to pull it in.

She'd worked so hard to block out the end of their lives-- but in doing so, she'd also pushed aside the living of them; the timbre of Danny's voice, the musical sounds of Zoe's laughter, the silkiness of the fur beneath Payton's ears. Thousands of incredible moments that she'd allowed grief to steal away.

"God, I miss you so much," she whispered, taking in the mountains of boxes that contained their lives. Nostalgia tugged hard, but she shook her head. "But I can do this. I *need* to do this."

She tugged a dusty sheet off the rec room couch and sighed deeply. How many times had they crowded there, Zoe sandwiched between her and Danny, Payton's head nestled in her lap? Grace closed her eyes and let the memory come.

"Family cuddle time, Mommy," Zoe would pout to begin the ritual.

"I don't think we can all fit up here--you're getting awfully big," Danny would say, grunting comically as he wriggled Zoe between her loving parents. Always, he would slide his hand over the back of the couch to link with hers.

"Make room for Payton," Zoe would giggle, and Danny would scooch them in tighter while the Lab waited patiently, tail wagging, for Zoe to pat the empty spot.

Grace lay down and pressed her face to the soft fabric, inhaling a whisper of buttered popcorn, wet dog, and the spray that never quite masked either. She plucked a few strands of shiny black hair from between the cushions and pressed them to her cheek. Payton...the spark that pulled her from her dark place the first time; the hero who'd given his life trying to save his family from a madman.

It ended here--the self-pity, the denial...existing, instead of living. Every day she didn't live her life was a day she let the bastard who killed them win, and that was no longer acceptable.

One tote. Maybe if she found one that contained linens, or dishes; something she could easily part with; the rest wouldn't seem so daunting.

She tugged the sheet off the coffee table to clear a work area, then stopped and stared. Perched upon it was a shoebox, covered with gold paper.

The One Box

Grace recognized her sister's handwriting, and lifted the lid. An envelope lay atop Payton's Bears bandana, and she opened it with trembling fingers.

Dear Gracie,

I know that you'll come here eventually, and that you'll be alone when you do. God knows you don't want to burden anyone with your problems. There's a lot of stuff here. None of it is valuable, except in the sentimental sense, and you know better than anyone that wallowing in all that you've lost is counterproductive. None of the important things are in this place. We've packed those away separately, but you know that you already carry all the important things in your heart.

No life can be adequately held in any container, and trying to fit three such beautiful ones into this box was a nearly impossible task. Things, however, hold no memories. They are only sparks...as you well know. I've taken the liberty of collecting a few of those sparks for you, in the hope that you might find the strength to let the rest of it go and set about the task of living again. You know that's what they would want for you, and it's what everyone who loves you wants, as well.

Love, Mandy

Grace sat and pulled the box into her lap, lifting Payton's bandana to reveal a treasure more valuable to her than gold. She pulled out the items one at a time, examining them from every angle, pressing some to her cheeks, some to her heart, and a few to her lips.

Her eyes welled as she slid a stack of photos from an envelope—on top was the picture her Aunt Karen captured on their wedding day—Danny's look of pure adoration as he got his first glimpse of his bride. Slowly, she sifted through the images that defined their lives—Payton as a pup, Zoe's baby pictures and first ballet recital, family trips and picnics, lazy days at the beach. Some were formal, some candid, and each conjured a precious memory of the joy and love her family had shared. The last one was taken just a month before the murders; Danny grilling steaks, and Zoe caught in the act of sneaking a piece of hot dog to an elated Payton.

There had to be thousands from which Mandy could have chosen, but these really did sum up all the things she wanted to remember about their life together. Grace set them aside, and reached back into the box.

Danny's wedding ring she brushed over her lips, then held it up to read the inscription on the inside of the band. *Until the end of time.* She took a breath, held it, then slid off her own ring and tucked them together into the velvet pouch.

Grace lost all sense of time as she let the past back in. She lay the treasure out on the table—Zoe's bronze-dipped baby bootie; Payton's favorite football toy, full of tooth holes; his Bears collar; a plaster cast with Zoe's hand print and Payton's paw. Every item brought a joy in the remembering, and the tears that streamed down her cheeks held a mixture of delight and sorrow. Her breath caught when she pulled out a letter Danny had written to her years ago. She knew what it said, but didn't have the strength to read it just yet.

Mandy was right. It was impossible to fit the sum of three lives into one shoebox, but she'd done a damn fine job.

She lay back on the couch and closed her eyes, letting her mind drift over the many happy memories they'd made as a family. Then, Danny was there, his fingers trailing over her skin, his voice in her ear.

"Hey there, Amazing Grace," he whispered.

"I miss you," she croaked. "So much."

"We miss you, too, love," he said, twining his fingers through hers, "but you've mourned enough. It's time to find your new spark."

"I don't want a new spark. I want you."

He pressed his other hand against her heart. "We're right here...and we always will be." He brushed a kiss over her lips, feather light. "You can't stay here," he said, his voice fading. "It's time to go."

Grace woke with a start, the scent of *Cool Water* in her nostrils. "Danny," she whispered, but in the next breath, it was gone. She sat up, pressing her fingers to her lips.

Danny was right; it was time to go. Time to get her head on straight, her life on track, and, hopefully, soon, back to the business of helping others heal. She had to fix herself, first, and make peace with the world again. It wouldn't be easy, but she needed to make it happen.

The first step was acknowledging that although a few lingering scents remained, her family was not in these boxes--they were in her heart, and that was where she would keep them.

Grace pulled her journal from her bag, and set it in her lap. She carried it out of habit, mostly, but hadn't opened it since the murders. She knew its contents--or the gist of them, anyway--every line was filled with moments of joy.

The final entry she knew by heart. *October 10th moment of joy...heading out to NYC for my biggest convention yet, watching Zoe's video and basking in the love and support of my incredible family.*

Grace opened to a fresh page. *April 18, moment of joy,* she wrote, *dreaming of Danny's kiss, and deciding that this is the day I start a new journey of healing.*

Sweeping her eyes over the mountain of totes and boxes, she made the decision. The One Box would be enough. Wherever, however, she decided to start a new life, it wouldn't be with any of these things. From this day forward, the life she forged would be fresh.

She carefully replaced each item, then plucked a few more of Payton's shed hairs from the couch and slipped them into the box. Closing the lid, she flicked off the light and walked out the door.

The clouds had rolled away, and the smell of fresh earth was in the air. Spring was coming, and with it, a rebirth--what better time to be reborn herself? *Maybe a road trip,* Grace thought as she climbed behind the wheel--a real journey into wide open spaces and fresh air might help her gain a new perspective. If she headed south she could meet spring halfway, then go west, and meet summer head-on. Hopefully, with a bit of luck and a lot of determination, she might even find that new spark.

As Grace pulled out of the lot, she paid no mind to the beat-up Chevy with the blacked-out windows that was parked across the street.

The driver, however, took great interest in her.

∞ ∞ ∞

Shoes? the driver thought. Only a woman spends hours in a room filled with all her worldly possessions, and comes out with a freaking pair of shoes.

Through the binoculars, he studied her face, puffy from crying, and smiled.

He liked watching her suffer--in fact, her pain was the only thing keeping her alive at the moment. Still, he itched to end her, and the desire to scratch it was getting harder to ignore. He ran a scarred finger over the blade of the knife that rested in his lap, drawing a thin line of blood. If it weren't for all the cameras around the storage facility, he might have finished it here--served poetic justice by leaving her to rot with the pathetic remnants of her life. He wanted so badly to tell her it was her fault they were dead; then, send her to join them.

Soon, he thought, watching her tail lights blink around the corner before pulling away.

Chapter 2

"What are you doing?" Mandy asked cautiously when she found Grace folding clothes into suitcases.

"Um…packing?"

"I see you've got some of your smart ass back," Mandy smiled. "I've missed it. Where are you going, exactly?"

"I'm not sure yet. I just know it's time."

Mandy sighed and rested her hand on Grace's shoulder. "I kind of thought you might be leaning in that direction. I know you've been talking to Gwen."

"Yeah, and once again, she's helped me put things in perspective."

"I'm glad you have her."

Grace turned, and wrapped her arms around her little sister. "I'm glad I have you, too."

"Argh," Mandy grumbled, "I knew the time would come, but I didn't think it would be so soon. It's only been a few months, Gracie…are you sure you're ready?"

"I don't know that I'll ever feel *ready*," Grace sighed, "but I do know that if I keep sinking, it'll be that much harder to climb back out. I mean, look at me. Pretty pathetic, don't you think, the one who coined, "The Spark," hiding out in her sister's spare room, wallowing in self-pity? I'm a hypocrite, Man. How can I help others heal if I can't fix myself?"

"You can't live for your fans, Grace; or your book. You have to live for *you*."

"Exactly. I need to figure out who I'm going to be, and how I…*fit*."

"I get it." Mandy pulled a shirt off a hanger and added it to the suitcase. "But that doesn't mean I like it." She tugged a skirt from the closet and folded it. "Remember the time we snuck out to get crepes in Paris?"

Grace chuckled. "How could I forget? I swore I remembered the way to that café. Gosh, what were you, ten?"

"Nine. I freaked out when I realized we were lost, but you kept your cool."

"Are you kidding? I was in a total state of panic! I couldn't let you know it, though—I was afraid you'd tell Mom and Dad and I'd be grounded for the rest of the trip."

"Was I that bad?"

"You're an awesome sister, Man, but sometimes," she grinned, "yeah…you were that bad."

Mandy laughed. "I'll never forget what you said to me that night. You grabbed my shoulders, looked me hard in the eyes, and said that no one is ever really lost—sometimes they just lose their way. 'Life is an adventure', you said, and when you need to get home, you just put your head on straight and you'll find your way."

"I can't believe you remember that."

"Remember it? I live by it, Gracie."

Grace blinked back tears. "I don't even know what to say to that."

"I bring it up because you've lost your way, big sis, but you're not lost. You'll make this an adventure, and come back stronger than ever." Mandy squeezed Grace's shoulders, and looked her hard in the eyes. "My home will always be your home."

"I know it absolutely. You're the best, in so many ways. I found *The One Box* today."

Mandy smiled. "I wondered how long it would take you to actually go in there. Don't think I don't know how much time you've spent sitting in that lot. And?"

"You're right, as usual. It's perfect, and I'm so grateful. I'll keep it with me on this journey to remind myself that there is a reason I'm doing it; that they would want me to go on."

"I'm so glad. It's what we all want. Just keep your head on straight…you'll find your way."

∞ ∞ ∞

Memories are fickle things. They creep into your mind sometimes when you least expect them, demanding to be acknowledged. Outside of Indianapolis, Grace saw a billboard for a ballet, and Zoe's video began pervading her thoughts. How long had it been since she'd watched her precious girl spinning in circles, giving her mother a pep talk? How long since she'd heard her husband's voice, or watched Payton frolicking in the fall leaves? It was, she knew, the day they were taken from her--never to frolic, spin, or speak her name again.

Her mind took her back to that day, the last time she saw her family alive.

"All set?" Danny smiled.

"Ready as I'll ever be."

Calling herself a motivational speaker hadn't come easily. It was almost incomprehensible that people actually sought her out to listen to her talk--she was just an ordinary person who'd gone through an extraordinary experience and found a way to heal. Helping others gave voice to the life her first child, Briana, never got to live, and gave Grace a rewarding new career; especially when it landed her a book deal.

She fluttered her fingers nervously over her heart at the toot of a horn. The door flew open, and Zoe launched herself into Grace's arms. "You got a movie star car, Mommy!"

Danny grinned. "Mommy *is* a star, Zoe. Lots of people are going to New York just to hear her talk."

Zoe cocked her head, eyes narrowed quizzically. "No way," she said. "Mommy's a movie star?"

"Not quite," Grace chuckled, nuzzling her neck. "You know I'll miss you terribly while I'm gone, right?"

"I miss you already," Zoe pouted, "but Daddy says you'll be back in three sleeps."

"Three sleeps," Grace repeated. "That's exactly right. Now you be a good girl, OK? Listen to Daddy and eat all your vegetables."

Zoe squished up her face and stuck out her tongue. "I don't like vegie-tibles."

Danny scooped her up and turned her upside-down, blowing raspberries on her belly. "Oh, we're not going to be eating any vegetables," he bellowed in his 'Papa Bear' voice. "We're having nothing but junk food while Mommy's gone, right? Pizza, popcorn and jelly sandwiches!"

"Hooray!" Zoe cheered, giggling as Danny set her down to wheel the suitcase to the waiting car.

Grace gave her daughter one last kiss, then whispered in her ear, "I'll be back in a few days to make you some vegetables." She grinned at Zoe's pained look, then wrapped her arms around her husband. "Wish me luck," she said.

"You don't need luck," he smiled. "You've got heart, baby. You're going to be amazing, Grace, as always." He pressed a warm kiss to her lips. "Break a leg."

She bent to give Payton a kiss on the snout. "I'm counting on you to take care of them both," she murmured as she hugged his neck. He answered with an enthusiastic lick and a wag of his tail.

"Watch my video, Mommy," Zoe yelled as she dashed off after Payton.

"I will," Grace waved, blowing one final kiss.

It was all so clear, like it was yesterday, and by the time she saw signs for Louisville, she could think of nothing else. If this was truly going to be a journey of healing, she needed to focus on happy times. It was the little things she missed most—Saturday morning pancake breakfasts, Zoe cheerfully mixing batter while letting Payton lick her fingers under the table, Danny nuzzling her neck as she scrambled up some eggs. The Christmas morning when Zoe flew down the stairs and saw the dollhouse she and Danny had built from scraps of wood and fabric when money was tight; her eyes lighting up like they'd given her the Taj Mahal. So many incredible memories, even for the short time they belonged to her.

Grace swerved into the Henryville Welcome Center and booked a room. She wasn't going to make it to Mammoth Cave tonight...she needed to watch that video.

She checked in, choking down a greasy burger before digging through her bag for her tablet. Taking a moment to be mindful, she summoned a host of happy memories to lay over her anxiety about watching the video. When she felt calm and strong enough, she scrolled through her photos. There were just a few at the end that she'd taken in New York; happy pictures of her and Gwen, selfies in front of the sign advertising the conference. It was all so insignificant in the scheme of things; yet at the time, it had seemed like her whole world.

Crazy, sometimes, how minor snapshots got in the way of the big picture.

She took one more breath, then tapped the play icon.

Oh, God, their faces. They'd blurred around the edges of her memory over the past months, but seeing them again brought them back into sharp focus.

"Hi Mommy!" Zoe's angelic smile filled the screen. "We're proud of you, and we wish you luck! I made up a good luck dance for you!" She shook her hips and did a lovely arabesque, then put her hands in the air and began to spin. The hem of her dress twirled around her like a tiny pink tornado, and then Payton burst in, barking and leaping in the air as if trying to mimic her movements. Grace couldn't help but laugh at the music in her daughter's giggles.

"Payton's dancing for luck, too!" she said breathlessly as she fell to the ground, dizzy. Payton took the opportunity to worship her face with kisses, tail wagging furiously.

"Tell Mommy you love her," Danny whispered. Grace swallowed around a lump in her throat.

"I love you, Mommy!"

Zoe scooped up some leaves and tossed them into the air so that they rained down on the two of them. Payton dashed off and came back with his football, which Zoe happily threw toward the side yard; disappearing after it and the dog.

The camera turned, and Danny's beautiful face filled the screen. "I'm so proud of you, baby," he said, his smile tugging at her heart. "You are the strongest and most beautiful person I've ever known, and I know you'll be great. Have fun, get it done, and come home to me, because you know I'm a mess without you." He smiled wide and blew her a kiss. "Love you, Amazing Grace."

The arrow popped up over his frozen image and she watched it again; tears sliding down her cheeks.

She forced herself to close the screen and texted Mandy, letting her know she'd stopped for the night. Then, she emailed Gwen. "Watched the video tonight," she typed, "and you would've been proud. I'm hitting the road tomorrow with the specific intention of finding some joy. Can you squeeze me in for a chat Thursday or Friday? Nothing official...just would love to hear your voice."

Grace climbed into bed, the sounds of her family's voices pulling her down to sleep. For the first time in six months, she slept through the night, and had no dreams whatsoever.

Chapter 3

Mammoth Cave didn't hold a spark. It did, however, hold the glory of rebirth, as spring had clearly announced its arrival there. The air was fresh, trees were kissed with the first whispers of green, soft new grass was underfoot. It was early in the season, so there was a quiet serenity that settled on her soul, and she filled her lungs to bursting with the crisp scent of the breeze.

Grace meandered along the interconnecting trails with no particular destination in mind, taking time to notice all the wonders nature provided. She was looking up the name of a flower in the guide book she'd purchased when she heard a twig snap and looked up to see a man approaching on the trail. Immediately, her heart started pounding and dread flooded her gut. It had been this way since the murders—the only thing they knew about the killer was that it was a man...and he was still out there. She knew it was ridiculous, but couldn't keep the hyperarousal from overtaking her. Shaking, she stepped just off the trail and held her ground until he passed, chastising herself for not being able to return his friendly smile. Then, she hurried down the trail until she came into a large clearing and took a deep breath. The sudden openness of the space made her uneasy at first--aside from her trips to the storage facility, she'd spent the majority of the past months in seclusion.

She'd ignored her email, her blog, her social media--hadn't even turned on her laptop until she started researching a route for this journey. Her fans would be understanding, but she knew they wouldn't wait forever. Of all people, they expected her to be able to find her way--and if she wanted to maintain any credibility, she was going to have to do just that.

Her agent had been forgiving, as well, but Grace knew there were at least four emails from Teri that had as yet gone unanswered.

If she could finish her book--get it out there and start doing speaking engagements again--she could make a comfortable living for herself; build a life of which she could be proud.

One summer. She'd take these next few months to rebuild herself; reclaim her life; and then worry about rebuilding her reputation.

She moved off the trail and sat down in some longer, wilder grasses dotted with wildflowers. Closing her eyes, she focused on the late afternoon sun warming her skin and brought her focus back to the present.

So much beauty. So much incredible joy and beauty all around her that she was almost moved to tears. This was life. Despite her own suffering and self-indulgent dunk in the pool of self-pity, life went on around her and it was still beautiful, interactive, and incredibly, amazingly strong. In her journal, she jotted notes, recorded joyful observations, and sketched her surroundings. It had been a long time since she felt a sense of peace and belonging, and she realized just how much she'd missed it.

Hunger finally drove her back to civilization, and she decided to stock up on some essentials and have a quiet meal in her room. Enjoying the mild ache in her neglected muscles, she sat outside with a hearty sandwich and scrolled through her pictures, adding notes in her journal to help her remember the details.

As she gathered her bathroom bag in anticipation of a long, hot shower, her image in the mirror stopped her. The day outdoors had already bronzed her skin, and her mousy brown hair seemed to have regained some of its luster. Her hazel eyes had some sparkle back--a few flecks of gold danced in the copper sunburst than surrounded the pupil-- and the dark circles were already fading. *Like a butterfly emerging from her cocoon*, she thought, smiling at her reflection.

Grace climbed into bed; looking forward, for the first time in a long time, to what tomorrow might bring.

∞ ∞ ∞

"Hey, Grace…how's the trip going?"

Gwen's familiar face brought a comfort that even the woods hadn't been able to muster. Mid-thirties, short dark hair that fell gracefully around full cheeks, expressive dark eyes, and a captivating smile…it was no wonder Gwen brought comfort to so many. After the first tragedy, Gwen had guided her through the therapy that helped reshape her life. Now, Grace felt lucky to call her a friend.

"Good…so far. It's great to see you."

"You, too. I'm interrupting your dinner, though. Want me to buzz back later?"

"No, that's OK," Grace said. "It's actually good to have some company. I didn't think I'd miss my niece's constant chatter, but it's been kind of lonely the past few days."

"It doesn't have to be, you know. There's a difference between being alone and being lonely. A big difference."

Grace shrugged. "I know. It just feels weird going into restaurants alone."

"What's different? You used to do it all the time."

"Yeah…but I feel a bit like a loser with no friends this time, instead of a professional with a message to share. I'm not sure I can handle the polar shift just yet."

"Oh, Grace," Gwen said, a touch of sadness in her voice. "You have lots of people who love and support you. It's you who turned away; not the other way around."

"I know," she conceded. "I was just spending some time…communing with nature."

"Communing with nature is great…but if you're really going to move on, you need to commune with the human race, too."

"I'm never going to see these people again, Gwen. Plus, I have serious trust issues. You should've seen how I freaked out when I saw a strange man on the trail."

"All the more reason. You can enjoy light conversation with people who don't know your backstory. You're in one of the friendliest places in the country--Southern hospitality can really lift your spirits. The trust will come, but you have to give a little, first."

Grace nodded. "You're right, as usual. I have to push the envelope a little. And I will."

"Of course you will. So, tell me about the video. You said I'd be proud."

Grace smiled, recalling the story.

"That's fantastic," Gwen said. "You can do this, Grace; you're already taking the first steps. That's got to be the most genuine smile I've seen in a long time."

"I'm a bit stronger every day--it feels really good."

"Good enough to start working on the book again?"

Grace frowned. "It's not that I don't feel strong enough to write...I think it's more that I'm not in the right frame of mind."

"How so?"

"Well, for one thing, I'm not the same person I was when I started it. I'm kind of in a reinvention stage, and the new 'me' might go at the topic from a completely different angle. I think I need to figure that out first."

"Maybe it'll end up being a second book," Gwen suggested. "You've gone through two very different trials, and you're healing in a completely different way this time."

"Ha. Finishing the first one is a daunting enough task."

"What if you eased into it...gave your followers on social media an intimate look at your healing process? You could blog about your experiences...kind of take them along with you on your journey."

"That's a great idea," she agreed, wheels already turning. "It'll be good for me, too...a way to track my progress."

Gwen smiled. "I thought you might agree--I look forward to reading them. I'm really proud of you, Grace. You're obviously on the right path."

She clicked on Mandy's image next, and smiled when her sister's face filled the screen. "How's the healing coming?" Mandy asked.

"Definitely making progress," Grace answered. "I'm amazed at how much better I feel after just a few days."

"I can hear it in your voice, and you're looking better, too. Keep the selfies coming—it's good to see you smiling again."

"It feels good, I must say."

"We miss you around here, though. Eva keeps asking why we didn't go with you—especially after seeing the picture of you and the chipmunk. It's been doing nothing but raining here—send us some of that sunshine, will you?"

"On its way...I'll send it along with a few souvenirs I picked up for you guys."

"Can't wait. I'm proud of you, you know." She blew Grace a kiss. "You're going to get through this, sis—there's another spark out there for you, I can feel it."

Grace held her hand up to the camera, fingers crossed.

Grace woke refreshed and determined. She headed into town and stopped at the first local diner she saw, then took a seat at the counter next to a slightly older woman. "Hi, I'm Grace," she smiled, holding out her hand.

She stayed for over an hour, lingering over coffee and chatting with locals and other travelers. Those conversations opened a door, and Grace stepped through it eagerly. Each outing boosted her confidence, and by the time she packed the car to head for Memphis, she was feeling more optimistic that she might actually find a way to heal on this journey.

Chapter 4

Brady Cash looked over the tips of his freshly shined shoes through the floor-to-ceiling windows of his corner office, down to the busy street below. Hundreds of heads bobbed up and down as little worker-bees rushed off to their next meetings, briefcases in one hand and cell phones in the other. Horns pierced copper-tinged air, as hundreds of people went nowhere fast. After all, this was LA, where cars spent more time idling than they did actually moving.

He wondered if he'd miss it.

His office phone chirped--something he definitely wouldn't miss.

"Hey, Shady Brady," his soon-to-be former partner grumbled. Jared didn't sound like his usual chipper self, and Brady thought he knew why.

"What's up?"

A long sigh rustled in his ear. "I was just reminiscing about our Wall Street days, when we had all these dreams about making it big. Then, I looked out my window, and realized they all came true."

"Yeah, it's been a great ride, my friend."

"I don't know why it just hit me that you're leaving," he said flatly. "I've ignored it, I guess, because I was sure you'd change your mind. Damn it, I just got out of a meeting with Lindsey, and it should've been you in there, man. It just doesn't feel right."

Brady frowned. Jared Little, he would definitely miss. "You'll get over it," he said, surprised at the crack in his own voice.

"I don't want to get over it. Let's grab dinner—I'll take you to Nick and Stef's."

"Pulling out the big guns?" Jared knew Brady's weakness for their aged steak, but for Brady, the venue didn't matter. He had precious little time to spend with his best friend before he left, and would take advantage of every opportunity.

"It's just dinner with a friend."

"With a bit of business mixed in, as always. You're not going to talk me out of this, Jared, but I'm flattered that you'd try."

"The last thing you need, Pretty Boy, is flattery…your head's big enough as it is. I do have an idea to run past you, however."

Of course he did. "I'm not saying no if you're buying. Seven?"

"Seven's good."

The hostess greeted Brady by name, and led him to a private table in the corner, where Jared was already waiting. An untouched gin and tonic sat in front of him, and what Brady knew to be a dirty vodka martini perched before the empty seat. Jared was a stickler for details, and would have ordered the drinks to be delivered precisely as he arrived. Yeah, he'd definitely miss Jared.

Brady caught the brief flash of discontent in his eyes as Jared rose to pull him into a brief hug. "Ah, hell," he said, when Brady looked at him with raised eyebrows, "I'm going to miss hanging with you, man."

Brady could see it; the realization that the amazing journey they'd begun together was coming to an end. It was in the way Jared held his shoulders, the way his lips curved down at the edges, and in the resigned sigh he breathed just before they sat.

"Me, too."

Jared lifted his drink. "First, a toast. To, Little, Cash…"

"Little, Cash makes you big money!" They sang their company slogan in unison, tapping the rims of their glasses together before taking a healthy first pull.

"I've been thinking about the old days, man. We've come a long way from the cocky bastards we were back at NYU."

Brady smiled. "That's for sure. Thanks to good old Professor Bender."

Jared sat up straight, grabbed the knot of his tie in imitation. "You know, boys," he said in a deep, accented voice, "you both have a lot of promise and a boatload of attitude. I can't help but wonder what you could accomplish if you pooled your talents and worked together, rather than always butting heads."

Brady laughed. "It sure was easier working with you than against you."

"And together, we've built an empire. You sure you want to give up your throne?"

"Lindsey's great," Brady countered. "You're lucky to have her. She would've been here from the start if she hadn't fallen in love with the Big Apple."

"I know, and I have no doubt she'll do a fantastic job— but she isn't you, Cash. I just don't get it. We built this place together, and I never even imagined it wouldn't be you and me 'til the end."

"I know."

"I mean, you give tons of money to that place, and you've been going there at least once a month since your mom died...do you really have to live there?"

Brady looked him in the eye and nodded. "I *want* to live there."

"She'd be proud of you, you know. Of the legacy you've built here. Hell, you made your first mil at what, twenty-six?"

"Twenty-five," Brady smiled. "And I know she'd be proud. *Is* proud."

"Then help me understand why you feel the need to go live at the animal shelter."

Brady shook his head. "You'd have to go there to really understand. It's not a shelter—it's a sanctuary. And it's one of the most amazing places I've ever been." Jared opened his mouth to protest, but Brady silenced him with a hand. He'd never really shared the details of his young life with Jared, mainly because there were too many parts about which he wasn't proud.

"I was fourteen when my parents split. My dad had been having an affair with his secretary for over a year when my mom found out, but she never told us that. She just packed us up and left.

"I was a typical teenager, and I blamed her for ruining my life. What I saw was her taking us away from everything we knew—our friends, private school, our swanky apartment. Suddenly I was in some rural public high upstate, living on my grandparent's sheep farm. No museums, no Michelin star restaurants—and I hated her for it. I saw her downward spiral, but a nasty little part of me thought she deserved it, for what she did to her kids. I was a little shit, basically."

"Weren't we all at that age?"

"I'm pretty sure I was the president of that club," Brady continued. "Anyway, about a year after we moved, this mangy mutt started coming around. It was covered with ticks, half-starved, and had to be about the ugliest dog I'd ever seen. Mom started feeding it, gaining its trust, and pretty soon, it was our dog. She made a bed for it in the barn, cleaned it up, and made it part of the family. She turned out to be an awesome animal, but she was old when she came to us, and didn't live long.

"The week after Ginger died, my mom dragged to me to the animal shelter. 'Don't go for the cute ones,' she said. 'The cute ones always get adopted. Look for the homely ones, the ones that try to disappear in the crowd. They're the ones that need us most.'"

"I loved Eliza Cash. God, I miss her," Jared said.

Brady blinked away a tear and nodded. "We brought home four dogs that day, and it completely changed her. The sparkle was back in her eyes and she was smiling again. Working with those dogs brought her back, and I finally realized what an ass I'd been. I helped her with them every day, and when one of her friends from church adopted two of them, I just had this feeling, man. I can't even really explain it—I just knew I'd something good.

"See, she didn't just save those dogs…they saved her, too. And in a way, me, as well."

Jared pursed his lips and nodded.

"My brother and sister helped out, too, but it was kind of our thing, and it brought my mom and me closer than ever.

"When I found out about the affair, it gave me a whole new respect for her. I figured out that she'd given up the life she knew, too, and had to crawl back to her parents with three kids in tow. It had to be so hard, but she forged something new for herself—she had a purpose again."

Jared smiled. "I never saw her without a grin on her face. She really loved those mutts."

"That's what the sanctuary is like, every time I go there. The people are selfless, committed…amazing. They do what they do for the greater good, not for themselves; and definitely not for money. I feel my mom there, and every time I go, it's harder to leave.

"I'm good, financially, and I know how to keep my money working for me. I'll miss this place, and you, especially, but it's time for me to do something for the greater good. My heart's already there, and I need to follow it."

Jared dropped his head. "How many did she save over the years?"

"Dozens…hundreds. She never kept count; she just kept going."

Jared let out a long sigh. "And you'll be keeping her mission alive. It's admirable, man, really. I guess you are more than a wheeler-dealer with a pretty face." He motioned to the waitress with a swirl of his finger for another round. It arrived quickly, and he raised his glass. "To new beginnings," he said, his voice hoarse.

"Here, here," Brady agreed.

"I do have one bit of business tonight, though. A proposal that would benefit us both."

Brady couldn't help but smile. Jared always had 'one bit of business.' "Of course you do."

"Just hear me out. You have loyal clients, Brady, and some of them are already pitching fits. I was thinking…what if you stayed in the loop? Kept some of the feistier ones, with Lindsay doing the work under your guidance. You could do consults a couple times a month—most of it from home— and still collect a paycheck. You could give it all to the dogs, if you want, and I wouldn't have to change the sign. Little, Hildebrand, just doesn't have the same ring, know what I mean?"

He did. In fact, he'd considered making Jared the same offer. He could do most of the work with a computer and a phone, and he'd maintain ties with people who needed serious tax deductions. Few people could say no to Brady Cash or the adorable animals at Best Friends.

"I assume you've already run this by Lindsay?"

Jared nodded. "She loves the idea."

Brady raised his glass. "Then everybody wins," he smiled.

"Awesome. I knew you'd say yes." He pulled an envelope from his inside pocket, and slid it across the table. "Your first assignment."

Brady laughed out loud. "Not wasting any time, are you? I'm not even gone yet."

"It's a waste of time to waste time," Jared grinned. "I got a call from this guy named Roberto Alvarez. He's got an office in Vegas, and way too much cash for a guy who owns a couple mini-marts. Kept asking about Swiss bank accounts. I trust your instincts, and want you to check him out for me."

Jared had given him the nickname, "Shady Brady," not because of a fault in his own character, but because he had an uncanny knack for separating the serious investors from the dodgy players. If Brady didn't feel good about a potential client, they wouldn't do business with Little, Cash.

Another thing he'd miss.

Brady swept up the envelope. "I can always use a little Vegas."

∞ ∞ ∞

Jared's radar was spot on. Alvarez was a scumbag, alright--he
had the stink of a drug dealer about him, and fidgeted when
Brady asked about the sources of his "outside income." He
was forty pounds overweight--fifty, if you counted his thick,
gold chains—with greasy black hair pulled into a short tail.
Definitely not what Brady would call a straight shooter.

Pictures of dogs hanging all over Alvarez's office had a
whole other radar pinging--photos of beautiful, strong Pit
Bulls wearing wreaths of foliage and ribbons around their
necks. When Brady asked if he was a breeder, Alvarez
frowned, his head jerking briefly and his eyes locking on
Brady's--sure signs dishonesty, in Brady's experience. Finally,
Alvarez shrugged, said the dogs were 'just a hobby', and
changed the subject. Hobby, my ass, Brady thought, as he
barreled home on I-15.

Brady's intuition rarely failed him, and he had more than a
sneaking suspicion that the dude was into dog fighting; which
didn't sit well with him at all. He drove back to Cali thinking
that he was going to have to do some digging into Roberto
Alvarez.

Chapter 5

"Hey, Doreen," Grace said cheerfully.

"Hi, Grace," the waitress answered. "Back for another slice of chocolate ambrosia?"

The café in Little Rock had become one of her favorites-- honest home cooking, great service, and the best cake she'd ever eaten. "My last one," she frowned. "I'm heading out today."

"Sorry to hear that," Doreen smiled, "I've really enjoyed chatting with you. Where you off to next?"

"I think I'm going to poke around Texas for a bit."

"Texas is beautiful, but I bet they don't make cake as good as ours."

"Does anyone? I'll take a cappuccino with my last piece."

"Coming right up."

Grace found a quiet table and logged on to the café's wifi. She opened her blog; something she hadn't done in months; and her heart leaped as she read through the posts of support from her followers.

It still amazed her that complete strangers found strength through her, and it was comforting to know that so many cared about her own well-being. She polished off her cake and opened a fresh post, her fingers itching to dance over the keys.

My Dear Friends,
It's been a long absence, and for that I am sorry. As you know, life has taken yet another tragic turn for me, and the road back from depression has been a long one. I've avoided visiting this page, once again foolishly believing that I had to do this on my own, despite my preaching that

you need to tap into your support networks to help you along the road to recovery. How wrong I was not to have known that you would be there for me! The outpouring of support on this thread has blown me away; humbled me; and made me feel honored to have you on my side. I've been reading through your messages, and am so very grateful to each and every one of you for your prayers, thoughts, and encouragement.

There is no easy way to heal, but heal we must— because those who've left us would expect nothing less. I've embarked on my own road to recovery—a real road trip that I hope will help me find peace in my heart and perhaps even, with a little luck, a new spark.

This is a beautiful country filled with amazing people, and in getting back to basics, I'm rediscovering myself and my place in this world. I invite you to join me, and hope that you will find inspiration from my journey as I seek inspiration at every destination. I've only just begun, but already feel as if I've come a long way on the road to reinvention. Let me tell you about Mammoth Cave...

∞ ∞ ∞

Dusty Pitts paced the worn, shabby carpet of the place he currently called home. His real name was Dustin, but only his crack whore of a mother had ever called him that. His big brother, Dale, had called him Dusty from the day he came home from the hospital, and it had stuck. Dusty sounded way more bad-ass, anyway, and he definitely considered himself a bad-assed dude. Some would go so far as to call him a monster--but hell, that wasn't his fault.

The Scanley Hotel wasn't much to look at, and it sure as hell wouldn't earn any stars for its amenities, but the owners took cash weekly for rent and didn't ask questions. The cops swept the place about once a month, and Dusty planned to be far away when they made their next visit. He would have been gone already if Grace hadn't given him the slip.

Why hadn't he finished her off sooner? He'd been asking himself that question since she vanished, but he knew the answer. Her suffering made his own anguish less sharp, somehow.

He could hardly believe Dale had been gone almost a year--Dusty still sometimes expected him to walk through the door, cigarette dangling from his cocky smile. Of course, it'd been nearly six years since he was locked up--but at least then, they could still talk once in a while, and there was hope that Dale might someday get parole. Or at least let Dusty visit.

God, he wished he could kill Jimmy Legs all over again. He smiled, remembering how the little prick begged for his life, spit running down his chin and piss dribbling down his namesake limbs. It was Jimmy's fault that Dale got locked up, and Dusty made sure he paid the price.

Dale's death, though, was firmly on Grace's head. The other two who'd pointed fingers had already met Dusty's wrath, and sending Grace to hell would finally close the chapter.

He should have been gone already. If there was one thing Dale nagged on, it was that when you were living above the law, you needed to stay one step ahead of it. He thought he was one step ahead of Grace, but somehow, she disappeared under his watch. Stupidly, he'd assumed she'd spend the better part of a month going through all the shit in the storage unit. There was a lot--he'd jimmied the lock a few times, to check that everything was still intact--but aside from a ratty sheet that no longer covered the couch, nothing appeared to have been touched.

Dusty sank onto the old flowered couch that reminded him of the one he'd watched his mother die on, lit a Kool, and logged into the less-than-reliable wifi for his daily check of Grace's website. There hadn't been any activity in months, but suddenly a new picture popped up on her homepage, and he danced in his seat. There was a link to a new blog...*My Journey of Healing.*

"Gotcha, bitch," he said aloud as he clicked on the link and skimmed the first post. *My dear friends*, it started, and about halfway through, *Let me tell you about Mammoth Cave.*

In Dusty's line of business one never knew when they'd need to go on the run, and he was always prepared for such an eventuality. He slid his lock box from the hole in the back of the closet and punched in the combination, pulling out the contents and laying them out on the bed. Nearly fifty thousand in small bills (not like he could put his money in the bank, he liked to joke), a fake driver's license and passport in the same name, a pair of false (and noticeably straighter, whiter) teeth. He tucked the items back into the box, restowed it, and headed for the drug store.

Two hours and half a pack of smokes later, he smiled at his image in the mirror. His hair was neatly trimmed and two shades darker; his unruly beard tamed just enough to hide the jagged scar on his cheek. With a generic pair of glasses perched on his nose, he barely recognized himself.

He took meticulous notes of her route, adding details that were in the blog post--favorite restaurants, trails she'd hiked, activities she recommended as "not to be missed." He stuffed his possessions into a duffel, and tossed it in his car.

"Ready or not, here I come," he snarled as he left The Scanley behind and headed south.

Chapter 6

Grace rolled into Phoenix in early June, after a beautiful drive through craggy mountains that jutted into the bluest, cloud-free sky she'd ever seen. She was feeling pretty good. Over the past weeks, she'd eaten barbeque in Dallas, watched the evening bat flight from Carlsbad Caverns, and flown in a hot air balloon over the Rio Grande. Most importantly, though, she really felt like she was healing; physically, emotionally, and spiritually.

Her skin had a healthy glow; constant activity and good Southern food had given her body tone and definition; and she'd let her mousy brown hair grow long, coming to like the soft waves and convenience of pulling it into a ponytail. Encounters with amazing people and places had greatly improved both her attitude and perspective, so instead of pushing herself through the days to guide her healing, she now woke early, looking forward to what a new day would bring. Record numbers of joyful moments were being recorded, and she felt really good about where she'd been; even better about where she was headed. Not bad for a woman who'd hid from the world for nearly half a year.

Tonight would be no exception. She'd been lucky enough to get on a sunset horseback tour up South Mountain, followed by an authentic "cowboy" dinner at a steak house overlooking the valley. Her stomach grumbled in anticipation as she grabbed her camera and headed out.

"Purple mountain majesties" gained a whole new meaning as Grace watched the sun begin its dip behind the ragged horizon, shadows turning rocks to a deep shade of eggplant before succumbing to the sunset. Just enough clouds had rolled in over the course of the afternoon to set the sky aflame, and she snapped dozens of photos--certain that she'd never quite capture the true scope or colors with the lens, but wanting the memory, anyway.

The guide was great and her travel companions enthusiastic--a young couple on their honeymoon, a family from Wisconsin, and another single rider--an older gentleman named Butch who'd recently lost his wife to cancer. Butch was a kindred soul, and he and Grace bonded immediately over the shared experience of losing a loved one. He was on a similar mission; vacationing in some of the places he and his wife had always wanted to tour, but never seemed to have the time to visit. Butch carried his wife's ashes with him in a wooden box, and sprinkled a few at each destination.

They dined together, Grace touched beyond words as they shared stories; Butch positively lit from within when he talked about the life he'd shared with his high school sweetheart.

After dinner, bellies full and butts aching, they made their way back down the mountain, handed over the reins, and said their goodbyes. Butch hung back as Grace snapped a few photos, then walked her toward the parking lot. "Would you have a drink with me?" he asked, nervously wringing his cowboy hat. "I don't often get to talk to folks who really get it, you know?"

"I do know," Grace whispered, "and I'd love to join you."

She followed him to a pub with a large outdoor patio, and they settled at a quiet table near the back.

"I wandered into this joint on my first night here," Butch said, handing her a menu. "I've been a beer man all my life, but never went in much for these micro-brews. Until that night. Do you see it?"

Grace scanned the list of local beers, and it nearly jumped off the cardboard. "Fate," she whispered.

"Yep. It got me thinking. You can't escape fate, I guess, and you can't run from it. I think, though, that maybe you can alter it a bit; make it your own."

"I like to think so."

"We have to believe it, I think," he said, blinking back a tear, "or else nothing we do matters. And I need it to matter."

Grace smoothed the back of his wrinkled hand. "It all matters," she said softly. "Every minute. Don't doubt it for a second."

"Damn it, you'd think I'd be over it by now. That I wouldn't spend every waking minute missing the hell out of that woman. Almost a year she's been gone, and I still think about her with every breath I take."

"You'll never stop missing her--and you shouldn't. But you need to focus on the happy times you had together, without letting the sadness get in the way." God, she sounded like Gwen. "There must have been so many."

"More than I could ever count," he whispered.

The waiter arrived with their pints, the "Fate" insignia etched into the glass. Without even thinking, they turned their glasses so that the word was facing outward, then touched their "fates" together in a knowing toast. "Here's to fate," Butch said, his voice gruff.

"To fate," Grace sighed, "wherever it takes us. She's proud of you, Butch."

His eyes glistened. "I'd like to think so. It's been a long, hard way, though...you know."

"I do know. When my first child was killed, the first thing my husband did was send me to a shrink. All it gave me was a crutch--drugs, mostly--that kept me from falling completely apart. But I wasn't me, you know? The drugs had horrible side-effects--I was always tired, but couldn't sleep because I was anxious and twitchy. I was losing weight like crazy, but so nauseous that I couldn't eat."

"Yeah, they put me on those, too. My blood pressure skyrocketed, and I was dizzy all the time. I quit them after a month."

"I got off them pretty fast, too, but reality wasn't much better."

"Tell me about it. What finally helped?"

Grace smiled. "I found my spark."

"Your what?"

"I started hypnotherapy, which helped a lot, but then Payton came along." She grinned at Butch's quizzical look. "My husband surprised me with a dog."

"Puppy therapy," he nodded. "My daughter tried to convince me to get one, too. Figured it would give me something to worry about besides myself."

"Exactly," Grace agreed. "I wanted nothing to do with him at first, but my husband was at work all day, and the dog kept crapping in my house. He just wouldn't leave me alone."

"What kind of dog?"

"Black Lab mix. Danny rescued him from the shelter, so we didn't know exactly what he was mixed with. He was a beauty, though…all feet, ears and tongue."

Butch smiled knowingly. "How long before you fell in love?"

"About a week. It was like he was determined to win me over, and he wasn't going to take no for an answer.

"I insisted that Danny take him back, but he laid on a guilt trip; reminded me what happens to dogs in shelters. The kicker, though, was when Danny asked me to do it for *him*. Aside from therapy, he hadn't asked me to do anything since the day I came home from the hospital without our baby." Grace closed her eyes. "I was a nurse. I worked with newborns, but after I lost mine, I just couldn't go back. Danny was working overtime to make up the difference, so I had that guilt to deal with, too. That's why I couldn't say no. He knew that while he was at work, the dog would be my responsibility. Danny even refused to name him, thinking that if I did it, I'd be more connected."

"Where'd you get the name?"

"One day, he jumped on me and started whining, really insistently. I pushed him away, but he kept coming back. Finally, I got frustrated, and plopped him in the backyard." A smile split Grace's face. "He pooped."

"Well, now that's something," Butch teased. "Did you call CNN?"

Grace chuckled. "It was the first time he'd ever asked to go outside to do his business. I knew I had to reward the behavior, so I threw his toy football, and he ran like the wind to retrieve it. He came tearing back, expertly dodging piles of poo, and dropped it at my feet. Danny was a huge Bears fan…"

"So you named him after Walter. Good choice…best there ever was."

"So was Payton. He was the spark that made me want to live again."

She hadn't opened up to anyone like this in a long time, and it felt good to talk about it; to give voice to everything she'd lost. Butch was a great listener, too; patient, and asking just the right leading questions.

"After Payton and I bonded," she continued, "I had a whole different outlook. I put everything I had into therapy, meditated while Payton napped, and started working on getting my life back."

"I'm glad it worked for you. How long after that were the…" he paused.

"Murders," Grace said simply. It amazed her that she was able to say it without breaking down. "Five years."

"I'm so sorry. It's horrible to lose anyone you love, but to lose your whole family…in such a horrific way…"

"This is definitely a whole different kind of healing, but I'm convinced that there's another spark out there for me somewhere."

"I hope you find it soon," Butch said softly, reaching over to squeeze her hand.

"Me, too."

It was eleven when Butch announced it was past his bedtime. "Got a long road ahead of me tomorrow," he said, yawning, "and I haven't been out this late in darn near twenty years. I'm sure glad the fates brought us together tonight, Grace. It has been my pleasure making your acquaintance."

"The pleasure is mine," Grace answered, rising. "I hope you find as much healing on your journey as I have on mine."

"Just meeting you tonight has been the best medicine I've had in a long time."

"Same here," she said, pulling him into a hug.

∞ ∞ ∞

Dusty thrived on dirty streets surrounded by thugs and criminals, so found it downright nauseating being surrounded by happy families and shiny souvenir shops. He tried to block out the shrieks and giggles of little brats as he scanned crowds for Grace and asked subtle questions at information kiosks, but they assaulted his ears and made his skin crawl.

Did he really think it was going to be so easy? That she'd just be sitting at one of her favorite places, waiting for him?

He'd nearly given up after Memphis.

The days sucked--the constant laughter and excited energy of the tourists messed with his head and left a hot, sour rock in the pit of his stomach. Plus, it was hotter than hell, but he didn't dare wear a t-shirt—he couldn't afford to call attention to himself.

Nights, though, were nearly unbearable. Because at night, he had too much time to think...to remember.

Dusty had no memories of his old man. He'd only been two when his father walked out on his mother's downward spiral into drugs and alcohol; three when she moved them to a shithole in a rough part of the city.

He supposed he should be grateful that the old man stuck around that long, though...or else he might have met the same fate as his three younger siblings.

He'd been nine when his mother killed the first one--a pathetically fragile creature who never had a name. What it did have was a hellova pair of lungs and constant diarrhea, probably because it was born addicted to crack. It lived three tortuous weeks before she drowned it in the bathtub, forcing him and Dale to dispose of the wasted body in the dumpster of the Chinese restaurant down the alley. He could still hear the dull thud of the garbage bag smacking against rotting vegetables and moldering meat; could still smell the cloying odor of decay that made his and Dale's eyes water. Or at least that's what they told themselves at the time.

Twice more they dumped bodies into festering orange chicken and slimy lo mein—needless to say, he'd forever lost his taste for Chinese food.

He hated the bitch, wished her dead, so it was with a certain thrill that he came home from school one day and found her on the couch, choking on her own vomit. He could've saved her, just turned her head a bit to the side, but instead, he watched until she was still, then went outside to wait for Dale.

"Mom's dead," he'd said flatly when Dale strolled up.

"About fucking time." He plucked the cigarette from Dusty's lips and dragged deep. "Don't sweat it, bro. I'll take care of us."

"We'll take care of each other."

They'd done well enough. The "Pitt Crew," as they called themselves, became connection men, for the most part, and didn't dabble directly with illegal goods. If you needed a gun, they could get you to the right person; needed some blow for a big weekend, they knew a guy who could hook you up. Whether you wanted a hooker who looked respectable enough to pass for a date or one who specialized in anal, the Pitt Crew was at your service. Wanted someone offed? They could set up a meeting with a reputable disposal unit in a matter of hours. And because they were paid by both parties, they had a pretty consistent cash flow, but never dirtied their own hands.

Until the double-cross that changed everything.

Jimmy Legs was the only one who knew about the 50K deal. They only needed to hold on to the money for one night--six measly hours--so when they were jumped in the hotel parking lot, beaten nearly to unconsciousness, and relieved of the cash, they knew Jimmy had betrayed them.

In just a few short minutes, they found themselves solidly between a rock and a hard place. They owed fifty grand to Demetri Castov, and a truckload of drugs and guns to Julio Hernandez. Neither were patient men.

Still, he should've stopped Dale from going to that bank-- should've taken on a hit right then. Instead, Dale ended up in jail, and Dusty had to take out some rich dude's cheating wife and business partner to pay the debt, then some desperate woman's husband to get a decent lawyer.

Jimmy he took out just for the fun of it. And for revenge.

Which was why he'd never stop chasing Grace.

Dusty arranged himself into the only comfortable position on the lumpy hotel mattress and drifted off to sleep, dreaming of meeting her face-to-face.

He woke in a cold sweat. With shaking hands, he reached over to the night table and grabbed his smokes, lighting one in the dark and inhaling deeply. He flicked on the light, hoping it would erase the nightmare, but, as usual, couldn't shake it from his mind.

Dale's face was sheer horror, pain and fury tainted by helplessness. In the dream, Dusty took a step back and saw the man behind his brother. He was a burly bald dude, with a tattooed head and neck, his toothless smile almost ethereal as he thrust his hips to pound into Dale again and again. His eyes rolled back in his head as he came, then he grabbed Dale by the hair, forcing him to his knees and demanding that he suck it. Dale's eyes went wide as the filthy cock was shoved into his mouth, gagging uncontrollably as it was pushed down his throat.

He was no idiot. Dusty knew what happened in prison, and knew that Dale had suffered plenty before he was shanked in the shower. Dale had refused to let Dusty visit, refused to let his little brother see what the fuckers had done to him. "Better," Dale said, "to remember me the way I was, little bro." If only he could.

Only three people could positively ID Dale in court, and Dusty'd made sure they knew the debt they were paying when he took them out. A few months after Dale's murder, the mother of the kid he'd accidentally shot "committed suicide" by hanging herself with a phone cord. Oh, how he'd enjoyed watching her eyes bulge as she clawed at her neck, while he told her who he was and why she was dying. The teller who'd filled Dale's bag with cash drowned in his bathtub several months later after "slipping" and cracking his head. Dusty still got chills when he recalled the power he felt watching the last few puffs of air bubble up from the dude's lips.

He'd told Grace's husband and kid, too, why they were dying. The best part, though, was the look on the dude's face when Dusty told him what he was going to do to his wife when he caught up with her.

The nightmares had to end with Grace, they just had to. She was the last one, and the one, he learned in court, who'd hit the button that summoned the cops. With her death, his brother would be avenged, and he'd stop haunting Dusty's dreams.

Dusty cracked a warm beer, then lit another smoke. He wasn't going to sleep again tonight, so he pulled out the knife and slid the pad of his thumb down the sharp end of the blade. As the blood flowed, he pictured the life force spurting from Grace's neck, and smiled at the thought as he waited for morning.

Chapter 7

"Brady, darling, we'll always have Vegas." It had been a successful meeting, and Brady was satisfied that the client felt comfortable with Lindsey taking over her finances.

"We can always have Vegas, Linds. It's pretty much halfway between Kanab and LA, so we can meet here whenever we need to."

"Even if we don't need to." She rested her hand on his. "You know your mother's smiling down on you, right?"

"I do...thanks. How are Buttons and Obie doing?"

"Shedding all over the house, barking at every leaf that blows by the window..." Lindsey smiled warmly. "I wouldn't trade them for anything."

"Glad to hear it." Brady remembered well the day he'd saved the two mutts from being euthanized. Had it really been five years ago?

The cancer was already wasting Mom and she could hardly walk; but two dogs from her "pack" had been adopted that week, so there was room for two more. Buttons and Obie had been huddled together in the corner of a cage, trying their best to disappear. Brady knew the two mangy mutts would be her picks, and knew Mom would have their tails wagging in no time. When he returned a few months later for another visit, he invited Lindsey out, knowing she'd fall in love with them.

"I really admire what you're doing, Brady," Lindsey said, pulling him back to the moment. "You're keeping her dream alive, and honoring her memory. Selfishly, I also appreciate that you're keeping some of your feistier clients. You're good for Jared, and you've always been good for me."

"I appreciate that, Linds. I'm glad, too."

Lindsey's phone chirped, and she jumped up. "That's my ride to the airport," she said, brushing a kiss against his cheek. "I'll see you Monday."

"I can take you," he said, tugging out his wallet.

"You're in Vegas, darling." Lindsey smiled. "Make the most of it. Win big tonight."

Brady had planned to spend the evening at Bellagio's poker table, but his thoughts wandered to Mom, then to Roberto Alvarez and the pictures of the dogs in his office. Suddenly, an entirely different kind of gamble came to mind.

Mom had kept dozens of Pit Bulls over the years, and there hadn't been a mean one in the bunch. That they suffered the stereotype of being ferocious animals bothered him greatly, and the thought that Alvarez could be using them for fighting seriously pissed him off.

A satellite view of Alvarez's compound showed ambitious digs for a guy who supposedly made his money selling cheap beer and cigarettes--lots of property that backed up to a dirt road, a huge house with a pole barn behind it. Suddenly, Brady needed to know.

He felt slightly ridiculous going out, dressed in a black suit under the cover of darkness, for what could only be called a reconnaissance mission. Guys like Alvarez could be dangerous, though, and Brady wouldn't take any chances. He plugged the address into his GPS, and drove out of town.

A couple beefy dudes lurked behind the gated entrance, so Brady drove around the expansive property and found the dirt road, cut his headlights, and crept along until he spied the pole barn rising from behind a stone wall. He left the car running, then got out to investigate.

Immediately, he heard vicious snarls and horrific yelps of pain, followed by enthusiastic cheering. Brady's blood boiled, and he yanked out his phone just as he heard a faint whine from over the fence. He flipped it to flashlight mode, his stomach lurching when he found the source of the sound.

The dog had obviously been left there to die. It was filthy, painfully thin, and covered with blood and scab. One eye was swollen shut, and ear was nearly torn off, its neck was a mangled mess of raw pink flesh, and scars slashed across its body. Brady's heart nearly broke. No creature should be made to suffer like that.

In an instant, he made the decision; he had to get it away from here, and fast. Brady squatted, speaking in soothing tones. "Hey, buddy...I'm a friend. I'm going to get you out of there."

The fence was flimsy, just wires strung between poles, so he kicked at one until it came loose. He ran back to the car, laid an old blanket over the passenger seat, and went to retrieve the dog.

"Easy, now. I'm going to take care of you." He eased his arms under the animal, very aware of the proximity of the dog's jaws to his throat. But aside from a pitiful cry, there was no reaction.

It weighed close to nothing. Brady nestled the dog on the seat and sped off, putting a few miles between himself and Alvarez's house of horrors before pulling over to administer some first aid.

In the glare of a street light, he did what he could to assess the dog's condition and clean up the more glaring wounds. Then he dribbled water over its lips, glad to see the tongue poke out to lap at his cupped hand. It was a female, he noted, then he tucked the rest of the blanket around her shivering body, and pulled out his phone.

His first call was to the police, then he pulled a card from his wallet, crossed his fingers, and tapped in the number.

She answered on the second ring. "Dr. Mary Kay," the voice said clearly, as if he hadn't woken her.

"Hey, Doc, it's Brady. I've got another one, and she's in bad shape. A bait dog; she had to be. God, Mary, I can't believe the utter disrespect some people have for life. Please tell me you can take her."

"It breaks my heart every day, Brady. Of course I'll take her--what can you tell me?"

He took a shuddering breath and described the dog's injuries. "I got her to drink a bit of water, but she's barely breathing, Doc."

"I'll be ready," Mary said.

"Thank you," Brady said thankfully. "I'm coming from Vegas--I'm still two-and-a-half hours out."

"Meet you at the clinic."

∞ ∞ ∞

Once he got away from the city, Brady pushed the speedometer to 90. Every bump made the dog whimper in pain, so he spoke to her in hushed tones, trying to keep her calm and awake.

"Hey, sweetheart," he whispered, "I'm a friend. I know you haven't had many of those, but just hang in there, and I promise you'll have loads of them. The place I'm bringing you is like doggie heaven--you'll have a comfortable place to sleep, plenty to eat, and lots of people who'll take care of you until you're better. Just hang on, pretty pup...I'll make sure you get the very best."

Brady had never been much of a praying man, but he said a few on the long ride to Kanab. "By the grace of God," he whispered, "please help me save her." He looked back at her crumpled form; blood dripping from his leather seats. "Grace," he said. "That's a good name for you. Hang in there, Gracie; just a bit longer."

Doc Mary and an assistant were waiting with a soft stretcher when Brady pulled up. "She's still alive," he said as he gently cradled the crumpled lump of fur and arranged her onto the stretcher.

"We'll do everything we can," Doc Mary said. "I can call you…"

"I'll wait," he whispered, following them into the clinic.

Brady fidgeted in the waiting room, leafing through old copies of Best Friends Magazine and pacing; wondering how it was that he'd gone from an elegant dinner at Yonaka, working on a portfolio worth nearly half a billion dollars, to sitting in a veterinary waiting room at two-thirty A.M., his $2,000 suit crumpled and bloody.

Ah, but he knew. His heart had been at Best Friends for the better part of five years now.

He'd been the first to arrive after the nurse called, telling him that his mother had taken a turn for the worse. Mom's eyes said that she knew and accepted what was coming, but she found one last burst of strength when Brady took her hand.

"Promise you'll take care of my babies," she said, eyes blazing. "I task you with that one small request, Brady, and I won't apologize for it. You're the one who's always connected with them, and they with you. They can't go back to the shelter. Promise me."

Brady had taken her into his arms, rocked her gently. "I swear it," he'd whispered.

Two days later, Brady sat with his brother and sister as Mom took her last breath.

Over breakfast at the farm the day after the funeral, Tressa told her brothers about Best Friends, the largest no-kill animal sanctuary in the country. "We've mourned Mom's death, now we need to celebrate her life," she'd said. "We'll make a donation in her name, and volunteer in her memory. Maybe they can take the pack."

They'd all fallen in love with the place that summer—the people, the animals, the beautiful backdrop of Angel Canyon—but Brady had fallen hard. He'd never met a more selfless or determined group of people than those who worked at the sanctuary; many of whom had left good-paying jobs to devote their lives to the animals.

He returned whenever he could, squeezing out long weekends and extended holidays to volunteer in Dogtown. There was something extraordinary about the place; it brought him a joy and satisfaction that money never could.

Soon, he would call it home.

Brady glanced at his watch and groaned, then looked down at his suit and groaned louder. He ran out to the car to grab his duffel--considering he'd left his suitcase at the Bellagio, he was glad he always traveled with a couple changes of clothes. In the restroom, he scrubbed away blood and changed into faded jeans and a t-shirt, then took one discerning look at his Armani suit, wadded it up, and stuffed it into the garbage can. No way he was going to try explaining that to a dry-cleaner.

Then, he sat down to wait.

Mary strolled in an hour later and Brady stood, eyes hopeful. "She's got a chance," the doctor said, "but it's a slim one. You were right about her being a bait dog--her teeth were filed down so she couldn't even bite back."

"Damn it," he muttered, his hands balling into fists. "But she's got a chance?"

"A slim one," Mary repeated, "and a long road to recovery if she makes it through the next few hours. You know we'll do everything we can."

"I know you will," he whispered. "I named her Grace."

Mary cocked her head and smiled. "It's a perfect name. You're a good man, Brady...we're lucky to have you on our side. You also look like hell--you're not planning to drive back, are you?"

"Not tonight," he said, running his fingers through his hair. "I'll get a room at the Quail, and check back in the morning."

"It is the morning," she reminded him. He glanced at his watch, and saw that it was nearly four. "Listen, you're welcome to crash on the couch in my office. It's not fancy, but God knows I've slept like a rock there many a time. I don't think you should even be driving back into town."

"I'll take you up on that," he said, "but what about you?"

"I'm going to stay with Grace."

Chapter 8

Grace woke up energized. She grabbed a quick bite, posted a blog about Little Rock, and called Mandy to tell her about the evening with Butch. "It felt really good to talk about them without breaking down--to focus on the good things."

"I can't believe how far you've gone on this trip, Gracie...or how far you've come. I'm so glad you can reflect on the happy times again."

"Me, too. I spent most of the night thinking about them--remember the time Danny almost burned down the garage when he tried to fry the Thanksgiving turkey?"

Mandy laughed. "How could I forget? We had spaghetti with all the trimmings. He felt so bad."

"And we never let him live it down."

"How about the time he went out in that snowstorm to get you popsicles when you were pregnant with Zoe? God, he loved you, Gracie."

"He did, and I was lucky to have him, even if it was only for a short time."

"One of the things I remember best is how he used to take me out on little 'dates' while you were working--out for pizza, or bowling--and then I'd brag to you about them when we picked you up."

"You were his little sister...he loved you, too."

"I don't know if I ever told either of you just how much it meant to me. He gave me the confidence to be myself; to be a drama nerd, and a chemistry geek. You two made my awkward years a little less awkward." Mandy sighed. "I miss him, too, and I miss the two of you together. He'd be so happy to know that you're living again, Gracie."

Grace wiped a rogue tear. "I can almost feel him smiling. In a few hours, I'll be hiking the Grand Canyon. I really wish I could share it with them."

"They'll be there," Mandy whispered.

∞ ∞ ∞

Dusty bellied up to the bar, ignoring the bartender's narrowed eyes when he ordered two shots of Maker's and two Heinekens. It became a birthday tradition on the day he'd turned fifteen, and he would keep it until the day he died. It wouldn't be the first time he'd drink alone--on his past four birthdays, he'd wait for Dale's call, then describe to his brother in detail the tastes he'd never again savor---the first swallow of cold beer rushing over his tongue, the smoky burn of whiskey in his throat. Dale wouldn't be calling tonight.

Dusty touched the shot glasses together, then downed the first in one neat swallow. Lifting one bottle toward the heavens, he toasted his brother, the brew bitter in his throat. He finished the second round over a burger, then had one last shot before stumbling back to his room, singing a pathetic 'Happy Birthday' to himself.

He woke early, his head throbbing and a stale taste in his mouth. Three cities, three dead ends…but he had hope for Little Rock. Grace had bragged about a café she loved in her blog, and described the friendly waitress with whom she'd struck up a friendship.

Dusty strolled in just as the breakfast rush was clearing out, sat at the counter, and smiled at the server. "Doreen…I knew it."

The waitress narrowed her eyes. "Do I know you?"

"No, but you know a friend of mine. She just raved about this place. She described you to a t, actually…although she failed to mention how pretty you are."

Doreen smiled, showing a gap between her front teeth. "Well, that's officially the sweetest thing I've heard all day. Coffee?"

Dusty nodded, then browsed the menu as she set a chipped cup in front of him.

"What can I get you?"

"I'll do the biscuits and gravy. Grace also mentioned a fabulous chocolate cake...she said it was...to die for," Dusty winked.

Doreen's eyes flashed. "Wait...that wouldn't be the Grace that came through here a few weeks ago, would it?"

Dusty tried to hide his simultaneous elation and disappointment. Finally, he'd found someone who remembered her, but the fact that she'd been here a few weeks ago confirmed his suspicion that she was well ahead of her blog posts.

"Maybe," he said. "Early thirties; brown hair; kind of tall; good-looking..."

"Does she have really cool eyes? Like, with a sunburst in the middle?"

"Yep, that's her."

Doreen smiled. "Oh...tell her I said, 'hi,' will you? She's a real nice lady."

"I will. Was it really a few weeks ago she was here?"

She tilted her head, and counted on her fingers. "Three weeks yesterday," she said. "I remember, because my niece's baby shower was that afternoon."

He squinted, like he was trying to remember. "That's right...she was on her way to..."

"Texas."

Dusty smiled. "Oh, yeah...Dallas, right?"

"She didn't say--just that she was going to 'poke around' for a bit."

Texas...shit, he thought. So much for narrowing the gap.

"Oh, there's your breakfast," she said, swooping a huge plate of Southern cooking onto the counter. She went off to refill coffees while Dusty pulled up a map on his phone and tried to guess where Grace would go next. At least he knew she was still heading west--maybe if he took a straight shot on 40, he could make up some ground.

"How's everything?"

Dusty jumped, and pasted a smile on his face. "Excellent. Best I've ever had."

"We bake everything fresh right here," Doreen smiled proudly. "Did you save room for chocolate ambrosia?"

"Afraid not," he frowned, patting his stomach. "Those biscuits did me in." He dropped a twenty on the counter. "Keep the change."

"Thanks so much," Doreen grinned as Dusty stood. "Don't forget to say hi to Grace for me."

"I'm looking forward to seeing her soon," he smiled.

∞ ∞ ∞

Grace simply stood, staring, mouth open and eyes wide. The Grand Freaking Canyon. She'd seen it on television, imagined it in her mind; but nothing prepared her for the enormity--the immensity--of the spectacle.

In the distance, lines of mules snaked carefully down the zig-zag trail with eager tourists on their backs, and a few brave hikers tentatively picked their way down another trail toward the mighty Colorado.

The immense scope of the canyon put into perspective just how tiny humans were in relation to the universe, and Grace wanted some time to meditate and absorb it into the very fiber of her being. She hiked until she found a quiet spot, wandered to the precipice, and pushed her toes over the rim. She contemplated for a fleeting moment what it would be like to jump; wondered how long she would free-fall before crashing into the bottom. Then vertigo spun her on the dizzying edge, and she took an unconscious step back.

Some twenty feet below her, Grace spied a large, flat rock, accessible by a couple short descents and a fairly well-used path. She wanted to sit there; to feel as if she were the only person in the universe; so she eased her way down until she was able to dangle her legs over the edge and rest her back against the striated layers of ancient stone.

She closed her eyes, letting sun soak into her skin, air bleed into her lungs, and the mystic feel of the place permeate her soul. When she opened them, she looked down, and saw, far below her, the twisted ribbon of the Colorado; a scrap of silvery-blue still biting away at the canyon. She snapped a few dozen pictures, already disappointed that there was no way a photograph could ever capture the true scope of something so timeless and infinite.

Amazing, she thought, how small she felt--barely a grain of sand at the bottom of the deepest ocean. Her problems had always felt so huge--so cumbersome--but even they felt diminished in the midst of the grand spectacle.

Grace watched a bighorn sheep pick its way along the cliff face opposite her, and zoomed in with her camera. About twenty feet down, a pair of squirrels argued over a morsel of food, and a small gray bird that Grace didn't know darted into a nest built in a crack in the canyon wall.

All around her, life was going on; fighting for survival against great odds and despite incredible adversity. The sky was blue, clouds drifted lazily overhead, and the sun bathed everything in golden light. She could do this, too--go on. With the clarity she'd gained on this journey, she no longer needed to search for joy in the way the sunlight glinted off the wings of a bird or a bend in the river. Her own survival instincts had kicked in, and she knew in her heart that she was going to make it.

Staring out at the Grand Canyon made her think of her own life on a grander scale. She'd started this trip believing she'd eventually go back to Chicago, but now she wasn't sure. She was in the midst of a reinvention, and the thought of starting over in a place where no one knew her or her story suddenly became an option.

She felt more settled--connected to the Earth—and could no longer picture herself in the sprawling suburbs of a major city. Plus, she was getting pretty good at this independence thing.

Grace couldn't say why, exactly, but she felt as if her journey would soon be coming to an end.

Chapter 9

Brady woke up groggy and discombobulated, until a sharp bark brought him back to full consciousness. Immediately, he thought of the dog he'd brought into the clinic the night before. Gracie.

He stood and stretched his muscles, cramped from being folded onto a couch that was too short for his tall frame, then glanced at his watch. 7:08. He'd slept maybe three hours, and it was likely to be a long day. He slowly opened a door at the back of the office, saying a prayer of thanks when it opened to a bathroom.

God, he looked a wreck. His blonde hair was mashed flat on one side, and sticking out in all directions on the other. Major bags sagged under eyes that were more bloodshot than blue, and creases from the pillow lined his stubbly cheeks. He ran the water cold and washed his face and hair with the liquid hand soap on the sink; drying it with a paper towel. Brady scowled at his image in the mirror, smoothed the wrinkles in his t-shirt as best he could, and stepped into the clinic. It was already bustling with workers and volunteers.

"Hey, April," he said to the brunette behind the counter.

"Brady!" she smiled. "Great to see you. Doc told me to bring you back when you woke up."

"Thanks," he said, following her to the exam rooms. She held open a door and announced his arrival.

His heart caught when he saw her. Gracie was lying on a pile of blankets, the only signs of life the slight rise and fall of her ribs, and the bleeps and pings on a little screen Brady assumed were monitoring her vital signs. An IV bag dripped yellow liquid into her front paw, and her body was crisscrossed with lines of pink, puffy skin protruding through dark stitches. One wound on her shoulder was still open, a thick salve smeared into the cut. Her head was wrapped with gauze, and where her tail had been, there was only a stump, wrapped in fat bandages. His heart literally ached as he looked to Mary.

"She's a strong little thing," the vet smiled.

Brady exhaled a sigh of relief. "Does that mean she's going to be OK?"

"Much too soon to tell, but she made it through surgery and the first crucial hours, so it's a good sign."

"Thank God. And thank you."

"You did an amazing thing by rescuing her, Brady. I'd go so far as to call you a hero."

Brady grinned. "I wouldn't go that far."

"This is, what, like the fifth one you've brought us?"

"Who's counting?"

Mary smirked. "We'll talk more about that in a minute," she said, picking up Grace's chart. "Here's where we go next. We'll have to keep her sedated for a while...she'll need at least one more round of antibiotics. Luckily, the bullet passed right through, but there's still risk of..."

"Bullet?"

Mary nodded. "She was shot in the neck..."

"And that's lucky?" Brady bellowed. He was instantly sorry he raised his voice, but Doc Mary took it in stride, laying her hand on his arm.

"Yes, Brady...lucky. Lucky that it missed anything vital, that you found her when you did...and very lucky that she ended up here."

"I know that absolutely," he said with resignation. "Sorry...please continue."

"Well, her x-ray shows possible damage to her spleen, probably from blunt trauma, and she's got a couple fractured ribs. I'll have to do some tricky sewing on that shoulder wound, but don't want to do anything too intrusive until she's more stable. I'm fairly optimistic we can save the eye."

Brady pressed a fist to his lips and Mary stood, wrapped her arm around his shoulder. "The good news is, she's responding to fluids, and her heart rate is nearly normal. You know I can't give you false hope, Brady, but my gut tells me she's going to make it. You know I'll do my best."

Brady nodded, then pulled out his checkbook, grabbed a pen, and scribbled. "I do know…and I'm very grateful." He handed the check to Mary, whose eyes widened when she looked at it. "Use that for Gracie. I want someone with her 24/7 until she's stable, and I don't care what it costs. Anything left over, you can use however you want. And if this doesn't cover everything, just let me know."

"This is very generous, Brady, and I'll take it because you know we always need the donations. Once she's stable, I'll put her in a private run at Angel's Lodge. I'll make sure she gets the very best care." She looked at her watch, and then the check. "Another reason why you're a hero," she smiled, tucking it into the pocket of her lab coat. "One more thing…" She turned her computer screen toward him. "Would you happen to know anything about this?" Brady read the headline: "*Anonymous Tip About Dogfighting Ring Leads to Drugs, Guns, Cash.*"

"My name isn't 'Anonymous,'" he said, trying to tramp down a smile.

"No, but it is Cash."

He pressed his lips together, but was unable to hide the smirk. "I plead the fifth."

"That's what I figured. So, see? Hero. Not just to Gracie, but to over a dozen dogs." She saw Brady's expression change, and raised a hand. "We're already on it. Mason's contacting the police and the shelter that took them in. We'll get them here if we can."

"That is good news. You're the best, Doc."

"So you say. Now, I've got to go. It's spay and neutering day for a whole litter of Shepherd mixes."

"Can I call you later, to check up on her?"

"Absolutely," she said, "but maybe before midnight, OK?"

"Deal," he grinned.

"It'll be good to have you around here full-time. When do you move in?"

"A couple weeks...I can't wait." Brady pulled her into a hug. "Thanks again, Doc, so much."

"You're welcome. And Brady?" He looked back. "My lavender hand soap smells great on you."

He grinned, threw a wave over his shoulder, and sniffed his hand as he walked out the door. He did smell like flowers, damn it. He scooped up some sand, rubbing it between his hands to neutralize the smell. If the painters at his new place got a whiff of him, they might paint the whole place pink.

Chapter 10

Her phone rang as she came to the 'T' in the road just outside Page, Arizona. Grace checked the number, and quickly pulled onto the shoulder to take the call.

"Detective Milton," she said anxiously. "It's been a while. I hope you have good news."

He sighed. "Can you stop by the station? I want to give you an update."

"I'm out of town, actually, and I won't be back for a while."

"Oh. I'd really rather discuss this in person..."

"Please. I need to know."

She heard his long inhale, and held her breath. "OK," he conceded. "I need you to know that we're not giving up, Grace. Sooner or later, this guy's going to do something stupid, and we're going to nail him. Right now though, we've exhausted every lead, and turned over every stone we could find...I'm so sorry."

Grace willed her voice not to shake. "Are you telling me that my family's murders are now cold cases?"

"No...not cold, Grace," he said quickly, "chilly, but not cold. I'm running weekly checks through the system-- eventually, we're going to hit on DNA or fingerprints..."

"I see," she said flatly.

"No, you don't," he insisted. "This guy's hiding deep, but you have my personal guarantee that none of us here are going to stop looking for him. I'll be in touch, and you can call me anytime. You *will* have justice, Grace."

"Thank you for calling, detective." She cut the call, and dropped the phone onto the seat.

Grace wasn't a fool—over seven months without a lead meant the chances of ever finding the killer were close to nil. At least when Briana was killed, Grace had had the satisfaction of pointing out the murderer in court. Helping to put him away for life gave her some consolation, but even when the killer was shanked in prison, it didn't bring her unborn child back. She wouldn't exactly call it justice.

Through the windshield, she saw the big yellow sign with arrows pointing right and left, and realized that her whole life was suddenly at a crossroads. Maybe this whole thing had been a stupid idea, she thought. At the end of the day, her family was still dead, and she was still alone. Could she really find happiness again? The old fear was trying to break in, tear down the confidence she'd worked so hard to build. Tears burned her eyes, and she glanced into the rear-view mirror.

Who do you choose to be?

If she turned right, she'd head back to Illinois, to the relative safety of Matt and Mandy's. Left meant she continued her journey, and the search for a new spark.

Who do you choose to be?

"I don't know!" she hissed at her reflection. She gripped the steering wheel in frustration and stared at the intersection.

Then Butch's words sounded in her mind. *You can't escape fate, I guess, and you can't run from it...*

"But maybe we can alter it a bit, make it our own," she finished aloud.

As much as the news saddened her, it wouldn't break her...and it didn't change anything. She'd worked too hard to give up now. Fate would decide if she ever got justice--but damn it, only Grace would decide when her journey was over. She pulled up to the intersection, and swung a left.

A huge stone slab welcomed her to Kanab forty-five minutes later, and Grace pulled into the welcome center. A rack of tourist brochures boasted locations like Bryce, Zion, the North Rim, and a place called Coral Pink Sand Dunes...all of which held promise. She turned toward the information desk, but the man working was already behind her.

"Welcome to Kanab," he said, smiling warmly. "First time?"

Grace nodded.

"Let me guess...you're here to see Best Friends."

Grace furrowed her eyebrows. "No...I don't know anyone here..."

The man chuckled. "Best Friends—largest no-kill animal sanctuary in the country. This is peak season for volunteers, and you have the look of an animal lover about you."

"You guessed that right," Grace agreed, plucking a brochure for the sanctuary from the rack.

"Well, you won't want to miss it then. It's really an amazing place; my wife works over at Cat World."

"What can you volunteer for?"

"They've got about seventeen hundred animals there, so there's something for everyone. Are you a cat person? Dog? Horse? They've got birds, rabbits, pigs..."

"Definitely dog."

"You'd love it then. You can walk them, help with feedings--even teach puppy preschool. You can take them for afternoon outings into town, or even for sleepovers."

"Sleepovers?"

The man nodded. "I'm going to sound like a commercial, but I really can't say enough good things about the place. Their mission is to end the killing of homeless pets; to either find them good homes, or give them a safe and loving place to live out their days. Part of that is to get them used to being with people, riding in cars, going on walks...most of the hotels and restaurants in town are animal friendly."

"I'm sold," Grace smiled. "Is it in town?"

"Just a few miles out," he said, pointing to the map on the wall. "You'll see the sign once you get to Angel Canyon, and you can hop on a tour at the Welcome Center."

Grace scanned the brochure, pictures of smiling dogs tugging instantly at her heartstrings. Absolutely she'd be paying a visit to Best Friends. She desperately missed the unconditional love of canine companionship; it might be the perfect place to find some sparks. "It'll be my first stop," she smiled.

"My wife'll be glad I'm sending some folks her way, even if it isn't for the cats. I warn you, though…you will fall in love. Might even decide to adopt one or two," he said with a knowing wink.

Grace smiled, tucking the brochure into her bag. As much as the idea of rescuing a homeless dog appealed to her, she was homeless herself at the moment. She could certainly give some love and affection, though, and was already looking forward to visiting the sanctuary.

"You never know," she said, grabbing a Southern Utah Vacation Guide off the rack. *Recreating Memories*, the subheading read, and she thought this could be the place to do just that.

"Anyway, enjoy your stay. It's a great little town."

Grace munched on chips and salsa at Nedra's Too, skimming the guide and reading an article about the sanctuary. Unfortunately, she'd missed the last tour of the day, so she drove through the charming town, certain she'd enjoy spending time there. Drawn by some old-fashioned bicycles out front and the "vacancy" sign, she pulled into the Quail Park Lodge to inquire about a room.

"Just lit up the sign," the clerk said when Grace walked in. "Had a cancellation. Lucky for you--this is a busy time of year."

"I noticed that most of the hotels were full. Is there something big going on?"

"Nah, it's Best Friends," she answered. "Summer's the busiest time for volunteers. Best season for the parks, too, and this is kind of an in-between spot for the Canyon, Bryce, and Zion. You can do any one of them in a day from here."

"I'm definitely checking out Best Friends tomorrow."

"You'll love it," she smiled. "My boyfriend's a vet tech there."

"It says that you're pet friendly. Does that mean I can bring a dog for an overnight?"

The clerk scanned the registry. "This really is your lucky day. The cancellation was for six nights in a pet friendly room…how long were you planning to stay?"

"Six nights sounds perfect."

Shrugging off the heat of the day, Grace slipped into her swim suit and then the pool. She'd just gotten over her initial shivers when a car pulled into the lot and a family with a golden-colored Pit Bull climbed out. The two kids ran, giggling, to the small patch of grass alongside the lodge where the dog promptly squatted. The younger boy grabbed a bag from the car, and they disappeared into one of the rooms, emerging a few minutes later. The woman headed in Grace's direction as the rest of the family headed off on a walk.

"Ah, you've got the right idea…I've been waiting for this all day," she smiled, holding out her hand. "I'm Courtney."

"Grace." They shook hands, and Courtney lowered herself to the ground, dangling her feet in the water. "Were you at Best Friends today?" Grace asked.

"Oh yeah. Do I smell like dog?" She gave herself a playful sniff. "That's OK. Well worth it."

"Is the dog yours, or a sleepover?"

"Sleepover…second night. My husband is already trying to convince me to put in an adoption application. The kids have fallen hard for Pearl already." She splashed some water onto her legs and laughed. "Ah, who am I kidding? I love her, too. Such a sweet animal. Are you volunteering?"

"I plan to. I'm on the first tour in the morning."

"Be warned. You will fall in love. Not just with the dogs, but with the place. I've never met a nicer bunch of people than the ones who work there, and they perform miracles every day, I swear."

"I'm really looking forward to it," Grace answered, knowing it would be impossible not to fall in love.

Chapter 11

Angel Canyon Road curved around vermillion cliffs, statuesque rocks of crimson and rust twisted around brown and gray. There was a peace about the place--as soon as she lost sight of the main road the air seemed fresher, the sky bluer, the mountains more serene. By the time she perched on a bench by the Wishing Pond at the Welcome Center, Grace had already noted at least a dozen moments of joy-- two beautiful horses nuzzling each other in a pasture, the sun setting the rock of the canyon aflame, hummingbirds dancing gracefully around a feeder, a tall, thin plaque that read, *May Peace Prevail on Earth*. A waterfall spilled into the pond, adding to the ambiance.

She watched the introductory video with a couple dozen others, and by the time it ended, she was in tears. She hadn't even seen a single dog yet, but was already in awe of the work they did here. All the other attendees claimed volunteer pins and name badges, and Grace wished desperately that there was one with her name on it. They clambered into vans for the tour; their friendly guide, Annie, sharing heartwarming stories along the way.

"It was a group of friends who started the sanctuary," Annie said. "They had no experience and even less money, but believed that every animal should have somewhere to call home. They'd all been taking in strays and rescuing animals from local shelters, and wanted to create a place where they could further their mission. They pooled their money, did a flurry of fund raising, and purchased land in the canyon to build Best Friends."

Grace was smitten by the time they left Cat World, but when she got her first glimpse of Dogtown, she was officially in love.

The first thing she noticed were the large, spacious runs that sprawled out from two octagonal buildings. As the vans rolled up, four dogs scrambled for the best spots at the fence to greet the visitors. "Ginger" and "Jethro" were separated by a white picket fence, behind which were several smaller runs. In one of the larger enclosures, a dog Grace thought may have been Pearl, a yellow Lab mix, a shepherd mix, and a Jack Russell were enjoying the relative cool of the morning by jumping all over each other. A large head poked out of a roomy doghouse, and a black Lab that reminded her of Payton splashed in a kiddie pool under the shade of a tree.

There was no love in the world like the unconditional, loyal affection of a furry mutt, and Grace couldn't wait to be surrounded by wagging tails and slobbery tongues. She was already thinking that five days at the sanctuary wouldn't be nearly enough.

A woman strolled out to greet them--she was maybe five-foot-two, with an unruly mop of curly auburn hair barely held captive by a large clip at the back of her head. There was a light splatter of freckles tossed across her nose and cheeks, and her smile was genuine and warm. She wore faded jeans, worn thin at the front pockets where Grace imagined dogs often sniffed out treats, and a t-shirt the rusty color of the sand that covered the ground.

"I'm Jeanie," she said, "one of the primary caregivers here at Jethro. Welcome to Dogtown."

Jeanie led them into a large open space with a table in the center. There was an indoor area of each run for dogs who wanted to escape the heat, complete with cots for lounging. Several dogs had chosen this option, and they rushed to the barred doorway when the visitors entered, vying for attention. Others came in through doggie doors from outside to greet their guests, and Grace couldn't help but smile at the wide variety of snouts pushing through the bars.

Spilling off from a bulletin board along the soffit above the runs were pictures of dogs who had once called Jethro home, but had since been adopted. Her heart filled with hope for the dogs who lived here now.

"I'd like to introduce you to one of our dogs," Jeanie said, passing around a box. "You can take a biscuit, if you'd like, but don't be surprised if he doesn't take it from you. His name is Baxter, and he's really skittish. He'll be more comfortable if you sit on the floor and don't make quick movements." They complied, and Jeanie opened the door to the run.

A medium-sized tan dog with white spots peeked out, head down and ears flat against his head. It took Jeanie several minutes to coax him out, but he finally entered hesitantly, tail tucked firmly between his legs. Grace's heart ached as she watched the poor thing shake, then nearly broke as Jeanie shared Baxter's story.

"Baxter was found in the desert, most likely dumped by a family who no longer wanted him. We don't know how long he wandered out there, unsure about why his family left him and scared nearly to death. A woman who lives in the area goes out a couple times a week--a lot of dogs are dumped there, sadly--and puts out food and water. She does her best to catch them, fosters some herself, and brings some here.

"It took her almost two weeks to get her hands on Baxter, and by the time he got here, he was severely dehydrated, had intestinal worms, and was pretty much broken. It took three weeks to get his medical conditions under control, and now we're working on his psychological ones. Bax gets along well with the staff, but is wary of strangers. We're working really hard to change that."

Grace exchanged pained glances with her tour mates. How could anyone dump a family pet in the desert, where they'd be lucky to survive, much less find another home?

Jeanie continued. "I'm hoping that if you encourage him softly, he'll summon up some courage."

Grace focused her breath to slow her heartbeat, and made indirect eye contact. "It's OK," she said softly, holding the biscuit in her palm, "I've got a treat for you here."

His ear twitched slightly as Baxter sniffed the air. He looked back at Jeanie, who gave him permission with a slight nod. Shyly, hesitantly, he shuffled toward Grace, then sat down, pressing against her leg. He regarded her for a moment, then gingerly took the biscuit. Grace lifted her hand slowly, and Baxter allowed her to stroke him down his back. He sighed softly, relaxing a bit, then one of the teenagers on the tour reached out and he spooked, rushing back to Jeanie's side.

"Looks like we have a dog whisperer here," Jeanie smiled, giving Baxter a congratulatory pat. "Are you volunteering in Dogtown today, by chance? I'd love to have Bax get some positive attention and a good walk. He seems to like you."

"I'm signing up as soon as we get back," she said. "I'd love to spend time with him. He's such a sweetie."

"I'll make a call," Jeanie said, "and see if they can expedite your paperwork. It's been breaking my heart that he hasn't really connected with anyone yet. He hasn't had a single sleepover since he's been here, and I just know he'd be great if he could only get past the shyness."

As if to emphasize the fact, Baxter sidled back and nudged Grace's hand. The man squatting next to her handed her his biscuit, and Baxter gently swept it up.

Too soon, it was time to leave Dogtown. Grace was the first one out of the van when they got back to the Welcome Center.

"Jeanie called about you," the volunteer coordinator, Lori, said. "If I can get your paperwork done, could you make an orientation in the morning?"

"Absolutely."

"I can squeeze you in at Dogtown tomorrow, but officially, we're full there the rest of the week. Of course, if the staff puts in another request we'll work you in, otherwise, would you be interested in working with horses or pigs?"

Grace's heart sank. "I'm happy to go wherever you need help, but I'd definitely prefer the dogs."

"I understand," Lori said with a nod toward the big Rottweiler that lie sleeping in the corner.

Grace filled out the necessary forms, and Lori promised to call as soon as she was cleared. With nothing to do but wait, Grace decided to take a ride around the sanctuary; get her bearings a bit.

The people in every car waved as they passed, many with canine passengers enjoying the wind on their faces. Grace took her time, stopping to snap photos of the spectacular scenery and the artistic metal gates that marked the entrances to the different areas of the sanctuary.

Angel's Rest came up suddenly after a bend in the road, and Grace was immediately drawn. Large stones outlined a walkway that led to a metal gate, where a golden cat and dog lie as if sleeping. Grace caught her breath as she stepped inside and saw the rows and rows of stone slabs--it was a cemetery like nothing she'd ever seen. A large fountain trickled, the splashes blending with the delicate tinkles of wind chimes. There was a tremendous sense of peace here, and the grounds were meticulously tended. Trees provided shade, walkways were lined with small rocks, and benches were set about for people to reflect.

Each slab had a carved stone or plaque that held the name of the animal buried beneath--and set atop nearly all were polished stones, trinkets, and personal items, left behind by those who loved them. The sight moved her to tears. There was pure love here that knew no boundaries and no end…the kind of love only an animal can give.

A gust of wind blew through, and the chimes rang out in celebration of lives lived, love lost. Grace approached one of the metal trees, and saw that each chime was placed in remembrance of a beloved pet. The wind catchers were adorned with plaques, some with heartfelt sentiments, and many with pictures of faithful companions. Tears slid down her cheeks as her thoughts went to Payton. The dog who loved with abandon, who found joy in every second of life, who died protecting the family he adored. He was a hero, and she instantly thought that perhaps she could memorialize him here, in this place of peaceful rest.

She took two more steps before she lost it completely. A poem was carved into a slab of marble, entitled, *Don't Weep For Me.*

> Do not stand at my grave and weep
> I am not there. I do not sleep.
> I am a thousand winds that blow.
> I am the diamond glints on snow.
> I am the sunlight on ripened grain.
> I am the gentle autumn rain.
> When you awaken in the morning's hush
> I am the swift uplifting rush
> Of quiet birds in circled flight.
> I am the soft stars that shine at night.
> Do not stand at my grave and cry;
> I am not there. I did not die.

Of course she wept. She wept for Payton, the happy-go-lucky grin he so easily wore, the gentle sniffs he gave Zoe when they first brought her home from the hospital, the constant companion of Danny's nightly jogs. She wept for the joy in knowing that they were still together--they did not die. Grace said a little prayer of thanks that fate had brought her to this amazing place.

She sat on one of the benches under a tree and meditated, a peaceful calm settling on her like a soft blanket. There were more moments of joy than could ever be counted here, filled as it was with the whispered memories of loyal companions and the people who loved them. Grace filled two pages of her journal, and it was an hour before she wiped away the final tear and stood to go.

She felt brighter than she had in some time, her steps light as she headed for the gate. As she turned to exit, though, she crashed into the solid wall of a man entering. Immediately, her heart slammed against her ribs and she stumbled backward, gasping in surprise as he reached out to steady her.

"I'm so sorry," he said with a chuckle. "Crap...you scared me."

For a moment, Grace was paralyzed, but relief filled her when she forced herself to look up. He was holding a messy bouquet of desert blooms, and his employee name tag read, Jordan. "Me, too," she said breathlessly, forcing a smile.

"I see that. You OK?"

There was kindness in his eyes, and she took a deep breath. "I'm fine," she managed, feeling foolish.

"Maybe you should sit for a minute," he said, taking her elbow and leading her to a bench. He sat beside her, and tugged one of the flowers from the bouquet. "Here," he said, handing her a delicate purple bloom. "An apology."

"Thank you," Grace said shyly. She really needed to work harder on getting over her crazy reactions upon meeting strange men. Jordan seemed warm and friendly, and there was genuine concern in his dark eyes. He was good-looking, too-- strong features over sun-darkened skin, jet black hair that hung impossibly straight to very broad shoulders. She managed a real smile as another gust of wind pushed through and set off the chimes. "You work here."

"I do."

"I was wondering if I could get a chime to place here...in memory of my dog."

"You sure can. They have forms at the Welcome Center."

"Oh, my gosh," Grace said, suddenly feeling like an idiot. He'd come to the pet cemetery with a bouquet of flowers, obviously to lay on one of the graves. "You've lost someone special, too. I'm so sorry."

"Thanks." His eyes dropped, and he blinked rapidly.

"Was it an animal from the sanctuary?"

Jordan nodded. "A dog named Buster."

Seeing him well up over a dog with whom he worked nearly moved Grace near to tears herself. She knew all too well the overwhelming grief of loss. "How long was he here?"

"Almost five years," Jordan said. "he had a virus from a tick that could have been transmitted to other dogs, so it didn't make him very adoptable. He was such a sweet boy, though. He would've been a great addition to any family. I'm sorry he never got the chance."

"I'm sure he was very happy here. It seems like an amazing place."

"It is," Jordan agreed.

Grace reached over and lay a hand on his arm. "I'm really sorry," she said. "I know how it feels."

"I know you do," he smiled. "What was your dog's name?"

"Payton," she croaked. Speaking his name out loud in this place made her feel his loss more profoundly than she had in a long time.

"After Walter?"

"Is there any other?"

"Definitely not...he was the best. Are you volunteering?"

"I will be, hopefully tomorrow."

"I promise you'll love it."

"I love it already." She appreciated Jordan's kindness, but had also appreciated her own time to reflect, and wanted to give him the same. "Well, thanks for the info, and for not letting me fall on my butt back there. I should go so you can have your peace." She stood to go.

"There's a blessing tonight," he said, pulling her back. "We have one every month for all the animals who've crossed over the Rainbow Bridge, and everyone's welcome. It's a pretty moving experience...you should come. I'll be saying my farewell to Buster, and I'll get a blessing for Payton, too."

Grace felt her own tears welling up again. "What time does it start?"

"5:30."

"I'll be here."

Grace chose to inscribe her wind chime with, "In Memory of Payton…A Hero to the End." Then she sat at the Wishing Pond, wishing that she could spend the afternoon with Baxter.

Until her background check cleared, though, there was nothing else she could do at the sanctuary, so she decided to head back to town and check out Kanab.

She pedaled a bicycle along the main drag, wandered through the old movie sets behind the Hollywood Museum, and stocked up on some staples at the grocery store. It was a quaint little town, but her mind kept trailing back to the sanctuary, and the dogs she'd met on her short visit. It also wandered to Jordan, mourning a dog with whom he'd worked and fallen in love. She found herself hoping she'd get a chance to see him again in Dogtown.

Chapter 12

Quite a crowd gathered inside Angel's Rest. All the folding chairs were full, so Grace joined the group that stood around the edges. After a heartfelt blessing, staff members gave touching eulogies about the animals they'd loved and lost. Jordan caught her eye as he stood at the podium, his lips pressed in a thin line.

"I've been to so many of these over the years, and it never gets any easier to say goodbye," he said. "But, I imagine the greeting I'll get once I reach the bridge, and remember the joy these beautiful animals brought to us. Buster, I think, will be the first to greet me. He was so full of life, and man, did he love to give kisses. He would wag his entire body whenever he saw me, and would shiver with excitement at something as small as a smile.

"I'll never forget this one time I took him to Coral Pink-- he found a beautiful stone polished by the sand, and gifted it to me. I, of course, thanked him profusely and told him what a good boy he was. When we were leaving, I left the stone in the sand, but Buster kept looking back at it, whining, until I picked it up and put it in my pocket. I've carried it with me ever since, and he'd sniff it out every time he saw me, grinning whenever I pulled it out to show him I still had it." Jordan reached into his pocket, and pulled out the stone. "I'm leaving it here for you today, Buster, as a reminder that it was something special between you and me. It'll be here every time I visit, and it'll always make me smile." He walked a few feet, and placed the stone on the fresh slab.

"I came here earlier today, to say a private goodbye, and was reminded that the love of a dog is a love that never dies. A volunteer, puffy-faced from crying, was wandering here among the spirits of all these wonderful creatures. I promised her that I'd mention Payton, and get him a blessing, because it was easy to see that she carries his spirit with her, as we carry the spirits of all our beloved friends with us. I imagine him romping with so many of our friends in the fresh, green grass in front of the Rainbow Bridge, just waiting for us to join them. We don't say goodbye, today, because we know we'll be together again. Godspeed, Buster. I'll see you soon, buddy."

"Thank you," Grace mouthed as she wiped away fresh tears, then slipped out of the crowd.

Near the exit, she bumped into Lori. "Oh, hey, Grace...you just saved me a phone call. You're all set for tomorrow," she said. "Orientation's at 8:00 over at HQ."

Grace smiled. "Thank you...I can't wait."

∞ ∞ ∞

She strolled up to the Jethro octagon ten minutes early, and Jeanie greeted her with a smile. "Good to see you again, Grace."

"You, too. I'm so excited to be here."

"Baxter'll be glad to see you, too." She tipped her head toward the woman stepping out of the octagon. "This is Lara," she said. "She's Baxter's primary."

Lara was adorable in a pixie kind of way; tall and thin, with light skin and short dark hair. She smiled, and shook Grace's hand.

"Glad to have you. Jeanie tells me Baxter's taken a liking to you. It's about time the old boy realizes that strangers often come bearing treats. I'd like you to try and get a walk in with him before it gets too hot--as you can imagine, he doesn't much like being out in the desert heat. Plus, he's got some serious abandonment issues, and I want him to understand that he's not going to be left behind again."

"Poor thing. I can't even imagine what he must have gone through."

"I know. He's going to make it, though, I'm sure of it. I was surprised to hear how quickly he came to you yesterday, and I'm hoping that means his trust level is increasing. I'll go leash him up for you."

Lara returned a moment later, with Baxter shuffling, head down, behind her. His ears lifted when he saw Grace, and he approached her cautiously, touching his snout to her leg. "Hi, sweetie," Grace murmured, squatting to pat his head.

"All the walks start there," Lara said, motioning to the trail head marker across the street. "He gets a straight, second left, first left, and if you think he can do it twice, go ahead and take him…but I'd be thrilled with one lap."

"Got it," Grace smiled, taking the leash.

"How you doing, Baxter?" she said softly. "You ready for a walk?" His tail didn't move, but his ears perked at the word, "walk." Grace started toward the street, but Baxter looked back at the safety of the octagon, planting his paws firmly in the sand. Grace sat next to him, talking in a low, soothing voice. "I know you've had it tough, baby. I know it's hard to trust again. Believe me…I have issues with that, too. But I promise that you'll never be abandoned by anyone here; especially not me." The dog moved a bit closer, sat, and placed one paw gently on her leg. Grace took the paw and shook it gently.

"I'm Grace," she said, "and I was very proud of how you took that biscuit from me yesterday. It took guts, so I know you've got it in you, Baxter. Walk with me, and we'll get to know each other better." She took the tiniest flick of his long tail as a sign, stood, and started toward the trail head. It took some coaxing to get him to cross the street, but once she got him started, Baxter busied himself with sniffing bushes. They fell into a rhythm on the scenic trail, and Grace let him set the pace. When they reached the starting point, he looked once at the octagon, but licked her hand, and allowed her to lead him around a second time. About half-way through, his tail dislodged from its tucked position, and even twitched in a little wag. "Good boy," Grace said. "You're safe here, sweetie."

She waited with Baxter at the end of the trail head as Lara handed four leashes to other volunteers and sent them off in a different direction. Bax sat at her feet patiently, seemingly in no rush to get back to his run. Grace took it as a good sign.

"He made it for two, huh?" Lara said when Grace led him back to the octagon. "I'm impressed."

"I even got a little wag out of him," she said proudly.

"Well, who's a good boy?" Jeanie smiled, giving him a pat. "Baxter's due for a grooming this morning, but I have a couple other pups here who could use some exercise. Could you do a few more walks, then spend some time with him when he gets back?"

"Sounds great."

Lara came back a moment later, leading a pale yellow dog with thick, curly hair. "This is Sandi," she said. The dog wagged enthusiastically, and licked Grace's hand when she held it out for a sniff. "She loves to chase lizards, so keep a good grip on her. She'll go straight to the end, then three rights."

"What's her story?" Grace asked.

"Sandi's a runner. She's been in several homes, but always manages to escape, so her people get frustrated with her." Lara scratched the base of Sandi's tail. "You just haven't found the right pack yet, right, girl?" Sandi wagged and did a little back-shuffle, anxious to get started.

Grace couldn't help but laugh at Sandi's energy level and the great enthusiasm with which she chased lizards up from nearly every bush. By the time they got back to the octagon, Grace felt a bit winded, but Sandi was still raring to go.

Murphy was a chocolate Lab mix who'd been rescued from a hoarding situation, and was another bundle of energy. He lifted his leg on nearly every bush, and grinned for the entire walk. A few seconds after Lara led him back into the octagon, Grace heard a splash, and looked at Jeanie.

"He's in the pool," she smiled. "We're pretty sure he's part fish."

Next, Grace walked Leroy, a big Shepherd mix with a gentle soul and sweet disposition. He'd been left chained up with no water in the brutal heat of summer, and was near death when he was rescued by a concerned neighbor. Halfway through their walk, he lay down in the sand and rolled over for a belly scratch.

It struck her as she stroked the soft fur on Leroy's chest...these were incredible animals. So many had sad stories; pasts that must have broken them; but they were given a chance to start over--to find joy again--at Best Friends. Leroy licked a tear off her face, then nuzzled his head under her neck. Grace wrapped her arms around him and sighed.

Payton hadn't only saved her--they'd saved each other. In that most pure, most unconditional of all loves, they'd made the most of the chance they'd been given, and found true happiness. She knew, then, that if there was a place where she could cast away the last of her fears and find true peace, it would be here, among the amazing creatures and people of Best Friends.

"Come on, Leroy," she said, giving him one last squeeze. "Let's go beg Jeanie for a treat. You deserve it."

By the time Baxter returned from his grooming, Grace was determined that he would feel some true happiness. Her heart was open completely, and Bax seemed to sense it. She sat with him in his run until she felt him really relax, then found a ball and got him to play a few rounds of fetch. Grace was overcome with happiness when he grinned and wagged his tail.

"Wow, Bax, look at you!" Lara said, stepping into the run. Baxter loped over to her, and she scratched his chin. "Looks like you were just the ticket for him, Grace. I'm really impressed."

"They know a true dog lover when they meet one," Grace shrugged.

"You have any of your own?"

Grace stiffened. "I lost my boy, Payton, about eight months ago," she said, "but I'll definitely get another soon."

Her head tilted. "Wait…is that the Payton that Jordan mentioned at the blessing last night?"

Grace nodded. "I ran into him at Angel's Rest yesterday, and he told me about the ceremony. It was really beautiful, and it was so nice of him to include Payton. Is he as nice as he seems?"

Lara smiled wide. "Oh yeah, Jordan's awesome."

"I thought so."

"Well, you'll definitely fall in love here…it's impossible not to." Lara glanced at her watch. Well, the morning session's officially over…are you heading to The Village for lunch? You know about the all-you-can-eat buffet, right?"

"Yeah, I guess I am. What time can I come back?"

Lara smiled. "One o'clock. See you then."

∞ ∞ ∞

Grace could not believe the view from The Village. She piled a plate with fresh food, found a table near the railing of the deck that cantilevered out over the canyon, and simply stared. Beyond the deep rust of the vermillion cliffs, she could see the white face of the Grand Staircase stretching into the blue. The canyon sunk low beneath her, dotted with deep emerald trees and pastel flowers clinging perilously to its sides. Grace walked to the railing, finding the spot with the best view and taking a minute to just breathe and enjoy the scenery. A deep peace settled on her and she felt a profound sense of gratification, knowing that she'd made a difference already. This place was already making a difference in her, too, and for the first time, she thought she may have found a place that could feel like home.

She pulled back into the lot between Jethro and Ginger, refreshed and rejuvenated. She practically danced into the octagon; and pretty much tumbled into Jordan's arms.

"We seem to keep bumping into each other," he said, catching her fall, an easy smile sliding over his rugged features. Grace's breath caught, and her heart skipped a beat. Jordan was the dictionary definition of tall, dark, and handsome; sharp lines, warm eyes, and a strong body. There was no sorrow in his eyes this time, and the word "beautiful" popped into her head.

"Oh, hi," she stammered, "Sorry. Again."

Jordan leaned back against the table, folding his arms and giving her an appraising glance. "You can bump into me any time," he grinned.

"Um...I wanted to thank you for last night...I mean, for mentioning Payton at the blessing. The whole thing was beautiful, and peaceful, and just exactly right. I love what you said about Buster. It's obvious you loved him as much as he loved you."

"I can't help but love them all. I'm a sucker for sloppy kisses and wagging tails."

"Me, too. I'm volunteering here today."

Jordan tilted his head. "Wait a minute...are you the dog whisperer? The one who got Baxter to do two rounds on his walk and play fetch?"

"That would be me," Grace grinned.

"Jeanie told me that you had a way with him. With all of them. They can sense that, you know. They can tell when someone's genuine."

Baxter entered through the dog door of his enclosure, and gave a sharp yip. Grace went to him, and stuck her hand through the bars to get a welcome lick.

"Hey, sweetie," Grace crooned. "Are you happy to see me?"

∞ ∞ ∞

Indeed, I am, Jordan thought. In fact, he hadn't been able to get this woman off his mind since he met her at Angel's Rest. He'd hoped to talk with her after the blessing, but she'd disappeared before he could reach her.

There was something about her—something that had his protective instincts on alert. She had the most expressive eyes he'd ever seen; hazel flecked with gold, an explosion of copper around the pupil. When they'd collided, though, there'd been a flash of something else there; something he'd seen many times before in the animals he worked with. It was the deep fear and mistrust that came from being deeply wounded; the dark shadow of a difficult past. He made his living being able to recognize that look—and being able to change it.

Too bad she'd be gone in a few days, he thought as he watched her stroke Baxter through the door with long, delicate fingers.

When Grace tossed her long brown hair over her shoulder with a flick of her head, turned, and smiled, however, he saw something else in her eyes that he definitely recognized. She was already in love with the place, and something in his gut told him that she was meant to be at Best Friends.

The front door popped open, and Lara walked in, smiling. "Hey, Jordan…missed you this morning."

"Yeah, I got caught at the clinic," he said. "Doc Mary's got a new pittie over there who's in pretty bad shape, and a group of them coming in a few weeks. Looks like we'll be getting a few new residents."

"Well, adoptions have been good, so we'll have room. Hey—you going to be here the rest of the day? There's a big donation coming in this afternoon. I was hoping for some muscle to help unload it."

Jordan's formidable biceps rippled beneath his t-shirt, and Grace noted Lara's appreciative glance. "Isn't that what we have volunteers for?" he joked, looking at Grace. "You can help me out with that, right?"

"Um…sure," Grace smiled, "whatever you need."

It was too hot for walks, so Grace hung with Baxter, coaxing him into the pool to cool off while his run mate, Gummi Bear, bounced in and out of the water, making it a sandy mess. She filled and refilled pools in all the runs, pulled some weeds, and played some spirited games of fetch. She even scooped some poop, and didn't mind it one bit.

Grace enjoyed the atmosphere at Dogtown, especially with Jordan around. There was lots of good-natured bantering, and they all seemed to truly enjoy each other's company. Everything about the place was comfortable, and Grace worked hard, hoping they'd ask her to return tomorrow.

A golf cart pulled up around 3:00, towing a flat trailer loaded with food and treats. It was driven by a beautiful blonde, who jumped off the cart and wrapped her arms around Jordan.

"Welcome back," he said, grinning. "How was the trip?"

"Awesome," she answered in a thick southern accent, "but it's good to be back." She held up her left hand, and Jordan's eyes widened.

"No way! Is that what I think it is? It's about time Elliot figured out he'd better lock you in before you got a better offer." He scooped her up into his arms and gave her a hearty squeeze.

"Hold on," she giggled. "It's a promise ring, not the real deal. You think I'd say yes to this paltry little stone?"

Jordan smirked. "I've never been able to understand it, but you're crazy for that dude. You'd've probably said yes to one of those Ring Pops."

"You're right," she agreed, "but he's school-poor right now, so I'm just happy he's making the promise."

"How much longer?"

She sighed. "A couple years, yet. And he's got clinicals through the summer and into fall. I won't even see him again until Thanksgiving."

"Well, I'm happy for you both. I'll have to call him later and give him the typical guy crap about tying himself to one woman."

"You do that," she chuckled. "He'd love to hear from you. He misses you, you know."

"I miss him, too. My new roommate doesn't do dishes."

"I'll bet," she smiled, turning toward Grace.

Jordan handled the introductions. "Grace, this is Veronica, our other primary caregiver."

"Nice to meet you," Grace said, shaking her hand.

"Likewise," Veronica smiled.

Lara dashed out of Jethro and pulled Veronica into an embrace. "Hey! I didn't expect to see you until tomorrow." She got a glimpse of the ring on Veronica's finger, and squealed.

"It's about time, right?" Veronica said. "Although it's going to be a while before he can get back here to paradise."

"At least you know it'll happen!" Lara exclaimed. "I'm excited for you! But why are you here today? You're still on vacation."

"Yeah, well, when Jeanie texted that there was a big shipment coming in, I figured I'd better deliver it, or else I'd just end up rearranging it all anyway."

Jordan leaned toward Grace and whispered loudly, "Veronica organizes for a hobby."

"So what if I do?" she teased back, giving Jordan's bicep a squeeze. "Well, Hercules, this stuff isn't going to unload itself..."

Jordan tossed her a smile and easily hefted a fifty-pound bag of kibble over his shoulder. "And she's already cracking the whip. Don't worry, I'll get the heavy stuff..."

Lara leaned in. "And I'll enjoy watching," she said with a wink.

By the time they finished unloading the trailer, the afternoon session had come to an end.

"You've put in a full day, Grace," Lara said, "and a good one, too." She filled Veronica in on her progress with Baxter. "Are you coming back tomorrow? We'd love to have you."

"They told me they didn't have any dog openings tomorrow," she frowned. "I'm supposed to work with horses."

"No way," Jordan said. "You're great with Baxter, and it'll be good for him to get some more time with you. No offense to the horses, but you're obviously a dog person."

"I definitely am."

"Let's all grab a cold drink, and I'll call Lori."

Lara shook her head. "I've got to go to the dog park and let the volunteers know they can bring their pack back. I'll join you in a bit."

"And I need to get this inventory sheet done," Veronica said. "I'll catch up with you in a few."

"Well," Jordan said, motioning with his head. "I guess it's just you and me.

"So, your first official day," he said as they settled at the table with ice cold bottles of water. "Was I right? Did you love it?"

Grace grinned. "Absolutely. You do amazing things here."

"We do our best," Jordan smiled back. So, where are you from, Grace? What do you do in the real world?"

"Chicago. I work in grief counselling."

Jordan nodded. "That sounds rewarding."

"It is, although it gets pretty sad at times. Mentally exhausting, I guess. You have a lot of that here, too, but you also get the physical exhaustion to go with it."

"Very true, but the rewards are more than worth it." He dribbled some water from the bottle onto his head, and Grace watched as it ran in trails down his neck and onto his shirt. It was almost disconcerting, how good looking he was. "So, how long are you staying in Kanab?"

"I'm kind of open-ended. I'm sorry to say that I stumbled on this place--I wish I'd known about it sooner. I'm booked for the rest of the week, but hope to find another room so I can stay longer. I really like it here, and I still want to get to the parks."

"You definitely need to do that…the parks are fabulous."

"How long have you been here?"

"All my life, pretty much," he said, propping his legs up on an empty chair. "My grandmother is Paiute, and still lives on the reservation. She raised me after my parents split up, when I was fourteen. I lived in Salt Lake before that."

He went to the fridge and pulled out two more bottles, holding one out toward Grace.

"Thanks," she said, "but I should probably be going. I'm starving, and I desperately need a shower."

He held up a finger, and picked up his phone. "Let me get you set for tomorrow." He tapped the screen a few times, and put it to his ear. "Hi, beautiful," he crooned. Jordan smiled, then laughed softly. "I'm good, how about you?...Glad to hear it…Listen, I have a volunteer here who says you don't have room for her in my neck of the woods tomorrow…that's right, Grace. I'm calling with a personal request to put her on my docket…thanks a lot, I owe you one." He chuckled at something Lori said, and tapped the screen again. "You're all set. I'll see you at eight."

"That's awesome, thank you. Not that I don't like horses, but…"

"You're a dog whisperer," he finished, knocking her a bit off balance with his smile.

"I'd sure like to be. Hey, can you recommend a good place for dinner?"

"I was planning to hit Rocking V--care to join me?"

"Who's going to Rocking V?" Lara asked, poking her head in the door. "I'm famished. What time?"

"Oh, yum," Veronica said, peering over her shoulder. "You joining us, Grace?"

"Um…sure. What time? I'll meet you there."

"Six?" Lara asked. Jordan frowned, and nodded.

"I'll text Jeanie," Veronica grinned. "See you all there!"

"Hooray," Jordan mumbled, looking slightly disappointed.

Chapter 13

Brady stood at the rail, watching the marina disappear as the yacht headed out to sea. Lights blinked on as dusk fell, and he felt a sort of melancholy as he took a private moment to bid it adieu, tossing a two-fingered salute in the direction of The City of Angels.

Lindsey strolled over and handed him a glass of champagne. "Jared's looking for you," she said. "He wants to make a toast."

Brady had asked him to keep it simple, but Jared couldn't resist the opportunity to throw a full-blown bash for his partner's farewell. There was a huge buffet, live music, and enough booze to float the boat. Brady appreciated it tremendously, but had, in his heart, hoped to wish his old life a more silent goodbye, with a lot less fanfare. The life he was moving on to, after all, was not one that had such lavish roots.

Ah, well, he thought, *may as well go out with a bang, then.* There would be plenty of quiet in his future, and he didn't know when he'd get to see these friends again. He felt the change in himself already and knew that when he did, it wouldn't be the same.

When he and Lindsey reached the top deck, Jared stopped the band, then took the mic.

"Here's the man of the hour," he grinned as the several dozen revelers applauded Brady's arrival. Brady scanned the group as he mounted the platform--Armani suits, designer sequins balancing on sky-high heels--was he really giving it all up for dusty jeans and sturdy shoes? Indeed he was, and knew he wouldn't regret it.

He would enjoy this last hurrah, however, and tipped his crystal flute toward the crowd.

Jared held up a hand, and waited for the group to quiet. "When I first met Brady Cash," he began, "he was hitting on a girl that I'd planned to ask out. Of course she chose him over me, but I didn't hold that against him." There were a few wolf whistles from the crowd, and Brady took an exaggerated bow. "You see, I saw the potential in him--he was charismatic, charming, and he loved money almost as much as I did. We were juniors at NYU, and I knew, even then, that we'd take the financial world by storm. Together.

"When we decided to hang out our own shingle, we had a good laugh about calling our firm, "Little, Cash.""

"Little, Cash makes you big money!" the crowd exclaimed.

"And we did," Jared continued. "We made money for ourselves, and for you, but the best part is—we had a hell of a lot of fun doing it."

He turned to Brady. "It's been an honor having you as my partner, but an even bigger one having you as a friend. We're going to miss the hell out of you, Brady; none more than me…well, except maybe a few of the ladies…and even though you've decided to spend your formidable years begging for donations and scooping dog crap, I know you'll be the best shit scooper there ever was, because you never do anything half-assed."

Brady slowly and deliberately raised his middle finger, grinning all the while.

"Please raise your glasses and join me in a toast to one hellova guy. To Brady!"

"To Brady!" Glasses clinked, then tipped toward the stage.

Brady draped his arm over Jared's shoulder and took the mic. "There's a lot of love out here, and I appreciate each and every one of you. It's been a great ride, and I owe it all to you.

"There's also a lot of money on this floating tub, and you can be sure that I'll be in touch very soon to collect your generous donations for the animals of Best Friends."

The group chuckled, raised their glasses again.

"It's true I'm moving on to a simpler life, but I've enjoyed every minute of this one. Oh…and, if you're ever in the mood to scoop a bit of shit, be sure to look me up." He grinned, raised his glass, and the band broke into, "For He's a Jolly Good Fellow."

He stepped off the stage, accepted well-wishes and hugs, and headed for the bar to swap his champagne for a dirty martini.

"We need a shot," Jared said, grabbing a bottle of Macallan from the bar. They walked to the railing as the last scrap of sun turned the Pacific to fire. "To your success." Lindsey joined them for a second round, then Brady left to mingle, getting pulled into dances with the women and more shots with the men. Soon, his brain was humming.

He stepped out of the head, his own head sloshing with booze and the gentle rocking of the yacht, and ran into Alli Henderson. *Dangerous territory*, his brain immediately warned, but he was too buzzed to listen.

"I've been hoping to catch you alone all night," she said. "You're a popular guy."

"Yeah, well, it is my party," he smiled. "You look good tonight."

It wasn't a lie. Her short, red dress hugged every curve; ample fake breasts spilled from the neckline. But then, Alli always looked good. It was everything else about her that made him cringe.

"I'm not your employee anymore," she cooed, tugging down her lower lip with the rim of her glass.

Brady had taken her out a few times when she first started working for the firm, but when she got clingy and started telling people that she and Brady were a couple after just a few dates, he'd broken things off, spouting the dangers of dating subordinates. She'd backed off reluctantly, but never let Brady forget that she'd be available if he ever wanted to 'kick things up a notch.' She'd been drinking, too, which was neither a surprise nor a good sign.

"It's too late, Alli. I'm leaving."

"It's never too late," she smiled, sidling closer. "Utah's not so far away--I could come visit, and you said you'd be coming back. We've denied ourselves too long, Brady; this is our chance." She slid her arms around his neck and pressed against him.

Out with a bang, he thought again, although this time, in a much more literal sense. He knew it was a mistake, even with the fog in his brain, but he went with it anyway, taking her mouth and clamping his hand over one perky breast. Her leg came up to straddle him and he caught it, running his hand up her thigh to find that she wasn't wearing panties. No surprise there, either.

Alli gasped and pulled the kiss deeper. "I always knew we'd be amazing together," she hissed, biting his lower lip. "I can't wait to find out how amazing."

A short burst of clarity lit Brady's brain as she fumbled with his belt, and he pulled back, catching his breath. No matter what his body was telling him, his brain knew it was a mistake. "Alli, this isn't a good…"

"Oh, it's going to be good, Brady, I promise you that."

She took his hand, tugging him in the direction of the cabin. He almost gave in, nearly threw his hands up in surrender--God knew he'd likely have quite a dry spell once he moved to the little town of Kanab--but Jared's voice cut through the fog.

"Where's Brady? I need him for a shot," he heard Jared holler. He broke the connection, putting his hands on Alli's shoulders and pushing her back. He took two deep breaths, trying to force some clarity into his fuzzy brain. Absolutely she was gorgeous, and willing, and he was dangerously close to the point of no return. But he was done with this kind of life; this kind of woman. The last thing he needed was a complication like Alli, and she would never be anything more than that.

"I don't think so, Alli. It's not a good move for either one of us."

"There you are," Jared said. He saw Alli, and took a step back. "Oh, shit, am I interrupting something?"

"Not at all," Brady answered. "Thanks for coming," he said to Alli, then to Jared, "did I hear you say something about a shot?"

Chapter 14

Feeding time was happy chaos. The girls gathered at the table, swapping gossip and preparing meals. It was Grace's fifth day in Dogtown, and already she counted the girls as friends.

"Let me do Baxter's."

"Ya'll have some sort of magic touch, Grace," Veronica said. "That boy's a completely different dog."

"Evening, ladies," Jordan's head poked through the window and he smiled, eyes fixed on Grace.

"About time you showed up," Lara teased. "We're nearly finished over here."

"Yeah, I got stuck over at Old Friends, and then my volunteers took Honey Bear for an overnight, so I'm shorthanded. Can you spare me a volunteer?"

"I'm all yours," Lara quickly offered, casting Grace a sideways glance.

"Um...great. Thanks." They heard Lara's giggles drifting through the window as they disappeared into the octagon next door.

"Well, that was obvious as all get out," Veronica said.

"What, that Lara jumped so quickly, or that Jordan wanted Grace to volunteer?"

Grace stiffened. Jordan had been more than friendly over the past few days, and she wasn't naïve enough not to know when someone was showing her more than a passing interest. She had to admit that she kind of liked the attention--who wouldn't be flattered to have caught the interest of a guy as good-looking and kind-hearted as Jordan?--but that was as far as it went. It would definitely go down as one of today's moments of joy, but she was in no way ready for anything more. Besides, as awesome as Jordan was, there wasn't a spark.

"Why aren't any of you…well, with the exception of Veronica, of course…"

"Dating Jordan?" Jeanie smiled. "We get asked that all the time."

"Let's just say that Kanab's a very small town, and we all know each other too well," Veronica added. "See, Elliot and Jordan were roommates for a couple years, and Jordan was dating Jeanie's roomie."

"That's how Veronica and I met. Heather—my roommate—was working at Old Friends, and I was working with Jordan every day. He became kind of like a big brother to me."

"What happened to Heather?"

"She got a chance to do something different for the sanctuary—working with start-ups around the country and setting up adoption events. They decided to call it quits so she could follow her dreams. They're still friends, but they both knew they weren't in love."

"Lara has a thing for him, though," Grace said.

"She kind of always has," Jeanie said, "but then, she has 'things' for lots of guys."

"They've never pursued it?"

"You know," Veronica said, "I don't think they've ever been simultaneously single before now."

"I think you're right," Jeanie agreed, "but everything could change in a couple weeks when Brady gets here. God knows she's crushed on him a time or two."

"Or twenty," Veronica smiled. "But then…who hasn't?"

"True story," Jeanie conceded as she tucked a capsule into a Pill Pocket.

"I'm not sure that Lara could settle down with just one guy, bless her heart. When's Brady coming, anyway?"

"I ran into Pete the other day," Jeanie said. "He said the place is almost done."

Veronica looked at Grace. "That'll be quite a show—Brady Cash makes a girl's toes curl up, he's so good-looking. Sweet, too. It's too bad he's a confirmed bachelor. Maybe y'all should stay a while longer."

"Actually…"

Jeanie's eyes went wide as she caught Grace's spreading grin. "You're staying?"

"For a little longer, anyway. I got an apartment room at the Parry for two more weeks."

"That's great news!" Jeanie said.

"I had a hunch," Veronica smiled. "I'm glad I was right. Jordan'll be thrilled."

Grace shook her head. "I'm still a temporary fixture here. That is not even close to being on my radar right now."

"Sometimes things sneak up on you when you're not looking," Veronica said.

"Yeah? Well, I'll have to keep my eyes open, then." Grace winked, grabbed two bowls, and went to feed some hungry dogs.

∞ ∞ ∞

"I've got more good news," Jeanie told her the next morning. "There's an adoption application on Baxter!"

"That's awesome!" Grace exclaimed, feeling immediately guilty for the shadow that darkened her heart. That's what they were here for; to find permanent, loving homes for all their charges. "That's the hard part of this job, isn't it?" she sighed. "I mean, obviously you're excited when a dog is going to a good home, but you get attached to them, too, don't you?" She thought of Jordan, and how touched he'd been by the loss of one of the dogs in his care. It was hard to imagine saying goodbye over and over again, even when the end result was a happy one.

Jeanie nodded. "There are lots of sad farewells, but when you consider that one dog leaving creates an opening for another one in need, it helps a lot."

"I know you're right. Where's he going?"

"Ohio. Remember the couple who took him for a sleepover last week?"

Grace nodded.

"They were here about a month ago, and really connected with Baxter's story. They've been emailing me ever since, checking up on his progress. Bax'll have a great life…the one he deserves."

Grace choked back a tear; part joy, part sadness. "You'll be a great addition to the family," she said to Baxter, who wagged in oblivious agreement.

"You know, Grace, you're a big part of the reason Bax is ready to go. Even Gummi Bear has settled since you've been here…and when you come in, it's the highlight of Bonnie's day."

"It's easy to love these guys," she sighed, "and so rewarding knowing that you're doing something good every day. How long have you been here?"

"Four years. I volunteered here for three summers, I might add," Jeanie said, shaking a finger at Grace. "The first time I was here for a couple days, and was planning a return trip before I even left. The second was two weeks, and the third time I stretched it out to three. I finally figured, what the hell? This was the place I really wanted to be, and suffering through eleven months of work for a few weeks in paradise wasn't enough. I quit my job, packed up, and moved here. I haven't regretted it for a minute."

"What did you do, before?"

"I was a pharmaceutical rep. I made great money, but I was always on the go. That's what I loved so much about this place. I felt so grounded here--so connected to what really matters in life."

"So you went from big city to small town, huh?"

"Yeah…it was a bit of an adjustment, at first. In the city, everything I needed was within a five-mile radius. Here, it takes me an hour to get to a freakin' Walmart. But, I like my life a whole lot better now. I like *me* a whole lot better."

What really matters in life, Grace thought. *A sense of family and community; love, faith, hope, joy…this place had it all. In spades.*

Just as Baxter was a different dog, Grace felt like a different person. The people here made her feel like family, and she was amazed at how many of them had quit good, high paying jobs to spend their lives caring for the animals. No amount of money, it seemed, could compare to the intrinsic rewards the sanctuary provided. Without a doubt, she already felt connected.

∞ ∞ ∞

Grace had taken to heading over to The Village early, to grab a few minutes of solitude and enjoy the view before the lunch crowd hustled in. The scenery made for a great place to do some reflection on her morning, and sneak in a quick meditation. She was later than usual today, and needed the serenity more than ever.

She'd had Lara ask some volunteers to leave--a horrible woman with two beasts for children who taunted Willow, dragged Ranger by his tail on the trail, and had Zeke in a panic. The woman seemed oblivious to their behavior, and chewed Grace out when she spoke to the boys about proper handling of the dogs. When one of them threw a handful of sand in Bradley's face after getting him all riled up behind the fence, she marched in to get Lara. It hadn't been a pretty scene.

Grace desperately needed two minutes of peace, and there was already a group waiting for the buffet to open. She squeezed her way through the crowd and waved to Johnny behind the register, then headed toward the deck for a few quick breaths.

She saw him through the window before she got to the door, standing in her exact spot, and obstructing her favorite view. She stopped, irritated that her opportunity for solitary mindfulness was now gone.

In a flash of frustration, she imagined herself tossing him over the railing, and she stared hard, willing him to move.

Tall, with spikey blonde hair and wide shoulders, he leaned casually over the rail, weight shifted to one hip. Faded jeans clung nicely to a firm butt and over long, lean legs. Not hard to look at, but certainly not what she needed right now.

Whatever, she thought. She didn't own the view, and there really wasn't a bad one from any spot along the railing. Grace appreciated the man for another moment, then slipped out and made her way silently to the opposite side of the deck.

She closed her eyes and took a deep pull of the fresh air, held it, and exhaled slowly. She cleared her mind, letting positive thoughts push out her bad feelings about the encounter with the awful family. Focusing on being in the moment, she felt her muscles relax and the knot in the pit of her stomach loosen. When she opened her eyes, feeling calmer already, her gaze drifted back to the man, rather than the scenic vista. His eyes were closed, chin resting on his folded hands, so she took a moment to study his profile. Thick arms, full lips, perfect eyebrows—the word 'sexy' popped into her head.

He must have sensed her staring. He opened his eyes and caught her glance, and she had just a second to see that they were blue before she turned away, a blush rising in her cheeks.

"Hi," he said, his voice like honey. "I didn't hear you come out."

She turned back toward him, feeling her heartbeat kick up a notch. The front, she decided, was the best view of all. "Hi," she said shyly. "I didn't want to disturb you—you looked so peaceful."

He straightened, and started toward her. "It is a beautiful..."

"You!" The door flew open, and the horrible woman burst out, a scowl on her face and her finger pointing at Grace's chest. She closed the space between them, cutting off the man's advance. Her little monsters followed behind, and began chasing each other around the deck.

"How dare you?" she bellowed. "You've got a lot of nerve, lady. I came here, out of the goodness of my heart, and you have the audacity to yell at my kids and tell me to leave?" One of the boys pushed the other into a chair, knocking it over with a loud crash. Grace could see the lunch crowd that was filtering in watching through the window, hesitant to come out.

A completely different kind of heat rushed to Grace's face, and she balled her hands into fists to maintain her composure. The man's raised eyebrows and tilted head asked if she wanted him to intervene, but she shook her head slightly, and met the woman's hard stare. She wouldn't be intimidated. "Your children were harassing the dogs, and refused to stop when I asked them to." She kept her voice calm, even though she wanted to tell the woman just what she thought about the goodness of her heart. Namely, that there wasn't any.

"They were just *playing*. They're kids, for God's sake." She was still yelling, even though she was standing firmly in Grace's personal space.

"My primary concern is for the safety and comfort of the animals. Your children were behaving unsafely, and the dogs were incredibly uncomfortable."

The man cheered Grace on from behind the woman's back, assuming a boxing stance and throwing some jabs in her direction. Grace glanced at him for a second, trying to rein in a smile.

"Give me a break. Those dogs were vicious. You owe us an apology for the way you treated us. You've ruined Harrold's birthday. He was going to pick out a dog for his present, but now I don't think he wants one."

The thought of one of her dogs having to live with that family made her snap. "There is no way I'd let you have one of our dogs."

The man gave her a thumbs-up and a devilish smile, then stuck out his hands as if he was going to wrap then around the woman's throat. Grace couldn't help it—the woman was oblivious to even his presence, much less his actions—she laughed out loud.

The woman's face reddened. "Who the hell do you think you are? You think this is funny? I'll see you fired!"

Behind her back, the man raised his hands in surrender, wiggling his fingers and curving his lips into an 'O'.

"Go ahead and report me," Grace snarled. "I'm a volunteer, too. *You* are the reason you were asked to leave, not me. Look at them," she said, motioning to the boys. One looked at her, giving the other a chance to knock him into a table. A forgotten glass crashed to the deck and promptly shattered. "If your children had any sense of discipline or common decency, it wouldn't have happened. That's supposed to be your job--if only I could have *you* fired."

The man cheered, holding up his fist in victory, and just as the woman was about to explode, Johnny appeared in the doorway. "Excuse me, ma'am?"

"What?" she turned on him, hands on her hips. The sexy man leaned back against the rail, assumed a neutral posture, and watched with interest.

"You're either going to need to control those kids, or I'm going to have to ask you to leave. People want to come out here to eat."

"This place is unbelievable!" she growled, throwing her hands in the air. "Let's go, boys, if they don't appreciate our help, they can find other people to do their dirty work."

The woman pushed through the crowd, which was already spilling out onto the deck, applauding Grace and patting her on the back. She caught the eye of the man, who shot her a delectable smile and started in her direction. Suddenly, though, his head turned toward the door, and a woman in scrubs, probably one of the vets, was motioning for him to come quickly. He turned once more back to Grace, smiled and gave her a wave, and then he was gone.

Chapter 15

Grace had been to Angel's Landing before, but she'd never seen it like this. A short hike up from a pond teeming with fish and turtles led to an enormous natural amphitheater scooped out of a cliff, spilling onto a large, flat area of soft, green grass. Muted light danced over the twisted rock, pulling colors, shapes and shadows from the ancient stone. Beneath the natural canopy, picnic tables were laden with offerings of homemade food, and smoke wafted from a huge grill. It was a perfect evening for a Fourth-of-July staff party, and Grace felt honored to be invited.

Lively music drifted from beneath the overhang of rock, and a good number of staff members were already milling about, eating, drinking, and laughing with each other.

Veronica waved from a picnic table on the far side of the landing, and they added their contributions to the already overflowing tables before joining her.

"Wow…this is like an oasis," Grace said as they settled in. "It looks so different at night."

"Wait until they light the bonfire," Jeanie said. "It's really spectacular."

Jordan planted his cooler next to the table, then passed out bottles of beer before claiming a seat next to Grace.

"I just love it here," Grace said, "everything about it. I wish the whole world could be like this place."

"You know," Jeanie said, "you wouldn't be the first person who came for a visit and decided to stay." Her tablemates nodded consensus, and as Grace cast her eyes over the crowd, she realized that she already thought of them as family, and Kanab, as home. For the past four days, she'd been calling a long list of hotels, hoping for a cancellation.

"Seriously," Jeanie continued, "you've already extended your stay."

"And now that I'm down to my last few days, I'm starting to panic. You're right—I don't want to leave yet, but it's looking like my only option is to buy a tent and move into the campground."

The girls' faces simultaneously twisted into looks of distaste. Grace frowned and shrugged in agreement.

Veronica laid her head on Grace's shoulder. "You belong here, sweetie--there has to be a way. Maybe y'all should look into a rental...something more long term."

"I might be able to help you out with that," Jordan offered. "A friend of my grandmother's has a little place. He's keeping it for his grandson, who's deployed overseas. It's not luxurious...just a little secluded cabin, really, but he might be willing to rent it to you."

"Really?" Grace asked. The girls leaned in hopefully.

"Actually," he continued, "it might work out for both of you, if you're willing to put in a bit of elbow grease. Don really wants to fix it up for the kid, but he's not getting around too well these days and hasn't made a lot of progress. I've been helping him out with things here and there, getting the place solid, but it needs a lot of finishing touches—paint, trim, some landscaping, a good deep cleaning. I bet that if you were willing to do those things, he'd give you a pretty good deal. I'd be happy to help you with the work."

"We'll all help," Jeanie added.

"Oh, I'm definitely interested. Do you think he'd go on a month-by-month basis?" Grace could easily squeeze another couple months out of summer--especially in this part of the country.

"I'll call him in the morning. The place is sitting empty right now, so if he could make a few bucks and get it fixed up in the process, I don't see how he could say no."

"I can't even tell you what that would mean to me, Jordan," she said excitedly. "Thank you. I'm already crossing my fingers."

"Then I'll make it happen," he said, dark eyes fixed on Grace. "We all want you to stay."

The girls nodded their agreement, except for Lara, who pursed her lips and forced a smile.

They mingled their way to the food tables, introducing Grace along the way, and by the time they finished eating, it was full dark. The bonfire was lit, setting the rocks ablaze and creating an other-worldly ambience. A trio of staff members took the little stage with two guitars and a pair of bongos, and in the shadow of the mountain, people began to dance.

Lara grabbed Jordan's hand. "Let's dance," she smiled, tugging him up from the bench. He tossed Grace a shrug, and let himself be led away.

"Oh, Grace," Jeanie said, "I'm really going to cross my fingers for that cabin to come through."

"Me, too," she agreed. "That would be a huge weight off my shoulders."

"I know Jordan would really like it if you stayed."

Grace shook her head. "I told you, I'm not…"

"Hey, Dogtown." A girl Grace had met earlier in the evening—Deena, she thought—approached their bench. "Did Brady find you guys yet?"

"He's here?" Jeanie asked.

"I saw him about a half hour ago. He asked if I'd seen you, and I promised I'd send you his way if I did. He's helping Brett with the grill."

"Thanks—we'll head over. I was hoping to get one of Grace's brownies, anyway."

"C'mon, Grace, we'll introduce you," Veronica said, tugging her up from the bench.

"We should warn you, though," Jeanie said, taking her arm, "that women tend to swoon the first time they meet Brady."

Grace laughed. "I think I can handle myself."

"We'll see," Veronica said with a wink. "Consider yourself warned."

They were halfway across the lawn when Jordan and Lara caught up with them. "How about a dance, Grace?" Jordan asked, extending his hand.

"Not right now," Jeanie said. "We're going to introduce her to…"

"You've got all night for introductions. Please?"

"Um…OK." She caught Lara's narrowed eyes, but then Jeanie whispered in Lara's ear and the girls hustled off.

Jordan led her into the center of the group of dancers, then let his hand slide slowly down her back to rest at her waist as he pulled her close. Her heartbeat kicked up a couple notches and she suddenly felt disoriented, heady. She blamed it on the girls; on them planting the idea of romance in her mind. Although the mere thought of romantic feelings terrified her, it had been a long time since she'd been held by a man, and she had to admit that she liked the feel of strong arms around her, a masculine scent in her nose. She closed her eyes for a moment and let go, let someone else be strong in the moment so she could just be a woman.

"I'm really glad you're going to stay," Jordan whispered. "I like having you around."

He put their joined hands beneath her chin, and tilted her head. When she opened her eyes, Jordan leaned in and brushed his lips against hers, and for the briefest moment, she wanted to fall in.

But it would be for all the wrong reasons, and wouldn't be fair to either of them.

She put her hands on Jordan's chest and stepped back, apologies and embarrassment in her eyes. "I'm sorry, Jordan," she croaked, dropping her head. "You're an incredible man, but my life is complicated right now, and…it's just not good timing for me. I still have a lot of things to figure out before I…"

He gently lifted her face to meet his gaze. "I understand," he said softly, and she saw in his eyes that he truly did. She wondered if he saw the fear in hers; the uncertainty, guilt, and distrust that squashed the warm tingle. "I'm patient," he said.

"I'm going to find you a place to stay so I'll be close by when the timing is right."

Grace had no words, and could only nod as the last notes of the song trailed off and the band swung into a quicker beat. She managed a smile as he wrapped his arm around her waist and turned in the direction of their table.

She needed some air, some time to process this new information. "I'm going to…check out the desserts," she managed.

"OK. I'll meet you back at the table," Jordan said. Grace let out a little sigh of relief that he hadn't offered to join her. If the confusion she felt was even slightly visible, he probably realized that he'd just thrown her for a loop.

"Sure." She picked her way through the throng of dancers, feeling suddenly claustrophobic, until she reached the fringes and took a big hit of the cooling night air. She made her way to a clump of trees, and perched on a rock.

Cupping her hand over her still-tingling lips, she breathed slowly until her heartbeat pulsed in a normal rhythm, then promptly began dissecting it in her mind.

She'd been kissed. By someone who wasn't Danny.

Big deal, logic argued. People are kissed at least a few million times a day, and Earth still rotates on its axis.

Oh, no, her emotions chimed in. It was more than the kiss—it was the look—the darkening in Jordan's eyes. It was an invitation.

Grace pressed her fingers to her temples and sighed. Someday she'd feel settled enough to take a chance on love—it was naïve to think she'd live the rest of her life alone. Today, though, didn't feel like someday.

How would she know when she was ready? There was no operator's manual for this sort of thing, and her stomach tightened just thinking about it. Would it swoop down on her like some sort of divine intervention, or sneak up on her when she wasn't looking?

Jordan was a good man. He was a great man. Good-looking, big-hearted...but there just wasn't…a spark.

Maybe she shouldn't expect one. She knew plenty of people who'd started out as friends long before romance blossomed.

She really did have a lot of things to figure out.

Goosebumps rose on her arms, and Grace rubbed them vigorously with her hands. She'd been gone a while, and needed to get back before someone came looking for her. She swung by the grill, but didn't see the girls, so she headed back to their bench.

A small crowd had gathered there, and Grace heard Jordan's laughter rise from the group. "Here's to having another unneutered male around the place," she heard him say. She stepped up to the table just in time to see two bottles raised in a toast. The light from the fire reflected off one and Grace immediately recognized the label. Fate.

"There you are," Jeanie said. "We were about to send out a search party! We wanted to introduce you to..."

He turned toward her, and they instantly locked eyes. Jeanie was still talking, but Grace heard nothing except for the rush of blood that crashed in a torrent past her ears as she realized who he was. It was the man from the deck of The Village; the one who'd caught her staring and then witnessed her altercation with the disgruntled volunteer. He smiled easily as recognition widened his eyes, while Grace's knees threatened to buckle. Wow, he was even better-looking up close, especially with the combination of light and shadow playing over his extraordinary features. His smile was so perfect it was almost unnerving, and she suddenly had a hard time breathing.

"Isn't this my lucky day?" he said in his honey-voice. "I was really hoping I'd see you again." He unfolded himself from the bench and turned to face her. Tall. Gorgeous. Deep blue eyes dancing with light from the bonfire. It was almost as if he had a gravitational pull; Grace swore she could actually feel herself being drawn in. "I'm sorry I didn't get a chance to introduce myself earlier," he said, extending his hand. "I'm Brady Cash."

Of course he was. With the way the girls talked about him, Grace wondered why she hadn't connected the dots the first time she laid eyes on him. Few could rival Jordan for the girls' attentions, but this man certainly did; without even trying. He was absolutely beautiful, but in a whole different way than Jordan. Where Jordan had long, dark tresses, rich skin, and sharp angles, Brady had spikey, caramel colored locks, light eyes, a sun-kissed glow, and soft lines. And a seriously killer smile. Her body temperature rose instantly and her cheeks felt as if they were on fire—she hoped the shadows would hide the blush.

Grace locked her knees and took Brady's offered hand. She felt a slight jolt, a warm tingle that zipped up her arm. She tried to speak, but between the little jolt, the flutter she got from Brady's smile, and the tingle on her lips from Jordan's kiss, she was so flustered that she was afraid to open her mouth for fear of tripping over her words.

She pulled in a deep lungful of cool air and composed herself; recalling the look on Brady's face when he'd feigned wrapping his hands around the awful woman's neck. "I'm so sorry you had to see that," she offered weakly.

"Are you kidding? You made my day." Amusement twinkled in his eyes, and Grace's stomach turned backflips. "That woman deserved it, and more. You know, she went straight to HQ and tried to lodge a formal complaint against you."

"Oh, God." Grace realized her hand was still resting in his, and she took it back, almost embarrassed.

"That's where I was headed when she flew past me in a beat-up minivan--her kids were still beating the crap out of each other in the back seat. She was already ranting by the time I got in the door."

Grace shook her head. "How embarrassing."

"It was pretty comical, actually. She was still puffed up like a rooster, and poor Jill, the girl on duty, didn't know what to do. I interrupted, and told Jill that I wanted to lodge a complaint against *her* for accosting another volunteer, and being a piss-poor disciplinarian."

"You didn't!"

"I most certainly did. For a second I thought she was going to take a swing at me, but then she huffed out, saying something about Disney Land."

Grace laughed, feeling a sense of relief even though she knew she hadn't done anything wrong in the first place. "Unbelievable…thank you, I think. I'm glad I won't be bumping into her again, at least. I'm Grace, by the way."

His eyes widened for a quick second, then he took her hand again, and held it for a few beats longer than a handshake. Definitely warm and tingly. "I'm glad to finally meet you, Grace," he smiled, holding her captive with his gaze.

"You, too." *So this is what it's like to swoon,* she thought.

Jordan cleared his throat and Grace started, pulled back to Angel's Landing from wherever it was Brady's eyes had taken her. The first thing she noticed was the silence—there was no chatter at the table; just a lot of raised eyebrows as the group watched their exchange with surprised interest. Another wave of heat rushed to her face, and she forced a casual smile.

"Shall we sit?" Brady motioned with a flick of his head. Grace slid into the open spot, then Brady squeezed in to perch on the end of the bench. It was a snug fit, and Grace felt a tingle that was almost electric where Brady's body pressed against hers.

"We should call Disney Land and warn them," Lara finally said, breaking the silence. "Anyone wearing a character costume could be in grave danger."

Everyone laughed, and the chatter started up again. Grace let out a breath she didn't realize she'd been holding.

"Those kids were a menace," Jeanie added. "I can't believe she was defending their behavior."

"Oh, Grace handled it with class…and a few choice words," Brady smirked, sharing the story. As uncomfortable as the confrontation had been, even Grace couldn't help but laugh at Brady's retelling. He added embellishments that made her sound like a true heroine, and replicated his own exaggerated expressions. The roars of laughter brought more people to their table, and by the time he finished, a good-sized crowd had gathered. Grace couldn't help but notice how Brady held them all captive, or that Jordan's lips were pressed in a thin line.

"I knew those kids were going to break bad the second I set eyes on them," Veronica chimed in. "I'm glad you gave her the what-for, Grace."

"My favorite part, though..." Brady paused, and the group leaned in expectantly, "...was when the woman told Grace she would get her fired, and Grace responded by telling her that she'd like to get *her* fired from motherhood."

"You didn't!" Jeanie said, clapping her on the back. "Good for you!"

"It was an Oscar-worthy performance," Brady smiled. "I'm glad I got the chance to tell you how much I enjoyed it."

"Me, too," Grace smiled back.

"So, Brady, are you finally here to stay?" Jeanie asked.

"Very soon," he answered. "I'm heading back to coordinate movers on Thursday, and plan to start moving in Saturday afternoon."

"Another Golden Boy leaving the big city for wide open spaces," Jordan said. There was an edge in his voice that Grace hadn't heard before. "We don't have a Nordstrom around here, you know."

Brady smiled. "Vegas isn't so far away. Besides, I'm leaving most of my suits behind—and I'm looking forward to the wide-open spaces."

The two men sized each other up, more competitively than adversarial, Grace thought. It was easy to see why, and Grace grinned to herself as she realized she was getting her first glimpse at how things were going to change once Brady was here full-time. Brady was easy-going, quick to smile, and since he'd arrived, he'd been on the receiving end of lavish attention not only from the girls of Dogtown, but from seemingly everyone at the party--especially those of the female persuasion. Jordan, she guessed, was used to being the center of attention with the ladies, and Brady's presence put a kink in his style.

"Do y'all need help with the move?" Veronica asked. "I'm a great organizer. And if Jordan's able to get Grace a cabin, we'll be doing plenty of house shopping anyway."

"You're planning to stay in Kanab?" Brady asked.

"For a while, anyway, and it's getting expensive staying in hotels."

"Where are you staying now?"

"At the Parry."

"As am I. Maybe I'll see you around the pool."

Grace felt the flush creeping up to her cheeks again, and pressed her hands there to cool them. "Maybe."

Chapter 16

"Five minutes!" a voice hollered. Everyone moved to an area of grass where blankets had been laid out and there was a clear view of the sky.

"Do you have room for one more?" Brady asked.

"It'll be cozy, but you're more than welcome," Veronica smiled.

"Cozy's good," Jordan said, throwing one arm around Lara's shoulders and the other around Grace's. They each took a spot on the blanket and lay back, Grace firmly sandwiched between the two men. There was no denying the tingle she felt where her body pressed against Brady's.

Someone cut the lights, and they were plunged into near-total darkness. A million stars twinkled in a sea of black glass--more than Grace had ever seen. Then the first fireworks lit the sky, sending showers of sparks raining down on Best Friends. It was like a metaphor, and Grace couldn't help but think about all the sparks she'd already found since arriving at this incredible place.

After the finale, the lights blinked on and people rose to their feet, folding blankets and chatting about the show as they prepared to leave. "You ready to head out, Grace?" Jeanie asked.

"I'll drive you back," Jordan volunteered.

"Why doesn't Brady take her?" Lara interjected. "They're staying at the same place."

"I was just going to suggest the same thing," Brady said. "It would be my pleasure."

The girls shared curious looks, Jordan frowned, and Grace's stomach felt as if a flock of birds had just taken flight. Brady's smile remained unwavering.

"Have a good day off, then, and we'll see you Monday," Jeanie said, pulling her in for a hug. "Try not to ravish Brady on the way home," she whispered, bringing another burn to Grace's cheeks.

They said their goodbyes, Jordan pulling Grace in close. There was an obvious change in his demeanor, and it was definitely due to the presence of Brady Cash. Jordan looked mildly irritated; eyebrows more slanted than usual and arms crossed tightly over his chest as he watched the girls fawn over Brady. Grace smiled inwardly--it was easy to see why the girls said it would be tough to choose between the two men.

"Shall we?" Brady slung his cooler over his shoulder, took her bag, and offered Grace an elbow. The short hike took nearly ten minutes, as more people stopped Brady to welcome him back.

"Finally," he smiled as he started the motor, "a chance to get to know you. It was kind of crazy up there."

"You're a popular guy," Grace noted. "It seemed like everyone came over to say hello."

"Yeah, well, I've been a frequent visitor for years, and I'm about to become a permanent fixture. It's the novelty, I guess. How long have you been volunteering?"

"Almost three weeks."

"And you're looking to stay longer. It grows on you, doesn't it?"

"Oh, definitely. I absolutely love it here."

He braked at a stop sign and looked over. "It's pretty much impossible not to fall in love here." She'd heard similar words from so many people, but somehow, when Brady said them, it made her stomach roll over. Of course, he meant with the place, and the dogs...didn't he?

He gave her just enough time to wonder before asking his next question. "Have you been in Dogtown the whole time?"

"Pretty much. I've taught Puppy Preschool here and there, spent a couple days at Old Friends, and did a few afternoon outings, but Jethro and Ginger are my favorites. Not just the dogs, but the people. They've made me feel welcome from the start."

"They obviously think a lot of you. I don't remember another time a volunteer was invited to a staff party."

"I definitely felt honored. It's nice to feel like part of such a great family."

"Another reason I love hanging around Dogtown. So, what do you do, Grace, besides being a heroine?"

"I work in grief counseling, in my off hours," she chuckled. "How about you?"

"I'm a finance guy. Investments, money management, that sort of thing."

"Is that what you'll be doing for the sanctuary?"

"Among other things. But my heart is with the dogs, so I'll be spending as much time as I can with them." Grace's stomach rolled again, an instant stab of anticipation.

"I'm amazed at the work they do here. So many of the dogs have such sad stories; it's been really rewarding helping them realize that they get second chances."

"This place is all about chances…all you have to do is decide how many need, and what you're going to do with them." He rested his hand on hers for a brief moment, and she wondered again if there was another meaning in his words. "I guess, in a way, it's not so far from grief counseling."

"I hadn't thought about it that way, but I have to agree."

"So, any big plans for your day off tomorrow?"

"Not really. I haven't taken a day off since I got here, so I'll probably just relax by the pool and do a whole lot of nothing." She recalled his casual comment about seeing her around the pool, and hoped it didn't sound like an invitation. "I am hoping to get some news about this cabin Jordan is looking into for me. It'd be nice to have a place to call my own."

"I know what you mean. I've been kind of between places for the past few weeks, and I can't wait to get settled in."

"Where do you live now?"

"LA, officially, but most of my stuff is in boxes right now, so I've been shuffling between here, there, and Vegas."

"So you really are leaving a big city. Do you think you'll miss it?"

"In some ways, but I'm really looking forward to starting fresh—reinventing myself—and I couldn't think of a better place to do it than here."

His words could just as easily have come out of her own mouth, and Grace found herself wondering if she'd already decided the same thing. "There is something about this place."

"You're growing roots already...I can tell."

"A little bit, I think. I was originally going to stay for a week, and now all I can think about is how I can stay longer."

"I'm glad," he said, as they pulled into the Parry.

"Me, too. Thanks for the ride."

"Any time." He checked his watch. "You know...it's a beautiful night, and you don't have to work tomorrow...want to take a walk with me?"

"I'd like that. Give me a minute to change?"

Grace slipped into jeans and a flowery top, then checked her image as she pulled a brush through her hair. God, she felt like a teenager suddenly, flushed with the excitement of a first date. Her heart pattered, and her stomach twirled—she hadn't felt this way in a very long time, and there was a certain thrill in it.

No big deal, she told herself. *It's just a walk...he didn't feel like going alone, that's all.* She slid some gloss over her lips, took a deep breath, and pressed her hands to cool her cheeks.

The streets were quiet, and stars blinked on as they strolled away from town toward the rugged peaks in the distance.

"Wow, I love it here," Brady said. "It smells so much better than LA."

"Have you always lived there?"

"I grew up in New York City, actually, then moved upstate when I was a teenager. I lived on my grandparents' sheep farm, so I'm not a stranger to the country life, just a little out of practice."

"I bet that's where you got your love of dogs."

Brady grinned. "You'd be right about that. My mother ran her own little rescue there, and we'd go to the shelter, pick out the mangiest, ugliest dogs they had, and work with them until they were adoptable. Then Mom would guilt people into giving them homes."

"She sounds like an incredible person."

"She was."

"I'm so sorry she's no longer with you. It's hard to lose someone you love." God, did she know that firsthand.

"Thanks...you must have to say that a lot in your line of work. She's been gone a few years now, and is a big part of the reason I'm here. I promised I'd never forget her mission, and Best Friends has the same values. I came here as a volunteer, too, the first time."

"Really?"

"Yep. My brother, sister, and I were all with Mom when she passed, and we realized it was the first time we'd been together in a while. We wanted to do something in her memory, and my sister decided this was the place to do it. Of course we fell in love with the place, and I came back as often as I could. When it started to feel more like home than LA, I decided I needed to move here permanently."

"It's that way for so many people."

"Yeah, there's something in this part of the world that I haven't found anywhere else. Something...pure. How'd you come to be here?"

Grace had anticipated the question, and was ready for it. "I'm writing a book, actually, about how to reclaim your life after losing a loved one. I think it's important for people to seek out a sense of purpose, and thought a place like this— where there's so much healing—would make for a great chapter. It's far surpassed my expectations, though—being here has given me a whole new perspective. It's put me in a sort of reinvention stage myself."

"We're kindred spirts, then," he said. "You definitely came to the right place."

"Yeah, I think I could fill the whole book with Best Friends."

They stopped at a park and sat on a bench, chatting easily about the dogs of Dogtown, things to do around Kanab, and a variety of random subjects. It was after two by the time they got back to Parry.

"I'm so glad I met you tonight, Grace—I really hope you decide to stay." He pulled her into a hug, and Grace felt a sizzle that went all the way to her bones.

"Me, too," she replied, not sure if she was responding to one or both statements. Brady flashed her one last smile, turned, and walked away.

Wow. It had been an amazing night, but adding Brady Cash to the mix made it downright brilliant. Their conversation had been so easy; comfortable; and she was drawn to him in a way she couldn't quite put her finger on.

Damn the girls for putting thoughts of romance in her head.

She washed her dishes, then fell asleep thinking about Brady's smile.

∞ ∞ ∞

Grace lingered over breakfast, settling in a corner where she had a clear view of the door. She wasn't watching for Brady, she told herself—she was just enjoying a leisurely meal on her day off.

When he walked in, however, her vision clouded and her breath quickened. He scanned the room for an empty table and spotted her, waving as that beautiful smile spread over his face.

"You're up early for someone with a day off, especially when I kept you out so late. May I join you?"

"Absolutely."

He ordered coffee and visited the buffet, coming back with a neat breakfast of eggs, hash browns, and fruit. "I didn't thank you for last night. I really enjoyed your company."

Grace felt the burn in her cheeks again. "It was the best night I've had in a long time."

"Glad to hear it. So, you sticking around here today?"

"Probably, unless Jordan calls. If it works out with the cabin, I may need to go over there."

Brady pressed his lips together, then sighed. "There's no good way to ask you this, Grace, so…I'm just going to ask. Are you and Jordan…involved?"

"No," she said, maybe too quickly. The slight raise of his eyebrows and nod of his head sent a tingle through her gut.

"Good to know. So, I've got to check in on a few things, then swing by the new place. Maybe I'll see you later."

"Maybe," she said, more hope in her voice than she wanted him to hear.

Grace almost convinced herself that she wore her bikini because she needed some color on her stomach, and painted her finger and toe nails a delectable shade of pink because she hadn't had a manicure in months. But when she nearly jumped out of her skin every time the gate to the pool opened, and read the same paragraph of her book for the third time without any idea of what it said, she had to admit that she was hoping Brady would show up.

Just thinking about him raised her body temperature, so she took a quick dip to cool off. When she got back to her lounge chair, she put on her sunglasses and closed her eyes, taking a few minutes to enjoy the feeling of the sun browning her skin. She focused on her journey, her healing, and how incredibly far she'd come; especially since arriving at Best Friends.

Grace couldn't say exactly when the change happened, but she was looking at life so much more positively now—toward a real future with true happiness instead of holding on with vice grips to the past. She liked the feeling.

She reached into her bag and pulled out her compact, powdering her shiny face and appraising her image in the tiny mirror. Not half-bad, she thought, especially considering that just a few months ago she couldn't stand to look at her own reflection. Her skin had a healthy glow, her smile lit her eyes, and her mousy hair fell in soft waves around good cheekbones. She didn't have Veronica's model good-looks or Jeanie's natural cuteness, but she was…

Why was she even thinking about this? She snapped the compact shut, pulled her sunglasses over her eyes, and lay back. Brady was a great guy, but it was just a walk, and some good conversation…it didn't mean anything.

"I was hoping I'd find you here."

She jumped and opened her eyes, heat creeping toward her cheeks again--she was seriously going to have to find a way to put a stop to that. But how, when he looked like he did? A woman would have to blind not to appreciate this man…caramel skin, broad shoulders, sculpted chest with a light sprinkle of blonde hair…a smile that would weaken even the strongest knees.

"Oh, hi, Brady."

"Is this seat taken?"

"Nope." She pulled her bag from the chair next to her-- the one she definitely didn't put there to save a seat for Brady Cash.

"Wow, it's hot today," he said as he lay the towel over the chair. "I really need to think about putting in a pool at the new place."

Definitely hot, Grace thought as Brady squeezed sunblock into his hand and rubbed it over his chest. "They said 96 degrees, but it feels like a hundred."

"That's for sure. Would you mind getting my back?" he asked, holding out the bottle of lotion.

"Uh…sure." She felt the tingle in her fingers as soon as she touched his skin, and hoped he couldn't hear the quickening of her heart. "How's the house coming?"

"It's ready, and I love it--the colors, the landscaping, the layout—there's an amazing balcony where I'll get the best sunsets. I can't wait to move in. Have you heard anything about the cabin?"

"Not yet."

"Well, I have a good feeling about it." He turned to face her, and she handed him back the bottle. "Your shoulders look a little pink," he said, twirling his finger in the air. "Let me see." Grace turned in her chair. "Yep. Your back, too. May I?"

"Sure," she said, her voice thin. Her breath quickened and her stomach fluttered as his hands slid smoothly over her skin.

"The sun is really intense here--you need to be extra careful."

"I will, thanks," Grace murmured. His fingers grazed her shoulders, and a shudder ran through her entire body. "So, your furniture comes tomorrow?" She could feel the shake in her voice, and hoped Brady couldn't hear it.

"Yep…the new stuff I ordered, anyway. I have an apartment in LA, so I have more space to finish here. I don't even know what some of it looks like--I put in in the hands of a designer, so I'm anxious to see how it all comes together." He pulled off his sunglasses and tossed them in his bag. "Wow, I'm baking already. Join me for a dip?"

He took her hand and pulled her up, then took two giant strides and leaped into the pool. Grace jumped as the splash sprayed her skin, then sat on the edge, dangling her legs in the water. When Brady smirked at her, she smirked back. "I'll get in in a minute," she said. "A little at a time."

"Sometimes you just have to go for it, Grace," he smiled, shaking water from his hair. "Dive right in and take a chance." He walked toward her, while she tried to decide if there was yet another double meaning to his words. "Trust me," he said, holding out his arms.

Grace grumbled, but scooched to the edge, put her hands on the concrete, and pushed off. Brady caught her and held her for a moment before setting her on the bottom, his hands resting on her hips. "Cold," she gasped.

"Only for a minute."

She looked up at him, held captive by his gaze. Her hands rested on his arms, and she could feel the crackle between them, even in the water. His eyes darkened, and she swore she stopped breathing as he took a step closer. His lips parted slightly, and she had just a second to think, *Oh, God, he's going to kiss me*, before her phone rang shrilly, breaking the moment.

"I've got to get that," she stammered, pulling back and swimming hard for the ladder. She jumped out of the water, feeling more flustered than she cared to admit. What was she thinking? Her heart slammed against her rib cage; her voice was breathless and shaky when she took the call.

"It's yours, if you want it," Jordan said. "Can you meet us over here to check it out?"

"Oh, Jordan…wow…absolutely! Where is it? I'll change and leave right now." She scribbled directions on the inside cover of her book as Brady hoisted himself out of the pool.

"I can have the cabin," she said excitedly. "I need to meet Jordan and the owner there to work out the details."

"Congratulations…that's great news. Can I take you to dinner later, to celebrate?"

Grace was instantly torn. She already liked Brady way more than she had a right to, and had what felt like a *need* to get to know him better, which scared the hell out of her. There were as many goose bumps on her flesh from his touch as there were from the chilly water, and she really, really wanted to go to dinner with him. Which was exactly why she wouldn't do it.

Damn it, she needed to figure out her own life before she even thought about fitting someone else into it.

"I can't…I'm sorry. I have no idea how long this will take, and if I get the place, I'll have so much to do…"

"Another time then."

Grace nodded. "Good luck with the furniture tomorrow," she said as she went back to her room to change.

Chapter 17

Dusty stirred the pan over the cheap hotplate he'd picked up, the smell bringing back a thousand memories. No matter how much money they had, Dale's birthday was always celebrated with Hamburger Helper Cheeseburger Macaroni, without the hamburger. It was a kind of homage to the day their lives changed forever, the day Dale became his hero. Today would be no different.

They'd heard the sounds from the kitchen—the smack of a fist, the muffled cries of their mother. She always had an excuse for the black eyes, the dark bruises, the limp that came from a well-placed boot heel. At the time, Dale still thought he could save her, and squared his jaw before marching to Mom's bedroom door and kicking it open.

Dusty jumped immediately to rush to the scene as Dale stepped into the room.

His mother was naked, her skin paper thin from years of drug abuse. He remembered the thin blue veins on her breasts, bruises already marring the flesh there. She was on the floor, leaning against the bed, "Uncle Ted" looming over her fragile frame.

"Stop hitting my mom!" Dale screamed, in a voice that cracked with the coming of manhood.

"Get the hell out of here!" he snarled, before turning on their mother. "Tell that kid to mind his own goddamn business. Now."

"Go on, boys," Mom slurred through swollen, split lips. Dusty remembered the spray of blood that came with her words, recalled that she didn't meet her sons' horrified stares.

Dale puffed out his chest. "*You* get the hell out of here," he said, his voice menacing, "or I'll call the cops."

Without warning, Ted's fist lashed out and connected solidly with Dale's nose. The punch was so hard that Dale flew backward through the door, smashing into Dusty and sending them both crashing into the wall in the hallway. It was a couple seconds of wide-eyed surprise before Dale even realized that his nose was broken and bleeding.

They were still trying to figure out what the fuck happened when their mother and Ted stepped over them, barely sparing them a glance, and walked out the door.

When Dusty got home from school the next day, Dale was standing on a stepstool at the stove, stirring; both eyes beet red and rimmed in deep purple. "I don't know how long to cook this stuff," he'd said, "I should've swiped the directions."

Dale scooped up a spoonful, and blew on it before offering it to Dusty for analysis.

"I think it's done," Dusty said, trying to talk around a mouthful of overcooked noodles.

"Guess we'll eat early, then," Dale had smiled.

They ate in silence, until Dusty asked the question they were both considering. "Is she coming back?"

"I don't know, little bro. Either way, we'll make due. I'll take care of you."

"It doesn't seem right to say it, but, happy birthday, Dale."

They toasted with spoonfuls of mushy, coagulated goo. "Thanks, man."

It was a week before she came back, slipping into the house like nothing had happened. Dale's bruises were turning yellow by that point, and she refused to look him in the eye.

Everything had changed, though, and Dale became the man of the house. He made sure there was food on the table, that Dusty had clean clothes, and that he did his homework. Dale made sure that Dusty had some sort of life, but now, there was no one to care one way or the other.

Dusty scooped some of the glop into a bowl, sat at the table, and raised a forkful to the heavens. "Happy birthday,

Dale," he said, nearly choking on the food as well as his words.

∞ ∞ ∞

The place was tiny, secluded, and in need of some serious TLC. "It's perfect," Grace grinned.

"Don'll be your neighbor, so to speak. That's his place over there," Jordan said, pointing north. She could just make out a roof in the distance behind some thick, scrubby brush.

Don smiled. "It's real quiet here, except for the coyotes." When he took in her wide-eyed look, he added, "Oh, they won't bother you. Just, if you have small dogs here, don't let them wander alone at night."

Grace immediately decided that she was going to have really big dogs here--every night.

"I'm thrilled that you're offering to fix the place up. I want it to be nice for Tommy when he gets home, but this damned arthritis has other ideas. Jordan's been a godsend...fixed the roof, put in the wood burner, redid some plumbing...if you play your cards right, maybe he'll give you a hand."

"I definitely will," Jordan smiled.

She could handle Don's requests with minimal help--paint, trim, landscaping. There was even a huge shed that housed all the necessary tools--although Grace cringed when Don opened the door and immediately added reorganizing it to her list. Or, maybe she'd put Veronica on it.

"Keep the receipts, and I'll deduct it off your rent," Don said, handing her the key, "and feel free to stop by anytime if you need anything."

"I will," Grace smiled. "Thank you so much."

"We need to celebrate," Jordan said after Don left. "Rocking V?"

Two dinner invitations, from two incredible men, in one day. "What I really need to do is get to the store and buy some cleaning supplies. It's going to take me a couple days to get this place ready, and that's all the time I have."

"I'll give you a hand. We'll grab some dinner, then swing by the store, and I'll help with the cleaning."

The hopeful look in his eyes made Grace feel guilty. She wouldn't have this place if it weren't for him, and she was incredibly thankful. However, she didn't want him to get the wrong impression. It wasn't going to be a date.

"OK, but only if I'm buying. I'm so grateful that you helped me find this place, and that you put in a good word for me with Don." She took one look at his expression, and added, "I mean it, Jordan. Dinner's on me…to show my appreciation."

"A beautiful lady wants to buy me dinner? Not usually how I roll, but I guess I can live with it."

Jordan raised his wine glass in a toast. "Here's to having the chance to get to know you better. I'm really looking forward to it."

Grace raised her glass, but sighed. "Oh, Jordan…I'm so grateful for the place, but I…"

"Don't worry, Grace," he smiled. "I said I'm a patient man, and I meant it. No pressure. I am glad to have a chance to spend some time alone with you, though, so you can get to know me, better, too. We haven't really had a chance to just sit and talk."

She smiled. "The dogs are pretty demanding of our attention."

"As they should be. But for now, we have some uninterrupted time. Tell me about yourself—who is Grace Burton?"

The million-dollar question, she thought; one she really couldn't answer. She thought she was getting there, because of Best Friends, but until she permanently settled somewhere, and decided what she was going to do with the rest of her life, she considered herself a work in progress. "I honestly don't know," she said. "I'm working on that, I guess."

"Tell me about Chicago. Did you live in the city?"

"I was about an hour away—I'm definitely not a city girl."

"Do you have family there?"

I did. "My sister, her husband and my niece." Jordan was really just interested, but she felt uncomfortable under the scrutiny. There wasn't much information she was willing to divulge. "I worked in grief counseling, and I traveled a lot, going to conferences and things like that."

"You said that in past tense," Jordan pointed out. "Are you out of work, or on a sabbatical?"

"Sabbatical's the perfect word for it." And it was. It explained that she was doing some soul searching without having to explain why.

"Well, I'd say you landed in the perfect place."

"I completely agree. How about you? How'd you get here?"

His eyes drifted for a moment, and he sighed. "Best Friends saved my life." He sucked in a breath and let it out slowly. "When my folks split up, life got ugly. My dad took his new girlfriend and her two kids to Europe, and my mom pretty much checked out. I looked too much like him, she said, and she couldn't stand to look at me. She shipped me off to live with my grandmother on the reservation."

"That must have been hard."

"I was *pissed.* I didn't know much about my heritage, and I didn't want to know. I started running with the wrong crowd, acting out, drinking...I was heading for disaster and I couldn't wait to get there."

"But you never made it."

He nodded. "Thanks to the sanctuary. I was running with my so-called friends one day. This dude Keith had pilfered some cheap whiskey from his dad's stash, and we were out in the woods, up to no good. We heard the squeal of brakes and a horrible yowl, and ran over to see this dog that had been hit, lying on the side of the road. One of the guys laughed and grabbed a big branch off the ground, saying something about putting it out of its misery. I took one look at the pain and confusion in the dog's eyes, and grabbed the branch out of his hands. There was no way I was going to stand there and watch him beat it to death, and I was completely shocked that he'd want to. He got up in my face, and we had it out. The guy had three years and thirty pounds on me, but I was determined. When we finished, I had a split lip, a busted nose, and a hell of a knot on my cheek."

"What about the other guy?"

"Let's just say that I made my point, and he skulked off with his tail between his legs," Jordan grinned.

Their starter arrived, and they placed their dinner orders. Jordan scooped a healthy dollop of hummus onto a warm hunk of pita before continuing.

"I ran up to the nearest house and knocked on the door. I was dirty, bloody, and had already established a reputation as a hoodlum, so the old man who lived there stared at me through the screen suspiciously. I hated that look, and suddenly felt like I was ten years old again. I begged him to come, and finally, he did. He took one look at the dog, and said its hip was broken. When he pulled out a knife and said he'd end its suffering, I lost it completely. It was like everything that happened over the past few months—the divorce, the abandonment by my parents, my horrible behavior—all crashed down on me at once, and I started bawling. I pleaded with him, and he took pity on me. 'I know a place,' he said, and he got his truck and put the dog in the back. I rode with it, crying the whole way."

"He brought you to Best Friends," Grace whispered.

"He did. The people were amazing. They took her, no questions asked, and even patched me up. Then the vet asked me if I had the pups."

"Oh, Jordan…she was a mama…"

"I looked at the old man who brought me, and he shrugged. Then he looked at me, hard, and said…and I'll never forget this, 'You still got a chance, kid. You're not all bad.'

"It took me two days to find the puppies, in one of his neighbor's sheds. One of them was dead, but there were four clinging to life. I put them in a box, and carried them to the old man's house. This time, when he opened the door, his eyes were softer, and my heart literally swelled. He nodded, and we drove back with the pups. They'd had to amputate the bitch's leg, and told me that they didn't know if she'd make it, but that having her pups back might give her the will to live. They actually let me into the run, and I got to place the pups at her teats. Mama let out an anxious whine, and the puppies immediately answered, then started to nurse.

"'You probably saved all of them,' the doc told me, and I broke down again. The old man put his hand on my shoulder and I knew, at that moment, that my life had a new purpose."

Grace wiped away a tear, and leaned over to squeeze his hand.

"That old man--Mark, his name was--became a mentor to me. He drove me to Best Friends every Saturday so I could volunteer, and I got to see that mama and her babies recover and get adopted. Within a month, they gave me a job, and I was amazed that I was actually getting paid to take care of the dogs. I saved my money, and got my CPDT after I graduated high school."

"That's an amazing story, Jordan. I have to say that I have a hard time seeing you as a little ruffian, though."

He grinned. "Luckily, I grew out of that phase pretty quick."

"What about your parents?"

"We're pretty OK. It took a while, but they finally realized what jerks they'd been. My mom asked me to come back and live with her after a while, but I was already here, so…"

"I completely understand. It's not an easy place to leave."

"Small towns do have some disadvantages, though." He raised a hand, and Grace turned to see Brady strolling toward them. She instantly felt a blush burn her cheeks.

"Hey, Brady," Grace smiled. "I got the place. I'm buying Jordan dinner to thank him for finding it for me. Will you join us?"

Jordan's expression clearly said he wasn't thrilled with the intrusion, but he swept his arm over the table and smiled.

"I'd love to. I ordered take-out, so I'll just ask them to put it on a plate. It'll be much nicer having dinner with good company." He went to see the hostess, then took the seat next to Grace, draping his arm casually over the back of her chair. "I was hoping you'd make it back to the pool; but when you didn't, I figured you'd gotten it. Congratulations."

Grace saw Jordan's eyes narrow. "Thanks, although it's going to be a monumental task to get the place cleaned up before I have to be out of the Parry. No one's lived there for a couple years, and I don't even want to think about how many spiders have taken up residency."

"No worries," Jordan said. "I'll kick them out." He turned to Brady. "We're going to start cleaning the place up tonight."

"How nice," Brady said.

"The furniture's in decent shape," Jordan continued, "but we're going to need to get a lot of basic stuff to get her started. We're going to hit some shops before we go over there."

Grace felt a bit of a tug-of-war between the two men, and felt bad that she was the cause of it. She turned the conversation to the recent antics of some of the Dogtown residents, in an attempt to keep things light, but an underlying tension remained.

"Excellent as always," Jordan said when they'd finished dinner, "but we've got a lot to do tonight. We really should get started."

"You're right," Grace agreed, turning to Brady. "I'm glad we ran into you."

Jordan pulled out his wallet, and motioned to the server. "Absolutely not," Grace scolded. "I said dinner was on me."

"Actually," Brady said, "it's on me."

"No, it isn't," Grace argued.

"Already taken care of," he smiled. "In honor of you staying."

Grace growled, then pulled him into a hug. "Thank you—you shouldn't have, though."

"Yeah, really…you shouldn't have," Jordan added, dark eyes fixed on Brady.

"My pleasure. Good luck tonight," he said, eyes drifting to Jordan.

∞ ∞ ∞

What was he thinking? Brady sat behind the wheel, watching Jordan's Jeep roll behind him, Grace riding shotgun. They were going to spend the evening scrubbing floors and toilets—why was he jealous? He hated cleaning—a crew descended on his place twice a week in LA—but he knew that if he'd been invited, he'd have jumped at the opportunity.

He was drawn to Grace in a way he'd never experienced before; had what felt like an intense need to get close to her. He'd made an ass of himself in the pool…God, had he really almost kissed her? He had, and for a moment, she was right there with him. Everything in her body language told him that she wanted it, but then suddenly, she was gone. A flash of fear? guilt? sparked in her eyes and she went somewhere else entirely. He knew she was going to pull back a split second before the phone rang.

He closed his eyes for a moment, picturing her in the little pink-striped bikini, her face flushed with heat, lips curved in a shy smile.

Her shoulders hadn't really been pink, and he'd had all kinds of lascivious thoughts as his hands slipped over her body.

They'd had great conversation last night—she had a quick wit, a good sense of humor, and a vulnerability that made him want to protect her, somehow. Plus, when she'd hugged him, he'd felt a snap of what could only be described as electricity sizzle in his gut.

Grace intrigued him, and he wanted to figure her out.

Too fast. His instincts told him that he needed to take it slow, and, as much as he wanted to ignore them, he always trusted his instincts.

Jordan had been irritated by Brady's arrival tonight, and was obviously interested in Grace, himself; but it was no accident that he'd decided to get dinner at Rocking V. Brady figured she'd gotten the place, and that Jordan would insist on celebrating. That didn't worry him, though. There was some sort of magnetic attraction between him and Grace, and he was sure she felt it, too. Something was there, and he looked forward to exploring it a lot further.

Not tonight, though, unfortunately, and he had some work to do for Jared before he got wrapped up with the move. Brady headed back to the Parry, wondering how it was possible that he'd rather be scrubbing floors than adding a fat commission to his portfolio.

∞ ∞ ∞

He couldn't help but watch her. She was on her knees scrubbing the bathroom floor, softly humming to herself and completely lost in the work at hand. He smiled as, for about the hundredth time, she absentmindedly tried to toss back the stray strand of chestnut hair that had escaped the elastic band. When she carelessly chewed on her lower lip, he felt an invisible hand squeeze his heart.

She reached over to dunk the brush in the bucket, and he was treated to a glimpse of creamy skin where her shirt rode up. He wished he'd been the one with her at the pool.

Something happened between her and Brady. The atmosphere changed when he arrived—it was more heated, somehow; more tense. Even in the dim light, it was impossible to miss the flush on her face when he arrived, and the darkening of her eyes when Brady told her he was glad she was staying. Damn it.

It wasn't that he didn't like Brady—he did. Being surrounded by women had its perks, but it also had its drawbacks. Since Brady'd started coming around a few years ago, Jordan had always looked forward to his visits—he helped to balance out the estrogen levels, gave him someone to talk football with; and for a spoiled rich guy, he wasn't afraid to get dirty or too hoity to heft big bags of kibble. Jordan considered him a friend, and was looking forward to Brady being here full time.

But Grace had stars in her eyes for him. There was something when they'd first met—some sort of static charge that they'd all noticed—and that wasn't good. Brady wasn't a bad guy, but he was a self-proclaimed bachelor who liked women—many and often. Jordan had had to be a shoulder to cry on for more than a few women who thought they could tame Brady Cash, and the thought of Grace being one of them soured his stomach.

Brady was a player, and Jordan was a long-hauler. He hoped Grace would see the difference before it was too late.

He jumped when she put her hand on his arm, breaking his revelry.

"You're tired," Grace said, smiling. "I can't even tell you how much I appreciate your help, but you've put in way more than a full day. You should go get some rest."

"Not until I take care of the drain in that bathtub," he said. "Then we should both call it a night."

She tossed her head, and Jordan couldn't help himself. He tucked the wayward strand of hair behind her ear, and looked into her eyes. "Watch out for him, Grace."

Her head tilted in confusion. "What?"

"Mr. Cash with all the flash...don't be fooled. He's a heartbreaker—I know this from experience."

"I don't know why you're..."

"Because I don't want to see you hurt. I care about you."

Grace closed her eyes briefly, then met his gaze. "Look, Jordan. I told you that I still have a lot to figure out before I even think about putting my heart out there. I meant it."

"I know. I also know that life has a way of twisting things in knots. I'm just telling you to be careful."

"I will be. Maybe too careful."

He pulled her in and rested his lips on the crown of her head. "You can never be too careful," he said softly. Then he clapped his hands together and smiled. "Let's get that bathroom done, and then go get some sleep."

∞ ∞ ∞

"Jordan told us you got the cabin," Veronica sang when Grace walked into Jethro on Monday morning. "We're over the moon!"

"I know—I'm so excited to be staying I can hardly stand it."

"We should buy Jordan dinner to thank him," Jeanie said. "He gets hero status today. Plus, I'll take just about any excuse not to cook."

"I tried," Grace said, "but Brady showed up and ended up treating both of us."

The girls shared a look. "Speaking of Brady…the way you two looked at each other the other night…"

Veronica nodded in agreement. "I expected to see sparks flying when he took your hand…there was that much electricity between you."

Grace's eyes widened at Veronica's choice of words, and she blushed as she recalled the buzz.

"Wow," Jeanie said, "Jordan *and* Brady. Toughest choice a girl could ever have to make."

Now that she'd had a chance to get to know Brady, Grace had a whole new appreciation for the high regard in which the women held the two men. They were both amazing, but in completely different ways. Jordan's Paiute heritage gave him the dark hair, rigid jawline, the firm smile. He was rugged, intuitive, down to earth, and had the heart of an angel. Brady was blonde, educated, worldly, apparently wealthy…and a heartbreaker, if Jordan was to be believed. After their conversation the other night, however, especially the way Brady talked about his mother, Grace believed he had a good heart, too, despite Jordan's warnings. He'd certainly won the admiration of a lot of people at Best Friends, which said something about his character. Just that fact that he was giving up a good job to further the mission of the sanctuary spoke volumes. Plus, Jordan had his own outspoken reasons for wanting to keep her from getting close to Brady.

Not that it mattered. She'd struggled with it all night, and barely slept a wink. Her guilt intensified when she couldn't conjure a clear picture of Danny in her mind—Brady's smile kept getting in the way. Finally, she'd pulled out her IPad and scrolled through some shots, amazed at how distant the memories were already becoming.

She couldn't deny that she was drawn to Brady, but getting involved with a man wasn't in the cards for her right now, so her answer was simple.

"Then it's a good thing I won't have to choose," she said. "I'm not even close to being in the right place to..."

"Look around you, sweet girl," Veronica said, sweeping her arms wide. "This is a place of miracles. I wouldn't rule it out."

"Me, either," Jeanie agreed. "So…nothing happened between you two?"

Almost, Grace nearly confessed, remembering the feel of his hands on her waist and the near-kiss. "Nothing like *that*," she said instead. "We took a little walk after the party, and hung out for a while by the pool yesterday…" The girls didn't even try to tamper their smirks, so she added, "That's it. Nothing happened, and nothing's going to."

"Uh huh," Veronica said.

"Seriously. End of story."

"Is there a happy ending, at least?" Grace jumped at the sound of Brady's voice, the damn blush rushing up again.

"How could there not be?" Veronica said. "We're at Best Friends."

"That's for sure," Brady agreed. He turned to Grace. "Did you get your cleaning done last night?"

"Quite a bit, anyway."

"Oh...we'll help with the rest," Jeanie volunteered.

"Definitely," Veronica agreed. "We'll make a night of it."

"I'd appreciate the help," Grace said, "Now that it's mine, I'm anxious to move in. I'll order pizzas...how about five?"

"I'll bring the pizza."

Three heads snapped in Brady's direction. "You're going to help clean?" Lara asked.

"Why not? You're all coming to help me on Saturday, right? I'm happy to do it."

Veronica tossed Jeanie a slanted look.

"Well, Grace," Jeanie said, "looks like your hosting your first party. We'll be there."

"Yay, my first party," Grace smiled, shooting the girls a warning glance.

Chapter 18

Grace was chopping carrots when Brady pulled up fifteen minutes early. Immediately, her stomach rolled, and the flutter set in. It no longer surprised her—like the uncontrollable blushing and the buzz she felt when he was close, it was just part of being around Brady. She skipped out to greet him, enjoying the hum as he wrapped her in a hug.

"Welcome to my humble abode," she smiled, leading him inside and sweeping her arm over the small space. "This is pretty much all of it."

"It's humble, all right," Brady frowned, "but it's got possibilities. A certain...je ne sais quoi."

"Something like that, I guess."

Brady's eyes darted to the corner of the small living room. "Holy crap--is that a wood burning stove?"

"It is, and it's only big enough for slivers. There's a huge pile of wood behind the shed, but most of it won't fit in there. I'm hoping Jordan knows someone I can hire to come out and chop it up."

"Let's have a look," Brady said.

When the girls pulled up, Brady was making an honest attempt at splitting logs. His bare back was shiny with sweat and covered with bits of wood, and the girls smiled appreciatively.

"Wow," Jeanie commented, cutting the engine.

Veronica whistled softly. "Wow indeed."

"Close your eyes," Lara teased. "You're an engaged woman."

"You'd have to be a dead woman not to notice that," Veronica smiled. "I'd say that Grace is a lucky girl."

Lara frowned. "Or a stupid one."

Brady raised the axe and brought it down on a hefty log. A small hunk shot off to his left and the log tumbled off its base, the blade firmly buried. When he heard the slam of the door, Brady turned and waved.

"Looking good, Cash," Jeanie teased. "Although, I think there might be easier ways to make toothpicks." She motioned to the litter of scraps that covered the ground.

"Thanks for the vote of confidence," Brady smirked. "It might surprise you to know that we didn't use wood-burning stoves in LA."

"You just keep working at it; we're happy to watch you learn."

Brady grinned and took another swing, sending the log flipping over twice in the air before landing with a thud a few feet away from the women.

"On second thought...we'll watch from inside," Veronica said, heading for the cabin. "Safer in there."

Brady shook his head, and swung again as the girls hustled dramatically into the house.

"Oh, wow, this place is...well, I guess it has potential," Veronica said, hugging Grace.

"I know. It's in sorry shape, but when I'm done with it, it'll be...quaint."

"Yeah...quaint." Jeanie moved to the window. "I definitely like the view."

"I'm sure Grace wouldn't have any interest in that," Lara said, tossing Grace a look before walking out the door as Jordan's Jeep rumbled into the driveway.

"What's that supposed to mean?" Grace asked.

"Don't you worry your head over it," Veronica said, wrapping an arm around her waist. "She's just jealous that Jordan seems to favor you. She'll get over it."

"Doesn't she know that I'm not a threat? I've told you guys..."

"It has nothing to do with whether you do or don't like Jordan," Jeanie said. "It's the fact that he likes you.

Really…she's a good person, just a little rough around the edges sometimes. Don't take it personally."

"I'll try to keep that in mind." Grace frowned, grabbing a beer for Brady on her way out. Poor guy…he'd been at it for twenty minutes, and there were only a few decent stove-sized pieces scattered among a pathetic pile of bark chunks.

"Hi Jordan," Lara crooned.

"Hey, beautiful ladies…Brady."

Brady grunted and tossed him a nod.

Jordan strolled over and laughed. "What are you trying to do, exactly?"

"What does it look like? She's got a wood burning stove in there."

"It looks like you don't have the right tool for the job. Big surprise there, city boy."
Jordan walked into the shed and dug around, coming out with a wood splitter. "Move over. I'll show you how it's done." He peeled off his shirt and raised the splitter, bringing it down in the center of the log and breaking it neatly into three pieces. "Voila," he grinned. He set the largest of the pieces, split it once more, then picked them up and started a pile on the side of the shed.

"You sure showed me," Brady smiled. "The job's all yours, man." Brady took a seat at the picnic table, and lifted his beer. "I guess I'll just sit here with the ladies, with my tail between my legs."

"I'll get the food," Grace said. "I figured we'd eat out here--there's no way we'll all fit inside."

Lara followed her in, and cornered her in the kitchen, and fixed her with a hard look. "What's your game, Grace?"

Grace set down the pizza box and leaned on the counter. "I've got no game, Lara."

Lara's eyes flashed, and she leaned in. "The hell you don't. You keep telling us that you're not interested in a relationship, but you're stringing Jordan along like a little puppy dog. I mean, he got you this place, and he's busting his ass to make it nice for you, and now you're stringing Brady along too, right in front of him? Who does that?"

Grace put her hand on Lara's arm, but she snapped it back, crossing her arms over her chest and glaring. "Oh, Lara," Grace said softly. "It isn't fair, especially to you. But I'm not stringing anyone along, and I'd never do anything purposely to hurt Jordan. He's a great guy."

"You don't have to tell me. I've known him a lot longer than you have."

Grace sighed. "I told Jordan exactly what I've told you; that I'm working on figuring out my life, and don't have room for any more complications; especially between us girls. I really like it here, and I adore all of you. But I'm still the outsider here, and believe me, the last thing I want to do is be the cause of trouble between any of you."

Lara pushed a breath through clenched teeth. "Why do you do this?"

"Do what?"

"Be so flipping nice. Damn it," she said. "I want to hate you, I really do, but I just can't"

"I'm sorry?" Grace offered, pulling a smile from Lara.

"You should be," she said, her posture softening.

"I like you, Lara, I really do. If I've done anything to hurt you, I really am sorry."

Lara dropped her head. "You haven't, really. Damn it. I can see why they both like you." Grace watched as she struggled with her emotions, then Lara smiled and put out her arms. "Oh, hell, come here," she said as she pulled Grace into a hug. "I'm trying, really." She rested her head on Grace's shoulder and whispered, "My money's on Brady, anyway."

The door opened, and Brady walked in with Veronica on his heels. "Are y'all bringing out that food? I'm itchin' to get this place into shape."

"Of course you are," Lara laughed, giving Grace one more squeeze.

"Actually, can I use your shower real quick?" Brady asked. "I'm kind of a hot mess."

"That pretty well sums it up," Veronica said, winking at Grace behind Brady's back.

"Ah…sure," Grace said, her cheeks warming.

As soon as he closed the door, Veronica whispered, "The least you can do is offer to wash his back."

"Ha ha," Grace said, her stomach aflutter as the water turned on.

By ten o'clock, the place was ready to go, and Grace couldn't wait to move in.

"You guys are the best," she said. "I can't tell you how much I appreciate your help."

"Oh, I almost forgot," Jordan said, "I brought you a housewarming present." He jogged to his Jeep, and came back with a paper bag.

"Aw, that's so sweet," Veronica said, exchanging a knowing look with the girls.

Grace pulled out a beautiful basket, a desert sunset scene with a howling coyote fashioned from tiny, colored beads.

"It's beautiful, Jordan, and yes, very sweet. I absolutely love it. Thank you so much."

"My grandmother made it," he said proudly. "The Paiute are famous for their baskets."

"That makes it even more special." She gave him a hug, and he gathered her in tight.

"I noticed you looked a little shocked when Don mentioned that coyotes might come around, so I thought this one might make you feel a little more secure."

"Coyotes?" Brady said. "I don't like the sound of that."

Jordan shook his head. "They don't bother people." He turned to Grace. "Give a holler when you go out at night, and they'll disappear." Just then, a howl rose up in the distance.

"I'm sure I'll get used to it," Grace said.

Brady shook his head "For now, I'll follow you back."

Grace put the basket on the little side table in the living area, and locked up. "I can't believe I have my own place!" she said. "Thanks again for all your help. And Jordan, for everything. I owe you a couple."

"I won't forget it," he smiled, pulling her into his arms.

∞ ∞ ∞

Brady opened the door to her room and flicked on the light. "Thanks again, Brady...for picking up the pizza, and for all your help."

"No problem," he said, wrapping her up in a hug. "I'm really glad you're staying."

Grace's stomach rolled over as the current between them intensified. His hand stroked her hair, then rested between her shoulder blades as the other settled on the small of her back. He held her for a couple beats longer than a friendly embrace; brushed his lips over the top of her head. "Goodnight, Grace," he whispered hoarsely, then he slipped away into the night.

Her heart was fluttering when she closed the door...she just didn't know what to make of the way she felt around Brady. She thought he'd been about to kiss her in the pool, but hadn't tried again since, so perhaps she'd misinterpreted. Still, so many of his words seemed to have double-meanings, his eyes often burned with an unsettling fire, and there was that crazy buzz between them. She wondered if he felt it, too.

Not that it mattered. She'd been going over and over it in her mind, but couldn't seem to get her head and heart to reach consensus. Being around Brady made her lose all sense of logical reasoning, and although she knew, unequivocally, that she was no longer a married woman, the feelings she had for him flooded her with guilt. Especially now that she was planning to stay in Kanab.

Staying changed everything, and she'd need to work things out in her own head...and in her own time. For the moment, she decided to focus on the excitement of having her own place, so she powered up her computer, and composed her next blog post.

My Dear Friends, she wrote.

When I started on this journey, I had no idea where it would lead me. It wasn't about the destination in the beginning, but now, I think maybe it was. I met a wise man along the way who told me that maybe we can alter fate a bit, make it our own. I'd like to think that's what I'm doing.

I've found the most amazing place, and I believe in my heart that this is where my journey ends. Even if I do go back to where it all started, I know that everything culminated here, at the Best Friends Animal Sanctuary in Kanab, Utah. If you haven't heard of it, you absolutely must look it up, and if you're an animal lover, you simply must plan a visit.

Moments of joy are immeasurable and there are more sparks than I can count here--like every finale of every fireworks show on Earth. One can't help but be healed when surrounded by so much unconditional love...

∞ ∞ ∞

Three-hundred-fifty miles away, a cell phone pinged an incoming email. Dusty Pitts grabbed it off the nightstand, swiped his finger across the screen, and grinned. He jumped out of bed, hastily tossing his possessions into bags. He dumped everything unceremoniously into the back of his car, screamed out of the parking lot, and headed north.

Chapter 19

Grace tied a Best Friends bandana around Baxter's neck and kissed his snout.

"It's your day, Bax," she said, her throat tight. "You're going home, buddy, and you're going to have the most amazing life." He answered with an enthusiastic wag and a sloppy kiss. "Yes, you *should* be happy," she said with a melancholy smile, "and I'm happy for you. I'm really going to miss you, though." With mixed emotions, she passed Baxter's leash over to Jack, who would take him to HQ for his final paperwork, then on to Vegas, where Bax would board a plane for Ohio.

All of the Dogtown crew had gathered to say goodbye, and even Lara had tears in her eyes. They stepped back, though, letting Grace have the last cuddle.

"Love you," she said softly. "Be a good boy, OK?"

Baxter looked back at her and yipped, then hopped into the truck. Grace waved, knowing the dog was oblivious to her trepidation, then fought back tears.

"That was so much harder than I thought it would be," she said to Lara and Jordan. Jordan held out his arms, and she stepped into them, wiping her eyes. "And…I'm an idiot."

"You were Baxter's angel," he said softly. "He'll have a happy life because of you. That makes it all worth it."

"Thank you," she croaked. "I'm being selfish, I know, but I can't help it."

"That's why you're so right for this place," Veronica added, patting her back.

"More like it's right for me," Grace whispered. She sniffed and squared her shoulders. "All right, then…I'm good. Back to work."

Lara clapped her hands together. "Glad to hear it, because it's going to get crazy around here. All our fences are getting replaced, which means we'll be down one or two runs every day. Thoughts?"

"We can send bigger groups to the dog park--switch them out throughout the day," Jordan suggested.

"We can push for more outings...and sleepovers. They're supposed to finish a section every day, but we'll need to be prepared, in case they don't."

"I'll definitely take sleepovers," Grace said. "Especially while I'm getting used to the new place. I'll take Leroy tonight, and Harry tomorrow."

"You're moving in today?"

"I moved in this morning...I'm now an official resident."

The door opened, and Jeanie strolled in. "Sorry I'm late--I got stuck at HQ. Did you say you're moved in already?"

"I am," Grace beamed. "It took all of fifteen minutes-- thanks to you guys."

"Happy to help," Jeanie smiled. "Oh...and Brady wants you to meet him at the clinic."

"Why?" Jordan snapped.

"Don't get your panties in a bunch, Jordan. He's with Doc Mary."

"I guess I'll run over there now," Grace said, butterflies already fluttering. "I'll be back."

"And we need to recruit some volunteers," Jeanie said, stepping out to greet the tour van. "Remember," she said, "encourage outings and sleepovers."

Jordan walked Grace out, an arm slung over her shoulder. "You know you belong here, right?"

"Yeah," Grace grinned. "I think I do." She waved at the van, then went to meet Brady.

∞ ∞ ∞

Dusty sat up in his seat and stared hard out the window. Holy shit--her hair was longer, and she was wearing some Indian-looking dude like an accessory, but it was definitely Grace. Fury rose like a volcano, and he clenched his fists to keep his cool. He'd chased her halfway across the damn country, and pictured himself jumping out of the van and ripping her throat out right there in front of the happy fucking families that couldn't wait to pet the puppies. That, he thought, would be his little moment of joy, and a very memorable experience for all.

He had issues with dogs--warranted ones--but he needed to know if this was where Grace actually worked, so he had no choice. He stayed near the door with his hands on the knob in case he needed to make a quick getaway, pretending to listen to the curly-headed girl's blabber about the wonderful things they did and sizing up the Indian. He was a big dude.

The girl let out a little ankle-biter, who ran from person to person, grabbing treats and licking faces. Fucking disgusting--they had to know the creature was licking its ass just a few minutes ago. When the mutt came at him, he stared it down and lifted his foot slightly off the ground in case he needed to kick it. Luckily, it got the message, and bounced back to a couple of kids, who gladly fed it more treats. He caught a cool stare from the Indian, but then the chick thanked them for coming, and he called the ugly creature back to its place.

"We're going to be replacing the fences in these two octagons," Jeanie said, "so if any of you are willing to help out with that project, it would be much appreciated. We'll also be looking to send these guys on outings and sleepovers during the construction, so I hope to see some of you volunteering with us here in Dogtown. Thanks for visiting, and have a great day!"

This could be complicated, Dusty thought on the ride back. Grace had established herself here, and had people who'd miss her when she disappeared. Judging by the way the Indian looked at her, she might even have a boyfriend. He'd hoped to swoop in once he found her and do the deed, but

he was going to need to do some recon—some planning.
He'd make sure she paid for it.

When he got back to the welcome center, he approached
the lady at the gift shop. "How do I volunteer?" he asked
with a grin, handing over his fake credentials.

∞ ∞ ∞

"Hey," Brady smiled. He waved over a woman in scrubs; the
same woman she'd seen him leave with the first time she saw
him at The Village. "Grace Burton, Doctor Mary Kay. Doc
Mary…Grace."

They exchanged pleasantries, then she led them into her
into her office. Grace and Brady sat on a well-worn couch,
and the vet pulled up a chair.

"Brady's told me a lot about you," Doc Mary said. "He
speaks very highly of you, and I respect his opinion."

"That's very nice, thank you." She looked quizzically at
Brady.

"He tells me you have a way with dogs, and that one of
your charges, Baxter, went off to his forever home today. I
understand you were a big part of his rehabilitation." Mary
caught the look on Grace's face, and flashed a knowing smile.
"I know the bittersweet feeling, when you nurse them back to
health and then they have to go."

"I'm sure you do. It was harder than I thought it would
be, but he's going to be great."

"He will be. You've been volunteering here for several
weeks, right?" Grace nodded. "Brady tells me you've rented a
house, and are planning to stay for a while?"

"Yes…I love it here."

"Then I'm hoping I have some incentive for you to stay.
Brady thinks it's time we put you on the payroll, and I agree.
It would be part-time, for now, maybe thirty hours a week.
We have a dog who really needs a tender touch, and he
thought you'd be just the person. You already have
something in common."

"We do?"

"Your name. She started out as Grace, but as we've gotten to know her, she's become, 'Princess Gracie.' We call her PG, for short. Brady brought her to us a few weeks ago, and she was in real bad shape."

Grace turned to Brady. "You rescued her?"

He nodded. "She was being used as bait in a dogfighting ring."

"Oh my God…how horrible."

"He was also responsible for the arrest of the ringleader," Doc Mary added, "and we've since taken in most of the dogs involved."

"You never mentioned it," Grace said, looking at Brady, who just shrugged. "That's amazing, Brady, really." Grace took his hand and gave it a squeeze. He turned his hand over, laced his fingers through hers, and rested them on his thigh. Grace looked up at him and smiled warmly. How could the things Jordan said about him possibly be true? Doc Mary was practically vouching for his character, and the fact that he hadn't even mentioned that he'd broken up a dogfighting ring and rescued the dogs involved was quite the opposite of flashy.

"We're hoping that you'll accept a job here, and be one of PG's caregivers. She's a sweet thing, but has no dog skills whatsoever. She's in a private run right now, but we want to get her into Dogtown as soon as possible.

"I just know you'd be good for her," Brady added.

He stroked the back of her hand with his thumb, and she felt the familiar roll in her stomach and hum in her bones. It just felt right. It would be good to have some money coming in, which would help to buy some of the supplies for the cottage that she had no intention of passing on to Don, especially with the paltry amount he was charging her for rent. Best of all, she'd be paid for doing work she already loved.

"I'd love to," she smiled. Brady draped an arm over her shoulder, and pulled her in. She leaned against him for a moment, bubbling with excitement and emotion. "This is amazing...thank you so much."

"Thank *you*," Doc Mary smiled. "I'll call HR and let them know you've accepted the position. You can stop over and fill out the paperwork, and start tomorrow, if that's OK with you."

"I could definitely do that."

"Excellent. We'll start in the morning, then." Doc Mary grabbed a clipboard off her desk. "Do you have any specialized training, or anything, that I should add to your file?"

"I'm a licensed RN," Grace said. Brady's head tilted in surprise, but Grace didn't meet his gaze.

"That's very helpful," Doc Mary nodded. "We think we've got a handle on PG's medical issues, but it's always good to have another practiced eye on her. We've got several caregivers and behaviorists working with her, so I'm mainly hoping that you and PG will bond, and that you can work some of your magic with her. Could you work six until noon, so you can have some quiet time with her before her trainer comes in?"

"Perfect." She could still spend her afternoons in Dogtown.

Doc Mary stood and shook her hand. "Welcome to the team, officially," she smiled. "Let's go meet the princess, shall we?"

"I'll catch up with you later," Brady said. "I've got to run over to the office for a bit." He wrapped Grace up in a hug. "I'm really glad you said yes," he whispered.

Mary led her to Angel's Lodge. "I should warn you that she looks pretty...scary. She's had extensive surgery, and it's taken weeks for her to heal. But I just know that there's a beautiful soul in there."

Grace's heart caught in her throat as she approached the entrance to Princess Gracie's run. The girl was beautiful once; Grace could imagine the shine her brindle coat must have once had; but right now everything about her was dull. Her coat lacked luster, and was crisscrossed with scars where the fur had yet to regrow; if it ever would. One of her eyes was bloodshot, hazy, and more jagged scars slashed the dog's face. She had a white belly and white 'socks' at the tips of three feet, and Grace wanted to pet her there, to show her she was loved, but didn't dare. Gracie was cowered in the corner, head down and glaring suspiciously, a stump of tail pressed against her back. PG pushed herself into the corner, putting as much distance as she could between her and her intruders. It was fear, not hostility that Grace felt, as well as an intense sadness and distrust. She unconsciously wiped away a tear.

"Hi, Princess Gracie," Mary said softly, slowly entering her run. "It's OK, sweetie. I've brought someone who wants to meet you. Her name is Grace, too, and she needs someone to look after." She came within a couple feet of the dog, but didn't move to touch her. Once Mary saw the shaking subside, she motioned with her hand, and Grace stepped into the enclosure. What little was left of the dog's ears flattened and she sniffed the air.

"Hi, Princess Gracie; aren't you a beautiful girl?" The dog was broken, and Grace's heart swelled with empathy. She moved to the wall and slid slowly into a sitting position. "If it's OK," she said softly to Doc Mary, "I'd like to stay for a while and get acquainted with her. I'll run over to HR in a bit."

Mary smiled. "More than OK," she said. "Check in with me tomorrow around seven?"

Grace sat on the floor and hummed softly. The dog perked slightly, then she tilted her head before dropping it back down. PG seemed to respond to the music--after a few minutes, she relaxed enough to rest her head on her paws and eye Grace cautiously. Finally, the dog let out a resolved sigh, and her features relaxed.

Grace kept her voice soft and low. "You've had a bad time, baby, I know. But you're going to pull through, I just know it. I see the beauty inside you, and I'm going to help you find it. I promise I won't give up until you find joy in the world again."

When PG finally closed her eyes, Grace stood slowly. The dog started immediately, but remained lying, and didn't shirk away. Grace took it as a good sign as she stepped out gingerly on tingling legs. It was another half hour of paperwork at HR before she was able to return to Jethro, bursting to share the good news.

Grace's heart skipped a beat when she saw Brady on his knees, scratching Leroy's belly. Lara and Jeanie were out front as well, handing Ginger and Willow off to eager volunteers for their daily walks.

Jeanie poked her head into Ginger, summoning Veronica and Jordan, and Grace jumped out of her car smiling, thrilled that all her best friends were together to share in her excitement. She immediately rushed to Brady, and threw her arms around his neck. "Thank you sooo much," she whispered.

He pulled her in tight, lifting her slightly off the ground. When he set her down, one arm draped over her shoulder, Grace got curious stares from the girls, and a sour look from Jordan. Their raised eyebrows told her that they hadn't yet heard the news. "Didn't you tell them?" she asked Brady.

"Of course not," he said, smiling. "It's your news to tell."

The others looked at her expectantly, and she nearly burst. "I got a job!"

"Here?" Veronica asked.

"Of course, here," Grace exclaimed giddily. "Would I be this excited if it wasn't here?"

Jeanie was the first to pull her out of Brady's grasp for a hug of her own. "That's awesome! I'm so happy for you--for us!"

"I knew you'd stay," Lara said, throwing her arms around Grace's neck.

Jordan wrapped her up next. "You seriously made my day."

"It's nothing permanent yet," Grace said. "It's part time, for now, and I'm not working *here*, exactly. I'll be working at Angel's Lodge, with a sweet girl that Brady rescued from a dogfighting ring."

"You were the one who rescued that pittie?" Jordan asked incredulously.

Grace nodded. "Doc Mary said Brady was responsible for shutting down the whole operation." Brady just shrugged as the girls showered him with admiration, then pulled Grace back in. "Her name is Princess Gracie--they call her PG--and she's so sad. She's going to be way tougher than Bax, but I'll do everything I can to make her wag again." She leaned into Brady, and smiled up at him. "I'm still in shock that I'm actually working here. Thank you so much."

"I knew you'd be perfect for her."

"Wait...you got her the job?" Jordan asked.

"One of PG's caregivers had to go take care of her sick mother. I told Doc that Grace was the perfect replacement, and she was on board."

"Now I owe you, too." Grace rose up on tiptoe, and kissed his cheek.

"One more of those, and you're paid in full," Brady teased. Grace smiled, stretching up again. Brady turned, just slightly, and her kiss fell on the corner of his lips. She swooned, but Brady caught her and bent his head to her ear. "Hmmm...I might need a few more, actually," he breathed. Grace felt her cheeks burn, and couldn't formulate a response.

"Yeah, but we'll miss you around here," Lara said.

"That's the best part," Grace replied. "I'm working six-to-twelve, so I can still come here in the afternoons. Plus, Doc Mary wants to get PG over here as soon as possible, so when that happens, maybe I'll be working with you guys even more."

Jeanie clapped her hands. "This calls for a celebration. As far as I'm concerned, Brady's hosting our next party, since we're helping him move in. We'll bring food and cook out after the work's all done." She looked at Brady. "You'll have a grill by then, won't you?"

He nodded. "Absolutely. I'd be glad to have its first steaks be in honor of Grace staying."

"We have so much to celebrate," Veronica said. "Grace's new place, her new job…and, we'll finally have Brady here full time. Life, y'all, is good."

"Yeah, freaking super," Jordan mumbled, leading Leroy back inside.

∞ ∞ ∞

Dusty watched the exchange from behind a bush on the trail across the street. He couldn't hear what they were saying, but he could sure as hell see the way Grace wrapped herself around the tall blonde dude. What the hell--two of them? The Indian was standing right there, and he looked none too happy to see her in the cowboy's arms. Was she doing the Indian behind the other dude's back?

It was good news, obviously, based on the way everyone jumped to hug her. Even Jordan got a squeeze before she jumped back into the blonde's arms like she belonged there.

Damn it, now he was going to have to put up freaking fences. That bitch would pay for every bead of sweat that dripped from his pores.

The group walked into one of the octagons and Dusty headed back to his car. He had some planning to do.

∞ ∞ ∞

"So, you're an RN," Brady said casually as he mixed wet meal into kibble. "I didn't know."

Grace felt the emotional walls go up before she could even fully process the comment, and she stopped, mid-pour, to try and knock them down. She felt the connection between her and Brady break—there was suddenly none of the usual hum and tingle she'd come to expect when he was close. She immediately missed it.

Pasting on a smile, she looked at Brady with what she hoped would be a casual expression, but saw instantly that it was too late. He'd seen her momentary lapse; she saw the confusion in his eyes and the tilt of his head...perhaps he'd even felt the break. "It was in another life," she said, her voice betraying her. "I just thought that if it could help PG..."

"Doc Mary seemed to think so," he said, walking out with Ranger's dinner.

Grace leaned against the table and breathed deeply. She didn't want Brady to think she was hiding something from him, but she also didn't want to open the proverbial can of worms that was her past. She was a different person now, and she liked the way her friends were looking at her...especially Brady. She didn't want their pity.

"Wow, that dog loves to eat," he said lightly when he walked back into the kitchen. He tossed her a wink and a crooked smile, then started on another bowl. "I guess they all do, don't they?"

It was obvious that he was making easy conversation for her benefit, and although she appreciated it tremendously, she didn't want it to be a rift between them.

"Brady...I..."

He came around the table and brushed his lips against the top of her head. "It's OK, Grace," he said softly, "you'll tell me when you're ready. Everyone's got a past."

All remnants of the wall crumbled as she leaned gratefully into his strong arms. "Thank you," she whispered.

"You're welcome," he whispered back. Then he broke the connection and grinned. "So, the landscapers came yesterday," he said. "There's a lot of empty property next to the house, and they're putting in a little secluded garden with a gazebo, and some winding trails. It'll be a great place for dog walking."

And just like that, her Brady buzz was back.

Chapter 20

"I don't know about these fence guys," Jordan said, looking out the window. "Guess which one is an actual fence installer?"

"The guy with the tool belt?" Lara commented, peering over his shoulder.

"Yep. I'm worried that Methuselah is going to keel over from old age, and the dude in the long-sleeves is going to die from heat exhaustion. What was he thinking?"

"The other guy's wearing flip-flops," Jeanie added from the kitchen. "He's going to regret that when the sun starts blazing."

"Smokers, too," Jordan said, wrinkling his nose as the smell drifted in through the window. "I'll remind them to pick up their butts."

"Well, they're going to be here for a while. May as well be friendly." Jeanie and Jordan went out to introduce themselves, cold bottles of water in hand.

"I'm Bill," the guy with the tool belt said, "from Great Gate. I'll be the foreman."

Jordan shook his hand. "I understand your company's donating the materials and labor for the job—it's much appreciated."

Bill smiled. "Glad to do it. I've always had a dog, and I respect what you people do here. Steve here's one of my guys, and Bryce and Kevin are volunteers."

"Nice to meet you…thanks for volunteering," Jeanie said, handing out the bottles. "The heat can really sneak up on you out here, so drink plenty of water. We've got a fridge and a bathroom inside—feel free to use them."

"We'll take advantage of that…thanks. We're planning to start early, take a long lunch, and come back mid-afternoon to finish up. Hopefully, it'll keep us out of the hottest part of the day."

"Sounds good. Let us know if you need anything. We're happy to help."

"Oh," Jordan added, "and if you're going to smoke, could you make sure you pick up your butts?"

"Yeah, sure," Kevin frowned. "No problem."

∞ ∞ ∞

"I see the wrecking crew's been busy," Grace said when she strolled into Jethro after lunch. Huge rolls of green plastic fencing were sitting on flatbeds, and parts of the old fence were piling up in a dumpster.

"They're making good progress, at least," Lara said.

"So, what's on the docket today, other than musical dogs?"

"That about sums it up. It's a serious pain, but the new fences'll be worth it in the end. They said they'd finish the first run today, so we should be able to tuck everyone in for the night."

"That's good news."

"Speaking of good news…Sandi's adoption was approved. Pearl's is looking good, too; we should know in a couple days." Lara said.

Grace smiled. "I'm so happy for both of them. I met Pearl's people at the Quail, and they were great. I really hope this'll be Sandi's last pack, too."

"Well, her new parents know her history, so that's a good sign."

"I'll miss them around here," Grace sighed. Her mind drifted to Baxter and the eight others they'd sent off to forever homes since she'd arrived at Best Friends.

"How's PG?"

"Not much to report, I'm afraid," Grace frowned. "The poor thing trembles like an earthquake every time I go in. She let me get a little closer today, though, so I'll call that progress."

"You'll make it happen," Lara smiled.

"Amy, her behaviorist, wants to start socializing her with other dogs fairly soon. Once PG gains some people skills, I'm thinking about bringing Leroy over to her. I thought if I put him in the run next door, maybe she'd gravitate toward him like all the other dogs do."

"Good idea," Lara agreed. "He'd be my choice, too, for her first canine introduction. That boy is as gentle as they come."

"Where is he now?" Grace asked. His was the run currently missing a fence.

"Last I saw, he was napping in the doghouse with Gummi. They were at the park most of the morning."

Leroy had become one of Grace's favorites--he was a handsome boy with one broken ear and wise amber eyes. He was still on medication for worms, which was why he was still here—once he was eligible for adoption, Grace had no doubt that he'd be snatched up right away. The fact that Gummi Bear was napping with him was a testament to his sweet disposition--the terrier mix was energy personified, but since they'd moved him into Leroy's run, he seemed a lot more settled. Grace hoped Leroy would have the same effect on Princess Gracie.

"They're all going to need baths," Lara added. "Murphy dug a good-sized hole trying to get at a lizard, and they took turns rolling in it. You feeling like some fun with suds?"

"Sure, why not?" Grace smiled. "I'll take Leroy first, so he can get a whiff of PG--I've got a towel with her scent on it. Maybe I'll bring him a special treat; butter him up a bit."

"He likes those bacon and egg snacks. There's a fresh case on the top shelf in the kitchen."

"Then that's what he shall have."

"I need to run over to the clinic and pick up Obie. Veronica just took a group to the park, Jeanie's filling in over at Old Friends, and Jordan's at HQ, so we're kind of shorthanded. Can you hold down for the fort for a bit before you start baths?"

"No problem," Grace nodded. She liked that she was able to take on more responsibility, now that she was an official employee.

Grace dragged the step ladder into the kitchen. A recent donation had stuffed the shelves, and naturally, the box she wanted was buried. She grabbed a pair of scissors, hoping she could get into the case without having to unload the whole shelf.

She had one seam cut when the door opened. "I'm in here," she called.

"Well, hello." Grace jumped when she heard the unfamiliar male voice, and turned sharply toward the sound. Panic shot through her as her foot slipped off the step, and she grabbed for a handhold where there were none to be found. She sent a box crashing to the floor, then tumbled herself; directly into the man's arms. Grace stood to face him, her cheeks red with the jolt of fear and the aftermath of embarrassment.

"You scared me," she wheezed, forcing a smile. "Thanks for catching me."

"Any time." He stuck out his hand, and Grace took it. "I'm Kevin," he grinned sheepishly, eyes narrowed in what must have been amusement.

"Grace." He held her hand a couple beats too long, and made no move to vacate her personal space. Grace had a quick flash of déjà vu, and suddenly felt woozy. "Um...I should..." she bent to pick up the dropped case, and he finally took a step back.

"Here...I've got it," he said, setting the box on the counter.

"Can I help you with something?"

"I'm on the fence crew," he smiled. "Jeanie said we could put some water in the fridge." He motioned toward a case of bottles sitting on the table in the other room.

"Oh, sure…sorry," she said, immediately feeling foolish. "There's a bit of room in there. You can leave whatever doesn't fit in the storeroom." She pulled out a pad of paper and a pen. "You might want to label it."

"Can do." His fingers brushed hers as he took the pad, and Grace felt an unpleasant shiver run up her spine. "It's a nice place." He was still standing too close, but when she tried to take a step back, her leg bumped the stepladder.

"Yes, it is." Grace heard a low growl, and looked over Kevin's shoulder to see Leroy's snout pushed through the bars of the gate, ears pressed against his head. She'd never seen the mild-mannered shepherd show any signs of aggression, and another wave of uneasiness washed over her. Leroy barked, and the man turned, startled.

"I've got to take Leroy for a bath," she said, taking advantage of the distraction to dart around him. When Kevin followed, Leroy curled his lips in a snarl, showing his teeth. Grace put her hand on the latch of his enclosure, and the man tensed.

"Uh…can I get the water in before you let him out? He doesn't seem to like me much."

In response, Leroy growled again. Grace nodded, and Kevin stowed a few bottles, slapping a sticky note on the rest.

"I hope to see you again real soon, Grace."

The instant he was gone, Grace felt as if she could breathe again. She let Leroy out of his enclosure, and he ran to the door, sniffing the handle and letting out a little whine. Then he turned and trotted back to her, tail wagging, all traces of aggression gone.

Grace sank into a chair and ran her fingers through the silky fur beneath his ears. "You were looking after me," she said. "You knew I was uncomfortable…you're such a good boy."

The door banged open, and Grace nearly jumped out of her skin.

"Sorry," Veronica said, balancing a case of canned food on her arms. "The shelves are packed over at Ginger. I figured we could use these for tonight's dinner."

Grace set them in the kitchen, then retrieved Leroy's treat. He'd definitely earned it.

As she worked up a lather on Leroy's coat, she thought about her reaction to Kevin. He'd startled her, then she'd nearly fallen off the ladder, and the adrenaline had her fight-or-flight instinct on high gear...that was all. He'd been in her personal space when she already felt vulnerable; added to her general distrust of strange men, her mind made it into more than it was. She was getting better. At least she hadn't had a full-on panic attack.

Leroy shook, splashing her with soapy water, pushing all thoughts of the encounter out of her mind.

Chapter 21

Grace huddled beneath the desk at the bank as the gunman's eyes scanned the room. There wasn't enough space to hide her pregnant belly--he was going to see her--but thankfully, his gaze passed over.

An explosion burst her ears. She thought maybe she screamed.

The security guard fell, his ruined head spurting a torrent of blood that rushed toward her. His face became Danny's, and he winked at her before the eyes rolled horrifically into their sockets.

She did scream then--wailed his name over and over but she couldn't get to him—couldn't traverse the river of blood.

The toddler in the Superman t-shirt charged the gunman. Grace begged him to lie still, but he spun in circles, his pink tutu a blur, and she saw that it wasn't the toddler at all—it was Zoe. The chair that hid Grace became the bars of a jail cell, imprisoning her. She watched in horror as the barrel of the gun rose, saw the flash of the muzzle, and screamed as Zoe dropped to her knees, wide eyes staring incredulously at the red bloom just above her belly. She looked accusingly at Grace as she collapsed.

Grace's hands flew to her own belly to find it flat and thin, a dark pool of blood spreading to fill the room. The chair was yanked back, the killer's malicious grin aimed at her. "You," he hissed, reaching for her with horrific, mangled claws.

Grace bolted upright in bed, gasping for breath. She hadn't had the nightmare since she'd left Mandy's--why was it suddenly back?

Leroy pressed against her, whining, and she cuddled him into her lap, pushing her face into his neck. "It's OK, LeeLee. I'm sorry I scared you, baby boy. I'm so glad you're here."

She snuggled him for a bit, hoping her heart would settle, but decided that rather than risk falling back into the nightmare, she'd make it an early day.

Grace slipped into PG's run and closed the door. "Hi, Princess Gracie," she murmured. "How's my beautiful girl?"

PG's head dropped, but she didn't cower, and Grace took it as a sign. "I brought breakfast," she smiled, holding up a bowl. Gracie sniffed the air and cocked her head. "Come eat with me." Grace set the bowl in the middle of the room, and sat on the floor next to it.

"You know, Gracie," she said softly, "the world's tried to knock me down a couple times, too. I know how hard it is to have faith when you feel like the universe itself is out to get you. There's something amazing about this place, though, and I really want to share it with you.

"I thought I was feeling pretty good when I got here, but the longer I stay, the better I feel. I think that's why I can't even consider leaving yet...I really feel like this is where I belong. Lots of us here have had tough pasts; but we're all healing in our own ways. We look out for each other."

Pins of numbness pricked at her legs and Grace nearly gave up, but then PG took a couple steps closer, her long tongue flicking.

"I want to introduce you to some new friends, PG; I want you to feel companionship from another dog instead of fear. I just know you're going to love Leroy--everyone does. In fact, I gave him a whiff of you yesterday, and I must say, he seemed very interested. Tomorrow I'll bring you something with his scent on it."

PG started toward her hesitantly, eyes drifting between Grace and the bowl. "That's a good girl," she encouraged as PG dipped her head. Grace held her breath to keep her excitement in check as the pittie took a hesitant first bite, then dug into her meal.

She wanted to jump up and cheer, but she fought the urge, and lavished praise in hushed tones. When PG laid down next to her bowl, close enough to touch, Grace felt positively triumphant.

"I can't wait to pet you, you know," she said, resisting the urge.

PG laid there for nearly half an hour before stretching and returning to her favorite blanket in the corner of the room. Grace stood slowly, unsteady on prickly legs. She limped outside to walk off the numbness, and let out a little cheer of victory.

"Hi, Grace."

Her heart lurched as she turned to face the voice.

"Brady...you scared me."

"Sorry about that...you OK?"

Grace broke into a grin and hobbled to the fence. "I'm awesome--we've just had a bit of a breakthrough, actually."

She adored the smile that split Brady's face as she told him the news. "I knew you'd reach her," he said, pressing his hand to the fence.

Grace touched her hand to his, and smiled back. "Still a long way to go, but it's a good morning."

"Definitely a good morning...I'm glad I stopped." He glanced at his watch and frowned. "Ah, I've got to run though--will I see you at Dogtown later?"

"Yep."

"Then it'll be a good afternoon, too." He flashed her another amazing smile, then Grace enjoyed the view as he walked down the path toward HQ.

Chapter 22

Grace was positively energized by the success she'd had with Princess Gracie over the past few days-- although she still hadn't petted her, PG no longer trembled when Grace arrived, and sat near her after every meal.

It was more than that, though. Gracie worked with a variety of caregivers and behaviorists throughout the day, but was really bonding with Grace. Much as it had been with Payton, Grace felt her own strength building as she guided PG on the path to healing. She'd found a true spark.

She arrived at Ginger full of excited energy, and was disappointed to see everyone huddled over paperwork.

"Who needs a walk?" Grace asked.

Veronica glanced up from her inventory sheet. "We're good, sweetie--we've got six volunteers today."

Grace fidgeted. "I need to do something," she said. "I've been sitting all morning. I've got energy to burn."

Jordan looked up. "Plenty of weeds need pulling." The stubborn desert brush was a constant nuisance, and had gotten a bit out of control during the fence project.

"Good idea," she said, "I'll be next door."

Grace had the weeding tool in hand when she felt the hair on the back of her neck stand up and turned to see Kevin standing in the doorway, watching her. His grin unnerved her...it was like it went too...*deep*, or something, but didn't seem to touch his eyes.

"Hi, Grace," he smiled. "It's a hot one today. I thought I'd restock the fridge."

"Here you go." She handed him the water, and forced a smile.

"You know…I've been meaning to ask you…There's a lot to see around here, but I haven't had much time for sightseeing yet. Any recommendations?"

"Well, the parks, obviously," she said, "but if you want to stay local, you can rent ATV's over at Coral Pink Sand Dunes."

"ATV's sound pretty cool," he said.

Grace relaxed a bit. Maybe the guy was a bit odd, but seeing his eyes sparkle at the mention of an ATV tour tempered her anxiety.

"When's your next day off? Want to go with me, and then get some dinner?"

Grace was taken completely by surprise, and tried to keep her eyes from widening. He wanted to take her out? Although she had no intention of doing so, knowing that he was interested actually made her feel less anxious—maybe he didn't have much experience with women; or was shy; which was why his actions seemed so awkward.

"I'm sorry," Grace said. "I appreciate the offer, but I really can't."

The fire in his eyes burned hotter. "You have a boyfriend, don't you?" he said, his voice flat. "Of course you do."

Grace looked away from his intense gaze. "Sorry, Kevin…I'm flattered, but I really need to get back to work…" She hefted the weeding tool and grabbed a garbage bag, then headed for the door to the first run.

"Sure…no problem," he said, looking disappointed. "If you change your mind, I'm free anytime."

Grace didn't answer. She exited the enclosure that led to the run, and breathed deeply when she stepped into the sunshine. Bill and a couple of new guys tossed her a wave and she raised a hand back, then started clawing at weeds.

Kevin rejoined the crew a few minutes later, handing out bottles of water and lighting a cigarette. Grace focused on the task at hand, trying to ignore the sensation that she was being watched, but after a while, she couldn't help herself. She glanced over at the crew currently stringing the fencing between runs three and four—Kevin's eyes were covered with dark shades, but they definitely seemed to be turned in her direction. She finished tugging up a particularly stubborn weed, added it to the bag she'd only half-filled, and started dragging it toward the octagon. She could find some inside work to do.

"I'll get that." Brady was walking toward her, and Grace felt an immediate sense of relief. Without even thinking, she threw her arms around him. She heard his sharp inhale as he pulled her close; the familiar current calming her instantly.

"Thank you again for getting me this job...I just love it," she said. It was a lame excuse for the unexpected hug, but it was all she had at the moment.

"I'm glad," he said, pulling her closer. Then he bent his head and whispered, "Mostly for selfish reasons, though." He let her go and winked before easily hefting the bag and walking back inside, leaving her wondering what his selfish reasons might be.

He dropped the bag into a can and turned to her. "I came to say good-bye. I'm heading out to finish up my packing."

"You'll be back on Saturday, right?"

"You gonna miss me, Grace?" He grinned, but his eyes weren't laughing.

Grace felt the slow burn redden her cheeks. Why did he have that effect on her? "Of course," she said as casually as she could muster. "I'm going to have to heft my own weed bags until you get back."

Brady chuckled. "You can save them for me. You're still coming over, right?"

"That's the plan."

"I'm already looking forward to it." He tucked a wayward strand of hair behind her ear and gazed into her eyes. "I'll miss you, too."

Grace felt her heart skip, and a delicious bloom spread in her middle. Brady took her hand, lacing his fingers through hers. "Come on...everyone's over at Ginger."

"I'm just saying that he's kind of creeping me out," Veronica was saying as Grace and Brady entered.

"Who's creeping you out?" Grace asked.

"Bill asked Lara out," Jordan said bitterly.

"That's not even the issue," Lara argued.

"Good heavens," Veronica agreed. "Guys ask her out all the time, Jordan--it's hardly a revelation. Kevin's the issue. He hangs around inside more than the other guys, probably because he's dressed more for Alaska than Utah. He's always a bit off, but yesterday he was asking a lot of questions about Grace."

Brady tilted his head. "What kinds of questions?" he demanded.

"He tried to toss them casually into conversation, but he was obviously trying to get some scoop," she said to Grace. "He asked why you were only here in the afternoons, if you lived in town, if you had any favorite hangouts...if you were dating anybody."

Jordan's hands balled into fists. "That's not cool with me...not one bit."

"Me either," Brady said firmly. "You didn't answer any of them, did you?"

Veronica looked stricken. "Of course not!"

"I think Kevin and I need to have a little chat," Brady said, lips pressed in a thin line.

"I'll go with you," Jordan said.

Grace blocked the doorway. "Wait a second," she said, laughing. "You can't go out there and gang up on some volunteers because they want to take us out. Do you realize how ridiculous that sounds?"

"Watch me," Jordan said. "They've only known you a few days--I can't believe they would..."

"Whoa!" Lara glared, folding her arms across her chest. "Really? You guys sure you want to go there?"

Simultaneously, Brady's and Jordan's eyes darted to Grace, then to the floor. Grace felt the blush rise in her cheeks again, and tried to tramp down her smile. Technically, they'd both asked her out after knowing her an even shorter time.

"Yeah, that's what I thought," Lara replied, moving her hands to her hips.

Jeanie shook her head. "We only mentioned it hoping you'd hang around a bit more; make your presence felt."

"Oh, it'll be felt all right," Jordan said, puffing out his chest.

Brady turned to Grace. "Has this Kevin said anything to you?"

"Yeah," she admitted. "He actually asked me out about an hour ago. He's definitely awkward, but maybe he just doesn't know how to flirt. You guys could give him some lessons." She'd hoped the little joke would lighten the mood, but the faces of both men seemed to darken, instead.

Brady shoved his fingers through his hair. "OK, I agree that both of us going out there is overkill," he said, "but I haven't met them yet, and I've got a knack for reading people. Let me introduce myself, and make my presence felt, too."

"Except you're not going to be here, are you Brady?" Jordan said.

"Shit." He looked at Grace. "Maybe you should come with me; give him some time to cool off."

Everyone's eyebrows raised immediately--except for Jordan's, whose brows nearly touched in the center as a frown narrowed his eyes to slits. "That's crazy. Grace just started her job--she can't just take off." he scowled.

"We'll see after I talk to him." Brady strode out of the octagon, the rest of the crew watching out the window as he made his way over to the group.

"I can take care of my girls without his help," Jordan murmured, shoving fisted hands in his pockets.

Veronica smirked, and turned toward the girls. "You know what? I think Jordan's jealous."

He scowled. "Jealous of what? The fence guys?"

"Among other things," Jeanie said.

"Like we need to be reminded of that," Lara hissed.

Jordan grumbled something unintelligible and grabbed a bottle of water off the table, yanking off the cap and taking a swig.

"Well?" Veronica asked when Brady returned.

He shook his head. "Bill seems cool, but I definitely get a weird vibe from Kevin," he said, "Something about him just isn't genuine." He looked at Grace. "Maybe you should come with me."

Grace put her hands on her hips. "This is ridiculous," she said. "You went out there with the assumption that something was wrong--of course you were going to find it."

Veronica spoke up. "Maybe you're getting a bad vibe because he's not here by choice. Community service, maybe?" She looked at Jordan. "Could you find out?"

"Absolutely," Jordan said, "and if he is, he's off the crew." He walked over to Grace, and put his hands on her shoulders. "I could stay with you, Grace. I'll make sure you're…"

"Absolutely not," Brady interrupted, glaring down his one inch height advantage.

"Knock it off," Grace commanded. "I'm going to have the last word on this, period. I'm not going anywhere, and I don't need a babysitter. I have dogs with me every night, and I like my independence. I traveled across the whole damn country by myself before I came here…I think I can handle a volunteer with a crush."

Everyone in the room stopped arguing and stared at her. She hadn't divulged that information before, and everyone, especially the men, looked surprised.

"I'll take Leroy," she said, before they could ask questions. "He's very protective."

The men struggled with their own thoughts and sized each other up. The girls waited, watching the testosterone-fueled posturing. Finally, Brady's shoulders relaxed. "Okay…" he conceded. "You're right, Grace…but I'm going to worry while I'm gone."

"I'll take care of her," Jordan said. "I've been doing it for a long time...long before you came, Cash."

Brady nodded tersely, and Grace could see the struggle in his next words. "I trust that you will." To Grace, he said, "Will you call me, just to let me know things are OK?"

Grace sighed. "Fine..." She couldn't be upset with them--it was good to have people so concerned about her well-being. "...but I still think it's over the top."

"We're always going to go over the top for you Grace," Jeanie said. "You're one of us now, so you'd better get used to it."

Grace smiled. It would be pretty amazing having these people in her life on a permanent basis.

"I really hate to leave on this note," Brady groaned, "but I have a plane to catch. Walk me out, Grace?"

As soon as the door closed, Brady wrapped his arm around Grace's shoulders. She could feel a fierce protectiveness in the intense current between them, which would also be easy to get used to.

When they got to his car, he held her arms and looked at her hard. "Are you sure you don't want to come with me?"

Adding the word, 'want' made it a whole different question—with so little distance between them, Grace could feel his gravitational pull sucking her in. It would be so easy to fall into his eyes and just stay there, and something inside her yearned to jump into his car, and drive off into the sunset.

But her thoughts went to PG, her friends, and the job she loved. She shook her head. "I appreciate your concern, Brady, but I can't leave right now."

He sighed, and pulled her into a hug. "Just be careful, OK? Regardless of whether you can take care of yourself, I'll be worrying. Promise you'll call me?"

"I promise," she smiled, resting her head on his chest.

"I'll see you soon." He pressed his lips to the top of her head, then let her go and drove away.

Chapter 23

Damn it, he'd gone too far, Dusty thought as he cruised through the parking lot of yet another apartment complex. He'd gotten so excited to be close to Grace that he lost his head. It couldn't happen again.

Asking her out was a huge mistake, but when he caught her alone, excited and bursting with happy energy, he couldn't help himself. He'd had a fleeting fantasy of taking her to dinner and maybe even to bed, then telling her his story before slicing her to pieces.

Brady was smooth, but obviously, the dude didn't come out for a casual chat. Dusty had played it cool, smiling and nodding in all the right places; letting Brady feel as if he had the upper hand. God, he hoped Brady'd be the one to find her body.

Dusty checked his map, and cursed. He'd been through every apartment complex in town, twice, but couldn't find her car. If she was staying with one of her boyfriends, it'd make it that much harder to find her. Actually, he really wouldn't mind if he had to take one of them out, too—especially the smug cowboy.

He rolled down the window, but refused to turn on the heat. He sweated his ass off all day working on the damn fences, and the cool nights were a welcome relief.

The fence crew was a mixed bag, really. It got him close to her, but since they started later in the afternoons, they were still working when Grace left, so he couldn't follow her home. Maybe he needed to think about quitting it all together--let her think he'd gone so he could stalk her easier.

Soon, he thought. For now, he was having too much fun watching her. She was uncomfortable around him, and although she'd narrowed her eyes when he encountered her in the kitchen, he was sure she hadn't recognized him. It was a dangerous game, but he'd waited so long for this that he decided he'd have a bit more fun with his little mouse before striking the fatal blow.

∞ ∞ ∞

Grace was refilling her third pool, enjoying the bit of mist that wafted over her from a small leak at the top of the sprayer. It was another hot day, so between the splashing of dogs and evaporation, the water didn't last long. Most were lounging indoors, but Grace had already seen Murphy poke his snout through the doggie door to check her progress, and knew that as soon as she was through, the Lab would make a dash for the fresh, cool water.

The fence crew was enclosing Jethro's last run, and Grace looked forward to having the octagon back to full operation.

Jordan had been driving them crazy all day, dashing between the buildings to make sure he was always at someone's side. Now, he rushed out the door from Murphy's enclosure and strolled purposefully toward her. "Why are you out here by yourself?" he hissed under his breath, casting a sideways glance at the crew.

Grace shook her head. "There's a fence between us, Jordan, and they haven't been staring. They're busy, I'm busy, and I'm sure you can find something more important to do than hovering over us all day."

"I'm not taking any chances," he said. "I know a way to shut him down."

"Really," she said. "What's that?"

In a flash, Jordan had his hands on her shoulders. Before she could protest, he bent both elbows and rushed in, pressing his lips to hers.

It took her brain a moment to process what was happening, but once she did, she immediately put her hands on his chest to push him away. He was prepared, though, and her shove barely shifted his position. "What are you doing?" she snarled against his lips.

He smiled. "If he sees us kissing, he'll think you're taken, and back off."

She crossed her arms in a 'v' over Jordan's chest and turned her head as he came in for another kiss. "Knock it off, Jordan," she said, ducking under his arm. She grabbed the nozzle, and aimed it at his chest. From the corner of her eye, she caught a glimpse of Kevin. He was definitely watching now.

Jordan put his hands up in surrender, then let his gaze wander to the crew. "I've made my point," he grinned, "and I'll finish this." He grabbed the hose, folding a kink it before she could pull the trigger. "Why don't you head to the park and tell the volunteers they can bring their dogs back? It's too hot for them to be out for long today."

"Whatever." It wasn't worth arguing over, especially since Jordan probably believed he was being chivalrous. She headed for the dog park, wondering how she would have reacted if Brady had come up with the same idea Jordan had. Fire rose to her cheeks just thinking about it, and it dawned on her…the reason that she couldn't help but blush every time she was close to Brady. Fire started with a spark.

Was she carrying a torch for him? There was no denying that she was attracted, but she'd been steadfast in her insistence that she wasn't ready to open her heart to anyone. When she started this journey, she hadn't even considered being with someone who wasn't Danny. And now?

Tomorrow, Brady would be here to stay, and she couldn't deny that she missed him. They'd gather at his house tomorrow after work to start moving him in, and she felt a hot flash of guilt at how much she was looking forward to seeing him. She stopped and sat on a log, pulled out her phone and tapped Brady's number.

∞ ∞ ∞

He really liked her. As Brady sealed the boxes that contained the last of his worldly possessions, he thought of Grace. Her wavy brown hair; incredibly captivating eyes; her long, sexy limbs; slightly upturned nose…her shy smile. The constant blush in her cheeks that he hoped was because of him.

There was little doubt that in his absence, Jordan would try to make his move, especially after his valiant offer to stay with her, but he was just as sure that there was something between him Grace that she didn't have with Jordan.

There'd been a little running competition between the two men from the start—just a guy thing, really, meaning it was mainly focused on women.

This, however, wasn't a game. He wasn't competing with Jordan for Grace's affections--he was trying to figure out if he wanted her to be part of his life. And so far, all signs pointed to yes.

Living in LA made him swear off relationships--he'd seen way more marriages crumble than he'd seen make it; and half of those were shams, anyway. Too many gold diggers were eager to get their claws into him and his money, so it was in his best interest not to get too involved. In his old life, he swore he'd be single until the end.

Now, everything was about to change. He was embarking on a path he hadn't even imagined all those years ago; and was starting to think that he'd like someone to share it with him.

Brady took one last nostalgic walk through his apartment, and knew for certain that he wouldn't miss it. The past few days in Kanab had shown him that he was finished with this life, done chasing the almighty dollar. He had enough to last, and being at Best Friends was proof that there was much more to life than money.

As promised, he'd keep a few clients and do some consulting—for a while, anyway—but he guessed that his connections to LA wouldn't last too long.

His phone rang, and he smiled when Grace's picture popped up. He wondered if she knew he was thinking about her. It wouldn't surprise him in the least.

"How's it going over there?" he asked.

"It's just fine—as I knew it would be. Except for Jordan peacocking all over the place. He's so busy making sure all of us are supervised that he's not getting anything else done."

Brady chuckled. "No more problems from the fence guys?"

"Well, Kevin did ask me to run away with him to Hawaii. I'm considering the proposal."

He grinned. She had a good sense of humor...one of many things he liked about her. "I think you should hold out for a better offer," he teased back. "I mean, Hawaii's great, but I'd put Bora Bora on the table, at least." In the short silence that followed, Brady could almost sense her balance shifting—he liked that he was able to keep her guessing.

"I'll keep that in the back of my mind," she said, "I've always wanted to stay in one of those little huts over the water."

"You'd have to promise to bring the pink bikini." Brady could almost feel the blush in her cheeks, and suddenly found himself considering a trip to Tahiti.

It was a moment before she spoke. "Yeah, sure. Ha-ha. By the way, Jordan did find out that Kevin's not here for Community Service. His record's squeaky clean."

"I'm glad to hear that." Although it didn't make him feel much better. He'd definitely had the feeling that the guy was hiding something, and his instincts rarely failed him. As much as he hated to admit it, he was glad that Jordan was there in his absence, watching over the girls.

Grace changed the subject. "Any second thoughts, now that you're back in LA?"

"Not a one. I've got big plans for Kanab." Maybe Grace didn't know she was part of them, yet, but he'd make sure she did, soon. He heard a deep bark, then voices in the background.

"Oh, I've got to go," she said. "Bonnie and Enzo are coming back from the park. I just wanted to…well, I promised I'd call, so…"

"I'm glad you did. I look forward to seeing you tomorrow, Grace."

"We'll be there around seven-thirty. I can't wait to see your place. I'll bet it's a little nicer than mine."

He stood there for a second after she ended the call, picturing her in his mind. Faded jeans, dusty t-shirt, sensible shoes…he liked the image he conjured up, and here, in the shadow of his old life, was grateful that he'd made the choice to follow his heart.

His phone chirped in his hand, startling him, and he checked the text. The moving truck was out front. He sealed the last box, and went out to greet them.

∞ ∞ ∞

Clouds rolled overhead on Saturday morning, but Grace doubted it would rain. She let herself slowly into PG's octagon, as always, with a few biscuits tucked in her pocket. Grace sat, placing one in her open palm.

"Today's the day, Gracie. You're going to take a biscuit from me today, I can tell. You know why? Because today I'm going to tell you about my family. They're watching over us from heaven, and Payton's going to find a way to let you know that I'm your friend."

She stretched out her legs, and settled in. "My story starts almost seven years ago, and I'm still working on the ending. This is a place of miracles, though, and I'm feeling more and more confident that there could be a happily-ever-after—for both of us." PG lifted her ears, and turned toward Grace. At least she was listening.

"I know suffering, too, PG. I was expecting a baby--I could feel her growing inside me, and I was so happy. We were going to name her Briana, and I just knew she was going to be a doctor. I went to the bank to open a college fund for her, and while I was there, someone came to rob it. He shot two people…one of them was just a baby."

She closed her eyes and took some cleansing breaths. Maybe the dream came back because she was supposed to talk about it--dogs were intuitive, and if she sent out the right vibes, perhaps PG would understand. Grace opened her eyes, and swore that PG was just a little closer.

"I was hiding under a desk, and I was the only one who could notify the police. I didn't want to take the chance, but when I looked into that mother's eyes, Briana kicked me, and I knew I had to try. I hit the silent alarm button, but my fat belly bumped the chair, and the killer caught me. He dragged me over the desk and kicked me, right where Briana was growing. I felt my baby die, PG. I felt the tear in my middle and knew, even before the blood started spilling out of me, that my baby was gone."

She heard the softest whine, and opened her eyes. PG was definitely closer.

"It completely destroyed me, Gracie. I fell into such a deep pit of depression that I couldn't even see the light anymore. My whole world crumbled, and I couldn't even imagine smiling again, much less being happy.

"Danny, my husband, brought Payton home one day, because he knew, better than I did, that the loveable mutt was exactly what I needed to smile again. I didn't want him, at first. I resisted that puppy in every way I could, but he wouldn't let me ignore him. Payton wouldn't give up on me-- and I'm not going to give up on you, either.

"Payton was my spark, PG. He taught me that it was OK to love life again, and I'm going to show you that, too, sweetheart."

Gracie scooted a couple more inches.

"When we went to court, I stood up and pointed out that killer. I wanted him to rot in jail for what he'd done. They sentenced him to life in prison, but a few years later, another inmate killed him."

Another inch, and another. Grace didn't make direct eye contact; just kept talking, hoping the dog would feel her raw emotion, even if she didn't understand the words.

"I got better, finally, and a year later, I had another baby. Zoe was the most beautiful thing in the world, and Payton was her biggest fan. We were such a happy family.

"I started helping other people who'd lost someone they loved, and I got even stronger. Then, I started writing a book to help people heal. It was about sparks, like Payton, and finding joy in the world again. It took a long time, but I finally believed that I would have a beautiful life."

Princess Gracie crept another inch, and Grace sucked in a breath.

"Nine months ago, I left them to go speak at a conference. While I was gone, someone broke into my house and murdered them, Gracie. Payton tried to save them—he ripped through the screen door and attacked the killer, but then, he got Payton, too. I lost my whole family that night, and fell back into the dark place. It was so hard to break out, but I finally realized that I needed to live again, and set out to find myself."

She was almost close enough to touch now, and Grace saw her nostrils flare as she inhaled the scent of dog biscuit.

"When I first got here, I figured I'd spend a few days, then go on my way, feeling like I'd done something good--but there's something so special about this place, Gracie-- something that makes me want to stay forever."

Grace felt warm breath on her hand.

"I came here, Gracie, because I was meant to—I really believe that. You're my new spark, PG, and I think maybe Brady is, too. He's the one who rescued you, you know, and he's such a great guy."

She felt the wet tongue on her palm as the biscuit was gently taken. "Good girl," she said softly, feeling triumphant. "Very good girl."

Grace tilted her hand slowly, and scratched PG gently behind her ear. When the dog pressed her head into Grace's hand, she scratched harder, then moved to gently rub the top of her head. Her tail moved slightly, more of a jerk than a wag, but it sent Grace's heart soaring to see it.

"There you go, sweetheart," she said as the dog rested her snout on Grace's leg. "Such a sweet, beautiful girl."

They sat for nearly an hour, Grace ignoring the tingle in her foot as her leg fell asleep under PG's head. Grace gently stroked the pittie's head and back, humming softly.

She shared more stories about her family, feeling joy for the happiness they'd brought to her life, and the intense satisfaction of feeling the dog relax under her touch. Suddenly, PG startled and got up, moving back to her usual corner, and Grace heard the door open. Sue, one of Gracie's behaviorists, peeked in.

"How's she doing today?"

"Excellent," Grace smiled, hobbling to the door as she tried to get the blood flowing back into her legs. "Absolutely excellent." She quickly told Sue about PG's progress, then rushed out the door…she couldn't wait to tell Brady.

Chapter 24

Brady's house was spectacular. A wrap-around deck circled the second floor, a large, cozy front porch graced the front, and enormous windows reflected the sun, just beginning its dip toward the jagged peaks of the vermillion cliffs.

The garage was full of boxes, reminding Grace of the storage unit in Illinois. Unpacking was meant to be the start of a new life, she thought, making a mental note to have Mandy give everything in it to charity. She trusted that her sister had kept all the important things, and she still had The One Box.

Her breath caught when Brady stepped out the front door, looking awfully relaxed for someone who'd just turned his whole life upside-down. He also looked really good, and Grace realized she'd missed him even more than she thought she had. She ran to tell him the good news, stumbled in the loose sand, and fell right into his arms.

"Well, that's definitely the best greeting I've had all day," he smiled, catching her in a hug.

"Gracie took treats from me today, put her head in my lap and let me pet her," she said breathlessly.

Brady froze for a moment while the information sunk in, then broke into a grin. "Seriously?" he said, scooping her up and spinning her in a circle. "That's awesome! I knew you'd do it."

Grace rested there a minute, inhaling his intoxicating scent and enjoying the hum in her bones. She heard the familiar rattle of Jordan's Jeep pulling in, and stepped back to wave.

"I had to tell you first," she said to Brady. "It almost killed me not to tell anyone today…God, I was so excited…"

"What's so exciting?"

The girls stepped onto the front porch, and waved to Jordan. She waited until he was in earshot before giving the news again.

"Haven't you figured out yet that y'all belong here?" Veronica asked.

"I do know it." Grace grinned, accepting hugs and congratulatory pats. Then, she swept her eyes over the house. "Wow...this is a masterpiece, Brady. I love the windows, and the deck--I can't wait to see the rest of it."

"It's amazing," Jeanie gushed, "I want to move in immediately."

Brady took Grace's hand. "Come on in...I'll give you the five cent tour."

Jordan started to follow, and Brady turned.

"This one's a *private* tour," he said with a wink. "Why don't you bring in a few boxes, and I'll take you next?"

Jordan fumed as he watched them walk in--was this the way he wanted to play it? There'd always been a bit of competition between him and Brady, but hell, they were friends. The competitiveness was harmless, really...a way to keep the testosterone levels balanced in a world filled mainly with women.

He'd assumed that once Brady was here to stay, they'd hang out even more, but now that Grace was part of the equation, he wasn't so sure. He'd watched Brady break more than a few hearts in his day, and he couldn't let Grace's be one of them.

It was different with Grace, but Brady was still playing like it was a game. He even had the audacity to wink over his shoulder as he led her into the house like he was claiming a victory in this round. Score one for The Golden Boy.

Ah, hell, he thought guiltily, *I've been no better.* He'd been mentally keeping score since Brady arrived, he realized, and the way he saw it, they were just about even. Grace met him at a vulnerable moment, when he was mourning Buster, which cast him in a good light. He'd mentioned Payton at the blessing, and had shown Brady up by chopping her wood and getting her the cabin. Brady earned props for rescuing Gracie, got Grace the job that would keep her here, showed *him* up by buying dinner, and probably got a huge tick in his column for the sheer amount of money he must have to afford this freaking mansion.

Yeah, just about even, except for the fact that there was some sort of chemistry between Grace and Brady that was impossible to ignore. She still had stars in her eyes for him, despite his warnings, and it killed Jordan that she was likely to get hurt. It wasn't a game for him when it came to Grace's happiness.

Players never win, and Brady was a player. Jordan was in it to win Grace's heart, and that had to count for something.

He jumped when Veronica grabbed his arm and gave his bicep a squeeze. "Come on, Superman; I'm dying to start organizing the kitchen, and those boxes are heavy."

∞ ∞ ∞

The place was stunning. The rooms were large and airy, with high ceilings and fabulous views from every window. Warm desert colors brought the outside in, and the decor gave the house a comfortable, lived-in feel. There was a huge fireplace, and the kitchen was a cook's dream, with lots of counter space and an oval ring to hang pots over the generous island.

"I can't believe this place, Brady, it's absolutely gorgeous," Grace said. Jordan had called him, "Mr. Cash with all the flash," but she'd had no idea that he had the kind of wealth to afford a place like this.

Brady shrugged. "I like it, even more than I thought I would. Designing houses is definitely not my thing, and I was a little skeptical about some of the plans. It really came together, though."

"That's for sure."

He threaded his fingers through hers, and led her up the stairs. "This is going to be my favorite room, I think."

The master bedroom was enormous, with a half-wall separating the sleeping area from a comfortable sitting/office space. The gigantic bed faced a wall of windows, with a sliding glass door that led to a large deck overlooking the cliffs. "Watch my first sunset with me, Grace," he said, stepping outside as the orange bowl exploded the sky before slowly sinking behind the mountains in the distance.

"So beautiful," she whispered, watching the last of the arch disappear, giving way to the moon and stars. "You get to see this every night."

"Oh, Grace," he said softly, and when she turned to him, more than remnant embers of the sunset blazed in his eyes.

She knew it was coming, knew that he would kiss her and that she should step away, right now, before his perfectly sculpted lips got any closer to hers. Yet she stood mesmerized as he put his hands on her shoulders, slowly running them down her arms while turning her to him; looked up at him helplessly as he leaned her against the rail, the first stars a halo around his head. She nodded wordlessly as he brought his hands to her face, brushing his fingers softly along her cheeks before cupping her chin in his palms. She gathered enough reason to put her hands on his chest, to gently push him away, but instead, found herself sliding them up to wrap behind his neck.

"So beautiful," he repeated, brushing his lips against hers, light as air. Her stomach rolled in soft waves with the delicious sensation of a first kiss, all thoughts of resistance gone as she sank into his arms. One hand slid behind her neck, the other, down her back to her waist, and he pulled her closer, molding her soft curves to his rigid frame. He deepened the kiss and electricity shot through her, fingers and toes tingling at the sudden rush of blood from her thumping heart. Her lips parted, and the soft crash of his tongue sweeping in, finding hers, nearly stole her breath.

Heat bloomed, rushing from her center to sing at every nerve ending, his touch like fire as his fingers grazed her throat.

She fell in, completely lost in the moment--the breathlessness and the urgency—and she slid one hand down his sculpted chest then around his waist, pressing closer, her breath ragged and her thoughts clouded. It was like a rebirth-- a reawakening--and she wanted this more than she could remember wanting anything.

A sudden crash, an explosion of breaking glass, caused them both to jump, and the moment shattered. Their heads turned toward the sound, and a curse pierced the air.

"Brady? I think y'all need to come down here," Veronica hollered.

"Forget it," Brady said, pulling her back into his arms and stroking her hair. He'd nearly reached her lips again when they heard Jeanie heading up the stairs, calling his name. "Damn it," he muttered, releasing her as Jeanie stepped into the room.

Grace saw the realization dawn on Jeanie's face, watched her cheeks redden with embarrassment. "Oh, my God," she breathed. "I'm really sorry to interrupt, but there's been an accident."

Brady growled and bounded down the stairs, but Jeanie grabbed Grace's arm before she could follow.

"You kissed Brady," she said, her eyes wide.

There was no denying it, she could see by Jeanie's look that it was written all over her face. "It was nothing," she said gruffly.

She took Grace's wrists and lifted them, studying her hands. "Nothing, my ass--you're shaking. It was that good?"

Grace could still feel the kiss on her lips, could still taste him on her tongue. Her whole body was singing, and she could barely breathe. It was that good.

It was also a mistake. She pulled her hands back, unnerved by the whole thing. She'd let herself get swept up in the moment, in the sunset, in the sexy package that was Brady Cash. It wouldn't happen again.

"It was...nothing," she said breathlessly.

Jeanie put her hands on her hips, tilted her head. "'Nothing' doesn't put that kind of look on your face."

Grace was flustered. "Please, don't say anything to anyone," she said. "Promise me."

"I won't have to," Jeanie said. "It's pretty obvious."

"That bad?"

Jeanie shook her head. "That *good.*"

"Oh, God. I'll be down in a minute…I have to…" she tipped her head toward the bathroom, and Jeanie nodded before heading down the stairs.

She stared at her image in the mirror. Her cheeks were flushed crimson, her eyes were hooded, and her lips definitely looked as if they'd been kissed. Grace splashed some cold water on her face and neck, pinched the inside of her arm, and took some deep, calming breaths. If it were up to her, she'd hide out here until they all left, but then she realized that would leave her alone with Brady, and she couldn't let that happen, either. She plastered what she hoped would be a genuine look of concern on her face, and went to join the group.

As soon as she walked into the kitchen, all eyes stared and conversation stopped. The look on Jordan's face and the shake of his head flooded her with guilt, and she grabbed a bottle of water off the counter to give herself something to do with her hands.

"What happened?" she asked, as casually as she could. A box of glasses was spilled on the floor, broken shards in a three-foot radius around it.

"Sorry," Jordan said, his eyes fixed on Grace. "I guess I lost my grip."

"Sure you did," Brady said, eyes narrowed.

"I'll buy you a new set," Jordan said with a shrug.

"No need. You have to expect things like this in a move. Unfortunately, I'm not sure which box the broom would be in. It's in the garage somewhere."

"I'll find it," Grace said immediately, hoping the night air would cool the burn on her cheeks.

"We'll help you," Veronica offered, and the three girls followed her out.

Jeanie held up a hand, stopping Lara and Veronica on the front stoop, then gently took Grace's arm and led her to the garage.

∞ ∞ ∞

"I saw her first," Jordan said, his voice low.

"I'm sorry," Brady smiled, "did you just call "dibs" on Grace? That's not the way it works, Jordan…not since fourth grade, anyway."

"Damn it, Brady, that's not what I meant."

"You mean you didn't just ask me to back off so you can have her?"

"I'm telling you to back off so she doesn't get hurt."

"Wait, are you asking me, or telling me?" He paused, looking hard into Jordan's eyes. "You know what, it doesn't even matter, because either way, you have no right."

"I'm looking out for her best interests. You don't exactly have a great track record when it comes to women."

"My track record has nothing to do with Grace."

"You're a heartbreaker, Cash, and always have been. Love 'em and leave 'em, and move on to the next one. Grace deserves better than that."

"On that, we agree…she deserves the best. It'll be up to her to decide what that is."

Brady turned, but Jordan caught his arm. "I kissed her, too."

Brady leaned against the counter, raised his eyebrows. "Did you now? And tell me, did she kiss you back?"

The slight lowering of Jordan's eyes gave him the answer.

"Look, Jordan…I like you. You're a good guy; maybe better than me in some ways. But understand that I'm starting a new life here, not just a new chapter, and right now, I'm thinking I want Grace to be part of it. Neither of us knows her well enough to make the call for her." He paused. "I'll tell you this, though...she definitely kissed me back."

Jordan balled his hand into a fist, and pressed his lips together. "This isn't a fucking game, Brady."

"It sure as hell isn't," he agreed. They stared each other down for a moment, then Brady relaxed his stance. "Listen. There are way too few men around this place to let this get under our skins. If you want to pursue her, I won't stand in your way, and you shouldn't stand in mine. It's always going to be her decision, and we'll support it either way. Agreed?" He held out his hand.

"If you hurt her, I'm coming for you, Cash."

"Fair enough."

Jordan grumbled, but shook. "Fine. Agreed."

∞ ∞ ∞

She tried to hold it together, but by the time they reached the garage, Grace's eyes were burning. "I'm sorry," she said, unable to meet Jeanie's eyes.

"Hey," she said softly, "What do you have to be sorry about?"

"I don't even know," she sighed, wiping a rogue tear. "I just am."

Jeanie frowned. "That's not the way most women react after kissing a hot guy."

Grace forced a thin smile. "I'm just not ready for this. I don't know if I'll ever be."

"Are you sorry you kissed him?"

"Yes...no..." she shook her head. "I don't even know what to think. It's...complicated."

"I think a very attractive, available man is interested in you, and that you're just as interested in him. What's so complicated about that?"

Grace hitched in a breath, but could only shake her head. Guilt stabbed her gut, worsened by the fact that she'd really, really liked the way Brady kissed her. Logic reminded her that she was only thirty-two, that she still had a lot of life ahead of her, and that she would probably, at some point, consider another relationship. Her heart, though, was still married to Danny.

Jeanie took Grace's arms, much the way she herself had once taken Mandy's, and stood on tiptoes to meet Grace's eyes. "What are you running from, Grace?" she asked gently.

Grace closed her eyes and took a deep breath. Part of her wanted to come clean; to tell Jeanie about how she came to be at Best Friends, and why it had become as much a sanctuary to her as it was to the animals, but she didn't want the people who'd become her new family to look at her with pity.

"You know you can trust me, right? All of us."

Grace met Jeanie's eyes. "Of course I know that," she breathed. "It's just…I'm not ready. I need some time to wrap my head around this. I don't want to hurt Jordan, I don't want to hurt Brady, but especially, I don't want to hurt myself. Please understand."

"Of course," Jeanie said, pulling her into a hug. "We've all got a past, Grace. It isn't going to change the way we feel about you. You're one of us, now."

"You have no idea how much that means to me," Grace whispered.

"When you're ready, I'll be here."

"I know you will. Thank you."

Jeanie grabbed a broom that poked out from one of the boxes. "Let's go clean up the mess, then call it a night. You've got a lot to think about, I imagine."

Grace nodded, and followed her back to the house.

∞ ∞ ∞

Dusty was pissed, as usual. He'd cruised the entire town of Fredonia, scouring every hotel parking lot, rental property, and apartment building he could find. It was the fourth town he'd searched that was within driving distance of Kanab, and he still couldn't find Grace.

It was after midnight by the time he got back to the hotel, and he had to be up at six to put up fucking fences in heat that would give hell a run for its money.

Still, he cracked a beer. He was too hyped up to sleep.

He was a professional killer, and he couldn't get his hands on one little chick?

That wasn't it, though, he knew. If all he wanted was Grace dead, he could've gotten a gun, taken her out from the desert while she was walking one of the freaking mutts. No, more than anything, he wanted to see the story her eyes told—fear, pain, regret, confusion—then the last glimmer of knowing before the lights winked out. First, though, he needed to tell her his story.

He pulled out the knife that he'd used on her family, ran the blade along the pad of his well-scarred thumb. Dusty squeezed until he had a nice bead, then pressed a thumbprint to the blade, just above the dark stains that still graced the cold metal.

Of all the scenarios he'd imagined when he started this epic journey, never had he considered that he'd find Grace so connected to a place; to people. Especially not to men the size of the two she was alternately pawing. She was so isolated back at home, jumping at shadows and hiding out at her sister's, and now, she was happy. Maybe even strong.

But he was smart. Would a stupid man think to randomly break in to some of her neighbor's houses months before storming hers, so he could leave some untraceable fingerprints behind to throw off the cops? He didn't think so.

No matter how long it took, he'd do this *right*. And, he'd do it soon.

Chapter 25

Grace drove back to the cabin, feeling unsettled and overwhelmed. It was one kiss, and as much as it knocked her off her feet, she could easily justify that with the fact that she hadn't been kissed in a very long time. Certainly not like that, anyway, she thought, remembering Jordan's kisses on Angel's Landing and at the back of the octagon. His hadn't left her wanting, wondering, smoldering.

She paced the cabin for a bit, which amounted, really, to walking in a tight oval around the tiny living room. After being at Brady's place, she felt kind of claustrophobic in her cramped quarters. The silence, too, was pressing in on her…even the coyotes seemed to have taken a night off from choir practice.

Maybe a bath—water as hot as she could stand it and flowery bubbles might calm her ragged nerves. She opened the closet to grab a towel and froze as her eyes fell on The One Box. Instantly, the guilt that had been gnawing at her rushed in, and she slid the box from the shelf and fell onto the couch.

What was she thinking? She'd said time and time again that she wasn't ready for this; that she needed to figure her own life out before even considering having someone else be part of it. Trouble was, Brady was already part of it, and she had to admit that she liked it that way. That she liked him.

Danny was gone, and there was nothing she could do to change that. Still, she loved him, and everything he'd been to her. She opened the box and took out the velvet bag, the rings tinkling together as they fell into her palm. *Until the end of time*, the inscriptions read. Danny's time had ended, but hers kept marching on. Grace wondered if she was really ready to change direction.

She needed an objective opinion--one that wasn't so close to the situation. She needed her baby sister. It was late in Chicago, but it was Friday night...and hey, sisters always had that prerogative.

"What's wrong?" Mandy answered breathlessly on the second ring.

"Nothing...sorry to call so late...did I wake you?"

"No, unfortunately. Eva's got a fever and a nasty cough, and managed to throw up on her new Cinderella pajamas. I just got her out of the tub, and now I'm doing laundry." As flustered as Mandy sounded, Grace couldn't help but feel a quick stab of jealousy that she'd never get the opportunity to do the same thing for her own daughter.

"Poor baby," Grace frowned. "You've obviously got your hands full, so I'll give you a buzz tomorrow."

"Absolutely not," Mandy said. A heavy sigh and the familiar squeak of the old sofa rustled in Grace's ears. "Matt's reading her a story, and her medicine should kick in pretty soon and knock her out. I'm all yours, and I need some female adult conversation. Besides, you're not fine if you're calling at this hour. What's going on?"

The concern in her sister's voice hurled Grace off a cliff into a churning sea of emotion. She held her breath for a few seconds before speaking. She'd start with the good news.

"I finally petted Princess Gracie this morning...she even rested her head in my lap."

"That's fantastic news--good for you, but especially, good for her. Finally, your spark becomes fire."

Mandy's comment hit a little too close to home. She'd told Mandy that PG was a spark, but, although her sister knew a lot about her friends at Dogtown, Grace had always kind of downplayed the guys. It just didn't feel right to talk about two incredible men who seemed to be vying for her attentions. It was time to put it out there. "Brady kissed me."

"Aw, that's…" There was a long pause as Mandy processed the information. "Wait…*what?*"

"We were watching the first sunset at his new place, and…he kissed me."

"Whoa, back up a second here," Mandy said. "This is the Brady you work with, obviously…the one from LA, right?"

"Yeah."

"You've mentioned him, but I never thought…when did this even become a possibility?"

From the first minute I saw him. "It's been a possibility for a while."

"And you never mentioned it? This is huge, Grace--I need a lot more details. Another spark…wow."

"I don't know if he's a spark yet. Maybe." *Definitely.*

"Oh, big sis…your voice betrays you—the very fact that you're calling to tell me about this kiss tells me that it meant something."

Grace took a huge breath, but was unable to answer, afraid her voice would completely give her away.

"You know it's OK, right Gracie?"

Danny's image flashed in her mind. "I guess that's what I'm trying to figure out," she croaked.

"Oh, sweetie, do you have any idea how badly I want to hug you right now?" Mandy whispered.

That did it. Grace felt the tears welling in her eyes, and let them fall. "I could really use your shoulder right now, Man."

"There's nothing to feel guilty about, Gracie. You're young, beautiful, and you're a great catch. I know it's hard, but you still have a life to live, and Danny would hate it if you passed up a good thing because you were feeling loyal to his memory."

"My head knows that—it's my heart I'm trying to convince."

"Why don't you let your heart tell me about Brady. Is he gorgeous?"

Grace felt the familiar blush rising to her cheeks, and smiled through her tears. "Beyond," she said, her heart lifting slightly. "I'll text you a picture." She was constantly snapping pictures of the dogs and the crew, but as she scrolled through them on her phone, she realized that Brady was definitely her primary focus. She was glad her sister couldn't see how just looking at his images reddened her face even more. Brady looked good in all of them, so Grace tapped a few to send. The first was Brady and Leroy, smarmy grins on both their faces; one was a candid of him, laughing at something Jeanie said; and the third was of herself and Brady, his arm around her shoulders and his perfect smile on his perfect lips. She waited until she heard the swoosh of the incoming text on Mandy's phone, then heard her gasp.

"Holy crap," she said breathlessly. "That's not a man...that's a god. Are you sure his name isn't Adonis?"

Grace snickered. "Pretty hot, huh?"

"I'm having a hot flash here," Mandy said. "Oh, wow. You look good together, too, in this next picture. He's tall."

"Yeah," was all she could say. She, too, was looking at the picture of them together, and wondering if was actually possible that they could *be* good together.

"Well, he's definitely got it all going on in the 'looks' department—what else does he have going for him?"

Where to start? When she started thinking about the qualities that made up Brady Cash, she realized that they added up to a pretty darn good package. "Well, he's *here*, which already makes him pretty great. He gave up a career in some financial field to come here--an awfully successful one, I'd say, based on the mansion he just built." She went on to talk about his sense of humor, his easy smile, the way she couldn't help but blush when he looked at her; the electricity that sizzled between them any time he was close.

"Sounds to me like this spark's already burning," Mandy said. "I'm thrilled for you, Grace. You deserve to be happy again."

"I do feel happy, just being here, but I don't think I'm ready for this."

"Did you feel ready when he kissed you?"

Grace touched her fingers to her lips. It hadn't been a case of being ready; more an inescapable feeling that she was supposed to be there, in his arms. "I knew it was coming...I guess I have for a while now. I've thought about it, even dreamed about it. It was an amazing kiss, but..."

"But what? There doesn't have to be a 'but,' Grace. Amazing is enough. Sometimes life just sweeps you away, and you have no choice but to go with it."

"But it's so soon after..."

"It's been almost a year. How long do you think you need to keep carrying a torch for Danny? You know he wouldn't want you to."

"I just can't wrap my head around it yet, I guess."

"Look. You have to do what you feel is best, and no one can tell you differently. In my humble opinion, however, you've mourned long enough--if Brady is the guy for you, then he is." Mandy paused. "Oh, Gracie...you can't deny yourself a life because theirs were taken. It sucks, and it wasn't fair, but you can't feel guilty for something that was beyond your control. Danny would want you to be happy."

Grace grumbled. "God...I feel like I'm on a teeter-totter. One minute I'm thinking I'm ready to move on, and the next...I'm just not sure how to handle it."

"Love isn't something to be 'handled,' Grace. It's something to be savored, treasured, unwrapped."

Grace couldn't help but roll her eyes. "You make him sound like a candy bar."

"Love is even sweeter."

Grace sat back when they cut the connection. Maybe Mandy wasn't as impartial as Grace thought she'd be. Of course Man wanted to see Grace move on—to find happiness again. Grace wanted it, too, but she hadn't anticipated it would happen so suddenly--or so intensely.

A few minutes later, she had pretty much an identical conversation with Gwen, who told her that she needed to live in the moment, and take advantage of every joy life had to give her.

Damn it all, she knew it, too, at least in her mind. The kiss was fantastic, but she still didn't know if she could give her heart away again. It hurt too much when it was broken, and she still had a lot of scars. She thought of PG, the scars that covered her entire body, and wished she could trust the world again.

She climbed into bed with every intention of sleeping in on her day off, going to see Gracie, getting some groceries, and stopping at a nursery to check out some landscaping ideas before heading back to Brady's.

Instead, she tossed and turned for hours, thinking about the kiss, and the feel of Brady's hands on her body. She dreamed of him laying her down on the big bed, stripping her naked, and running his hands over every curve before taking her at sunset. She woke in the middle of a Brady-dream-induced orgasm, and had to press the heel of her hand between her legs to stop the quaking there.

Damn it...she came on this journey to heal, to rediscover herself, and make peace with the world again. Could she reinvent herself, as well, and take a chance at love?

Grabbing her tablet from the nightstand, she watched the video of her family's last day on Earth, and decided the time wasn't right. Not just yet.

Chapter 26

Princess Gracie was huddled in her usual spot, but lifted her head when Grace peeked in. "Morning, PG," Grace said softly, grabbing some biscuits from the storage room. She let herself in slowly and held out a treat. "Look what I've got for you," she said, crouching. Gracie looked at her for a moment, stood, and sniffed the air. "That's the way," Grace said softly, "you know you love these." PG's stub of a tail was plastered firmly against her rump, but she slowly made her way over and accepted the treat. "Good girl, Gracie. Such a good baby." Grace scratched behind her ear nubs, and PG's tail wagged slightly. Grace took it as an omen. "I want you to come outside with me today, Gracie, feel the sun on your face."

She stepped out, sitting in the sand just outside the door and holding out a biscuit. PG slowly crept toward her, closing the distance, and Grace moved again, smiling when she saw the snout poke through the door, wrinkled in a tentative sniff of the outdoors.

"That's it, PG...you can do it, come sit with me."

Her head slid out hesitantly, and PG met Grace's eyes. There was fear there, but also something Grace thought might be hope. PG inched out slowly, made her way over, took the biscuit, and sat next to Grace in the sand. Careful not to get too excited, Grace reached out and ran her hand down the pittie's back. She was rewarded with a full flick of her tiny tail.

It took some coaxing, but once she was outside, Gracie decided she loved it. Within an hour she was running, wagging, and even rolling in the sand. Grace ran with her, encouraging her new-found freedom. Grace couldn't help marvel at how quickly, once they'd learned to trust, a creature could find joy again. If only the same could be said for her.

∞ ∞ ∞

"You want us to do what?" Lara asked, when they'd all gathered at Brady's for day two of what they'd dubbed, "The Great Move In."

"Look, I told you, it's not going to happen again. Just make sure I'm not alone with him."

Jeanie shook her head. "If you don't want to kiss him, just tell him."

"Although I can't imagine that," Veronica added. "Really, Grace, you know you want it as much as he does."

"Please," she begged. "I just need some time to figure this whole thing out."

Lara shook a finger at Grace. "You know that if you're alone with him, you won't be able to help yourself. Doesn't that tell you something?"

Grace burned red, knowing they were right, but was determined to follow through with her plan. One that didn't include kissing Brady again. "Please just do this for me," she whispered.

The girls looked at each other, engaging in an entire conversation without a word being spoken. Finally, Jeanie spoke for all of them. "We don't like it, but we'll do it. For you."

"Thank you," Grace whispered.

Brady was obviously frustrated by the girls' constant attention. When he invited Grace upstairs to help him decide which towels to put in the master bath, Jeanie followed. When he asked her to help him for a minute in the kitchen, Lara was there. When he told Grace that he wanted to show her the progress of the trails and garden, Veronica tagged along.

Grace could see the frustration in the roll of his eyes, and his constant attempts to motion her out of the room when no one seemed to be looking. Grace felt bad--not just for being the cause of Brady's annoyance, but because she was finding it hard to convince herself that being with him was wrong. Whenever she was around him, she found that she wanted to be closer, and it was incredibly hard to keep her distance. She knew she couldn't trust herself if she got too close--attraction would kick in, and she'd surely lose her head.

The girls kept their word, though, and it wasn't until the last box was unpacked, after nine o'clock, that he just threw his hands in the air and asked, "Can I have a minute alone with Grace, please?" The girls shrugged, shot apologies at Grace with their eyes, and walked away, leaving them alone in the kitchen. Lara wrapped her arm around Jordan and led him out reluctantly.

Brady looked her hard in the eyes. "Finally," he huffed. "It's like they've been on a mission to keep us from being alone."

"Brady," Grace said, holding out her palm to keep him from getting closer. "What happened last night..."

"Was amazing, and I'm looking forward to a lot more," he finished, causing Grace's determination to falter.

"There isn't going to be any more," she said, unable to meet his gaze.

He furled his brows. "What do you mean?"

"I don't even know how to say this," she said, more reluctantly that she'd anticipated. "I mean, look at you. You're...spectacular, actually, and I really like you. But I'm not in the right place to...to..."

"To kiss me?"

"Right. Or anything else. I'm trying to figure out my life right now, and I need as few distractions as possible."

"So, I distract you," he grinned sheepishly. "That's good to know."

"No...yes...I mean..."

He tried to take her hands, but she stepped away. "You were there, too, Grace," he said, "in the kiss. I felt it."

God, his voice was like music in her ears, his scent intoxicating, and she was starting to doubt her own words. She couldn't let herself even look at him, for fear she'd leap into his arms. Finally, she summoned her resolve, and started, "I'm just…I can't…"

Then his lips were on hers, and she was lost again, floating on a tidal wave of need, and falling into him. Wanting. Demanding. Exploring. The words tossed around her head, and she didn't want to push him away, didn't want the kiss to end. Her heart wanted to take it to the next level, regardless of what her brain had to say.

But it had to end, and she somehow found the strength, pushed against his chest and pulled away.

"Don't tell me you didn't feel that," he challenged. "You'd be lying."

"I'm so sorry." She rushed out, grabbed her purse, said a hasty goodbye, and drove away, blinking back confusion and hot tears.

∞ ∞ ∞

"Shady Brady, my man, how are things in the desert?"

Jared's voice was a welcome distraction, especially when he couldn't get Grace off his mind.

"They're good, man—it's great to hear from you! The house looks amazing. You were right about Lacey--she's a miracle worker."

"Glad to hear it. All settled in?"

"For the most part. I'm still waiting on a new set of glassware I ordered," he said, fully convinced that Jordan had dropped the box on purpose, "but I'm pretty much there. The sunsets are amazing here. You should come check it out."

"Exactly why I'm calling. I want to throw you a little housewarming party, bring the staff out. Everyone misses you, and it would be good to get together. Plus, I want to check out the new digs. There's a little airport not too far from you—I'll charter a jet--how about Saturday?"

It was amazing how far removed he already felt from California and the daily grind. Here, he spent a couple hours a day in the offices, a couple more on the phone, and one or two touring facilities to check up on renovations and upkeep. He was then free to spend the rest of his time as he pleased, usually hanging out in Dogtown or checking up on Princess Gracie.

Brady was in a completely different place since he'd left LA, but still, it would be good to see the old gang once again. "This Saturday?" he asked.

"Indeed. But don't worry--I've got it all planned--you don't need to do a thing."

"Saturday's good, but you don't need to throw a party. I can put something together."

"It's a gift, Brady; just sit back and enjoy. Say thank you, and we'll see you on Saturday. About 5:00?"

He was skeptical, but couldn't say no to Jared. "All right, thank you, but keep it simple," Brady warned. "I mean it, Jared...this isn't LA."

"Sure...no problem. Looking forward to seeing you. I miss you, man."

He should have known better. Jared didn't know the meaning of the word, 'simple,' and when a truck pulled in that night to deliver enough booze to stock a cruise ship, he knew Jared had already gone overboard. A caterer called in the early evening, and informed him they'd be setting up at 1:00, for 200 guests. Brady realized he'd better invite more people...and fast.

He typed up some flyers and went around the sanctuary, tacking them up on boards in every building. He made rounds, too, personally inviting everyone he saw. It wasn't often the workers from different areas got to mingle together, and it was always a good time when they did.

What the hell, he was going to have a party.

Of course his Dogtown friends got the first invitations, and they, of course, offered to come early to help set up.

∞ ∞ ∞

When Grace didn't show up at Jethro again on Tuesday afternoon, he took a ride over to Angel's Lodge, hoping to catch her. They needed to talk about why she rushed out on Sunday, and why she hadn't returned his calls. He tried to hide his disappointment when Molly, PG's afternoon caregiver, smiled up at him.

"How's she doing?"

"Oh, Brady…she's an entirely different dog. I just can't believe how far she's come."

As if to punctuate the point, PG made her way shyly over to the door of her enclosure. "May I?" Brady asked.

Molly handed him a biscuit. "Absolutely. These are her favorites."

PG backed up when he opened the door, but stayed on her feet. Brady squatted and held out the biscuit, talking to her softly. "I hear you're doing great, Princess Gracie," he said. "I knew Grace was the right choice for you."

PG's ear buds perked up at his voice.

"You're looking good," he said. "Got some more meat on your bones, don't you, and your eye's looking better. How about a treat?"

The pittie lifted her little stump, flicked it twice, then made her way over to Brady to take the biscuit.

"Good girl," he said, patting her head. "Listen," he whispered, "can you put in a good word for me with Grace? She's having a hard time admitting that she wants to be with me." PG lifted a paw, and put it on Brady's leg. He took it, and shook it gently. "Thanks," he said, "I'll take all the help I can get."

"You can leave her door open," Molly said when he stepped out. "She's actually coming out here once in a while when I'm working around the octagon."

"I'm so glad to hear that."

"Have you talked to Grace?"

"No, actually, I was kind of hoping to catch her here. She didn't come to Jethro today. Did she happen to mention where she was going?"

"No, she didn't, sorry. She may have gone to see Doc Mary--Grace had Leroy over here this morning, to test PG with another dog."

Brady raised his eyebrows. "Really? How'd that go?"

"It was awesome," Molly said, a twinkle in her eye. "Grace put Leroy in the run next door, and he immediately sensed PG's presence. He laid down right next to the fence, and whined. After about five minutes, Gracie poked her head out, and saw him. At first she darted back in, but Leroy kept calling her, coaxing her out. Finally, she waddled over, and Leroy didn't get up--he just lifted his snout and gave her a gentle sniff, then let PG sniff him all over."

"I love that dog," Brady said. "Everyone gravitates to him. He's going to get snatched up as soon as he finishes his next round of medication. We'll miss him around here."

"PG certainly gravitated to him. After a thorough scent introduction, she lay down right next to him."

Brady smiled. "That's fantastic."

"It was. They stayed like that for almost an hour. PG even pressed herself against the fence to get closer. That's why I said Grace may have gone to see Doc Mary. She wants to introduce them into the same run, and was going to talk to her about bringing PG over for visits by you."

"Best news I've had all day," he said, peeking back into Princess Gracie's enclosure. "I'm proud of you," he said to the pittie. "Leroy's a good choice for you, too. You'll love him." PG wagged her stump, and rested her head on her paws.

"Thanks for the report," Brady said to Molly. "If you see Grace, could you tell her I need to talk to her?"

"Will do."

Brady walked over to HQ, but Grace's car wasn't in the lot. He was about to head over to the clinic when he saw Jordan rushing toward him. "Hey, I'm glad I caught you," Jordan said urgently. "I've got to go to the reservation--I just got word that my grandmother's sick."

"Oh no," Brady said. "What can I do to help?"

"Can you hang out around Dogtown?" he asked. "That Kevin dude didn't come back today, but...who knows?"

"Done," he said, "Keep us posted, OK? I really hope your grandma's all right."

"I will...thanks." He hopped in his Jeep, and drove off.

Chapter 27

Grace managed to avoid Brady for the next couple days, taking PG for outings in the mornings and working on the cabin in the afternoons. She bought some new trim, and set up a work station in the shed on a huge sheet of plywood. Her evenings were spent with one or more of the girls, planting yucca, zebra grass and other native plants around the little cottage.

"You can't avoid him forever, you know," Jeanie said, tucking a butterfly bush into the ground and filling the hole with fertile soil.

They hadn't mentioned Brady the first night, but Grace knew it would happen, eventually. "I know," she said. "I just need to figure some things out before I can decide where this whole thing is going to go."

"We miss you," Veronica pouted, "and so do the dogs." Leroy was napping in the shade of an ash tree, but Grace was missing the rest of her canine charges. It was hard avoiding Dogtown, but she couldn't face Brady until she figured some things out.

"The housewarming party's on Saturday. You know you have to go."

"Of course I'll go," Grace said, wondering if she actually would. She needed to work this out quickly; needed to talk to Brady before the party. If only she knew how.

"I don't get it, Grace," Lara said. "You obviously like him, and he very obviously likes you. What happened to turn you off men?"

Grace stopped, a shovel full of dirt hovering mid-air, and almost told them. But she was a different person now, and she was done dwelling in the past. Except, of course, for her hesitation on moving toward a future. "It's complicated," she said. "I just have some personal issues I need to work on."

"Well, I sure hope you work them out fast," Jeanie said. "We're a group, Grace, and you're part of it. Besides, I don't know how much longer I can deal with Brady's cranky moods."

Grace looked up at her, eyebrows raised.

"He's been sulking around waiting for you to show up," Veronica said. "He keeps asking us if you're OK, what you're doing, why you're avoiding him. He's like a little puppy dog."

"It's kind of pathetic, actually," Lara added. "I've never seen him like this before."

"And of course he can't leave, because Jordan's not here. He's our new fierce protector."

Grace couldn't help but smile at the revelation. The fact that Brady was sulking because she was avoiding him made him even harder to resist. "I just need a little time."

"Please don't take too much," Jeanie said softly, taking Grace's hand and squeezing it.

Grace brought PG home on Wednesday for her first sleepover, following a fabulous afternoon at Coral Pink Sand Dunes, where PG actually wagged her tail and ran up the wall of sand, tongue lolling out her mouth and a smile on her face. PG was clingy when they first got back to the cabin, but as the evening wore on, she became more comfortable, lying on the kitchen floor or next to the sofa as Grace went about her business. When it was time to go to sleep, Grace lifted her onto the bed and climbed in beside her, curling PG into her and stroking her back. Grace woke in the middle of the night to find PG pressed up against her, feet in the air, snoring softly. *See, you can trust again*, she thought, wondering if the same would ever be true for her.

∞ ∞ ∞

By Friday morning, she couldn't stand it anymore. Brady was just as invested in Gracie's progress as she was, and he would be thrilled by the good news. Besides, she needed to talk to him before his party tomorrow--she had to go, and needed to clear the air with him before she saw him again. At least over the phone, he wouldn't be able to see how the mere sound of his voice affected her.

He answered on the first ring. "Grace," he said softly. Just that one word held so much sadness she thought her heart would break.

"Hey, Brady," she said, hoping he couldn't hear the shake in her own words. "I had to call you to tell you about Princess Gracie. She's really made a lot of progress over the past couple days, and I thought you'd want to know."

"I'm so glad you called. I talked to Molly, but I really want to hear it from you.

"Yeah. She's really doing great. She just loves Leroy."

"Who doesn't?"

"Oh, Brady—they played together today, and it was nothing short of awesome. I took her to Coral Pink yesterday and for a sleepover last night--she slept in my bed, and had an egg with me at breakfast. I'm amazed at how quickly she's healing. She actually wags her little stub, and comes to me when I call her. She's going to ace her Canine Good Citizen Test, I just know it."

He sighed. "I'm so glad to hear it--I knew you'd do it." He paused, and Grace could hear the uncertainty in his voice. "How about you, Grace…are you OK? I miss you. Don't think I don't know that you're avoiding me."

His words touched her heart, and she had a hard time answering.

"I'm OK," she said finally. "I miss you, too."

"I can't stand it," he said, his voice full of emotion. "I don't understand what I did wrong."

"Oh, Brady…you didn't do anything wrong. It's me that's all wrong, and I don't know how to fix it."

"Have dinner with me," he said hastily. "No kissing, I promise, unless you initiate it. You can tell me more about PG."

Grace's head told her to say no, but her heart intervened. "OK," she whispered.

Grace opened The One Box, and pulled out the items out one by one, laying them on her bed. When she got the bottom, she pulled out the letter from Danny that she'd never found the strength to read. He'd left it on the counter for her a few months after they'd lost Briana. Hesitantly, she slid it out.

My Dearest Amazing Grace, she read.

It is with a heavy heart that I write this letter. Seeing you succumb to sadness and depression pains me, and I wish, more than anything, that I had the power to take this grief from you. I know it isn't fair, losing someone you loved, but all we can do is make the most of the life we have left and carry the happy memories of that love in our hearts. No part of this was your fault, and it kills me, watching you struggle with so much guilt over something that was beyond your control.

The only thing I want in this world is for you to be happy. You have so much life ahead of you, and it can still be beautiful. Let go of the guilt and the pain and look to the future, instead of dwelling in the past.

Life gives us second chances, Amazing Grace, and third chances, and fourth...however many we need. Please take a chance and run with it, wherever it might take you. I'll be by your side the whole way, supporting you, cheering you on, and loving you until the end.

Forever yours,
Danny

Grace clutched the letter to her breast and blinked back tears. Danny had written it nearly six years ago, but the words rang so true today, that it nearly stopped her heart. Brady was her second chance--she'd be a fool to let it pass her by, but the thought of running with it still had her tied up in knots.

She packed everything back into the box, and prepared to meet Brady, still unsure of what she would do when she saw him.

She refused to let him pick her up, for fear she'd be powerless when it came time to potentially inviting him in at the end of the evening. They met at Rocking V, and Grace could see the uncertainty on Brady's face as he slipped in across from her. It was awkward, not greeting him with a hug, and she found it hard to focus on anything other than the sadness in his eyes.

They started with small talk, discussing the weather, Brady's new place, how he liked his new job. Light, easy conversation that didn't come close to anything either of them really wanted to say.

The server brought their wine, and he lifted his glass. "To your success with PG," he said, and Grace touched his rim with hers. "Tell me about your outing. You took her to Coral Pink?"

Grace softened. It was easy to talk about the scarred little pittie who was finally on her way to recovery. "Oh, my gosh…she's so good, Brady. At first, she wouldn't leave my side, but she really liked Coral Pink. We even had a little run up a dune, and her tiny tail wagged the whole time. She's got her own spots staked out in the cabin, and she's OK with being on her own for short periods while I'm outside or in the shed. She loves walking around the property, but still freaks out a little when she hears the coyotes. When they get close, she actually growls."

"So she does have a voice; that's good to hear," Brady said. "I've never heard her make a sound, except for the night

I found her. She's obviously smart, too. She doesn't want any other dogs moving in on her territory. I know the feeling."

Grace knew he was talking about Jordan, and she changed the subject. "I probably don't want to hear it, but tell me what happened. How'd you find Princess Gracie?"

"Well...now that's a sad tale," he said mournfully. Grace couldn't help but notice how his features softened, a sadness touching his eyes as he recounted the story. By the time he got to the end, Grace was crying. "Hey," he said softly, reaching over to catch a tear, "the story has a happy ending."

Grace forced a smile. "It's getting there."

"Because of you."

"And you."

"You were the one who made her happy again."

Grace shrugged. "It was in her all along; I just helped coax it out."

"Don't underestimate yourself, Grace," he said with conviction. "She's where she is because of your unconditional love and devotion--don't question it for a minute."

Grace dipped her head in thanks. "I know she responds to that, and I'm happy to give it to her."

"Nothing beats trust and unconditional love."

Grace sighed. The conversation had shifted again, and she owed Brady at least a small explanation for her childish behavior over the past few days. Brady had told her that he felt her in the kiss--that if she denied she felt something, it would be a lie. He didn't know just how right he was. It was the first time in almost a year that she gave everything she had...released all that she'd locked up so tightly inside her...and if he felt that, which she believed he did, it must have been intense for him, as well. Having her push him away, then avoid him completely, must have been confusing and, judging by the look on his face, perhaps even painful.

Oh, but having him in such close proximity squeezed at her heart, and she fought the urge to close the gap by throwing herself into his arms and giving herself away for good. Grace looked down at the table so he wouldn't read it in her eyes, and whispered, "Some creatures find it hard to trust, because they're too afraid of getting hurt again." Brady reached across the table, lifting her chin with his hand to meet his gaze.

"Trust is the first necessity," he said, eyes blazing, "the foundation for everything else." She wanted to look away, but his eyes held her captive. "You can trust me, Grace."

God, she wanted to. More than anything, she wanted to let go of the crushing fear that came with the thought of giving her heart away again. Everything in his expression told her that he meant every word, and slowly, the invisible hand that squeezed at her heart loosened its grip. She very nearly lost her tenuous hold on self-control and she he would, if he touched her again, spoke again, or if she looked too long into the deep blue pools of his eyes. Grace believed she'd made her decision, thought she was going to tell Brady she just needed a little more time to figure things out; but now, when she saw the earnestness in his expression when he asked her to take a chance with him, she wasn't certain about anything.

She needed some air so she could clear her head--needed to add this new information to the words in Danny's letter and see if she could come up with an answer she could live with--without guilt or regret. He wanted her, and she wanted him. If she let Brady go, it could end up being her biggest regret of all. Grace shook her head. "I need to go. I just…God, I'm so stupid…but I…I need time to… I'm so sorry." She grabbed her bag and slid out of the booth as Brady hastily threw some bills on the table and followed her out the door.

Her strides were no match for his long legs, and within a few steps, he caught up to her side. Grace caught his expression, and the invisible hand gave another quick squeeze. None of this was fair--not to Brady, or to her--she couldn't let things go like this. "Brady, I…."

"Don't say another word, Grace…just don't." The pain in his eyes stabbed her like a knife, and she felt horribly responsible for having put it there.

He walked her to her car, and as she leaned against it, he studied her for a moment, then took her hand, and softly kissed the back of it. "I hope I'll see you tomorrow."

Her heart cracked as she watched him walk away, and she felt torn in two.

"Brady...wait."

He spun on his heel, walked back in two long strides. "Yes?" Grace saw hope in his eyes.

"Thank you for dinner. I know it may not seem that way, but I had a really nice time." God, she didn't want him to go.

"You're welcome." He stood for another moment, and when she didn't speak again, he gave her a terse nod and turned. "Have a good night, then."

She couldn't stand it. Her heart pounded as she put her hand on his arm, tugging him back. He just stood, hands in his pockets, and waited.

"I have a hard time with trust," she said softly. "I just don't know if I'm ready."

"You can trust me, Grace, I promise you." His eyes smoldered, and her cheeks burned.

"OK." It was hard to say it, even harder to believe it, but right now, she'd do anything to make him stay.

He waited for a couple moments, then pressed a light kiss on her forehead.

Oh, God, she thought, feeling something inside her break free. Her vision narrowed, the edges clouding until there was a single focus of sight inside a fuzzy halo. In the center of the halo stood Brady Cash. Flashing lights from distant street signs danced in the haze, and her stomach rolled over and over. Sparks. Damn it, something in him was right...something in *them* was right. A calm knowing settled on her like a soft blanket, and she knew. Danny would want her to be happy--she'd be a fool to let Brady walk away.

Grace reached out before he could turn again, and grabbed his hand. "I'm initiating it," she said, her voice barely a whisper.

His head tilted, and he looked at her with narrowed eyes. "What did you say?"

She met his gaze, and matched it spark for spark. "I'm initiating it," she said more boldly, taking a step toward him. "Kiss me, Brady."

For a second he just stood there, and she worried that it was already too late. Then his eyes burned into hers, and the sparks turned to fire. "Are you sure, Grace? Because if I do, there's no going back. Not for either of us. I think you know that."

The fire consumed her, stealing her breath. All she could do was nod.

She was swept into his arms in a heartbeat, her hands curling around his neck as he wrapped her up tightly in his warm strength. His eyes blazed, then his mouth was on hers, and she felt as if she were bursting into a million pinpricks of light, tiny stars that could fill the heavens. He deepened the kiss, fingers tangling in her hair and the other hand sliding slowly down the side of her body, skimming her breast feather-lightly. She moaned softly and he pulled her closer still, until she could feel the frantic beat of his heart. "Oh, Grace," he whispered, tugging gently at her hair to tip her head and nibbling his way deliciously down her neck and back up again to her mouth.

God, she wanted him more than she wanted to breathe, more than she'd wanted anything in a very long time, and she let herself go. She ran her hands up the back of his shirt, soft warm skin over hard, tense muscles. He splayed a hand over the small of her back and pulled her closer--she could clearly feel how much he wanted her, too.

A loud chirp made them both jump back, and Grace opened her eyes to see a couple approaching a car two spots away from where they stood. A furious rush of blood flooded her cheeks as she read in their expressions that they'd clearly seen the hot make-out session on the public street. The man and Brady shared a knowing smirk, and the woman gave Grace an inconspicuous thumbs-up. They waved as the car pulled away, and Brady turned back, tucking a strand of her tangled hair behind her ear and letting his hand rest softly against her cheek.

"I love it when you blush," he smiled, trailing his thumb along her cheekbone.

"That's good, since I can't seem to help it around you."

"Even on that first night, I hoped it was because of me."

"It's always been because of you, Brady."

He slowly brought his mouth down to hers, kissed her softly. "No going back...right, Grace?"

Grace pressed her cheek into his hand. "No going back," she agreed. He pulled her into his arms and held her, resting his lips on the top of her head. "I'll follow you home," he said, opening her car door.

All the way back to the cabin, Grace debated the ultimate question. How far should she let things go with Brady tonight? Was she ready to take this from zero to warp speed in one night? The obvious conclusion was that she would be powerless to say no--her whole body was wanting; reawakened after a long hibernation, aching for more of what he had to offer.

She convinced herself that it was OK; that she'd be good waking up next to him in the morning. However, when they pulled into the drive, Brady stuck his hand out the window in a wave, flashing his lights as she got out of the car. Grace waved back and let herself in as Brady backed out of the driveway.

A gentleman, she thought, as she leaned against the door and kicked off her shoes. There was no question he wanted her, but he hadn't taken advantage of her vulnerability. She wasn't quite sure how she felt about it, as hungry as she was for more of him, but couldn't help but admire his chivalrous nature.

She pressed two fingers to her swollen lips and smiled. No going back, he'd said, and she found herself anxiously anticipating moving forward. It was time to start writing the next chapter of her life, and she wanted Brady to be part of it.

It was scary, sure, but when she went to bed--the feel of his hands on her body and his kiss on her lips--she was already looking forward to tomorrow.

∞ ∞ ∞

Damn, it had taken every shred of strength he had to drive away. The look in her eyes when she asked him to kiss her set him on fire, and the wanting in her kiss made him consider sweeping her up right there and carrying her off like some kind of caveman. Watching her walk into the cabin, knowing that she probably wouldn't be able to say no if he invited himself in, tugged at him so hard that he had to clench every muscle in his body to stay in his seat.

He could still feel the hum of her kiss on his lips, and strongly considered flipping a U-turn and going back. He pictured himself knocking on her door, scooping her up, laying her out on the bed, and stripping her slowly. It was an incredibly tempting scenario, but something inside him said it was wrong to rush her. She had some sort of baggage, something that made her keep pulling away; something that made it hard for her trust. It made him more determined to win her over.

Brady really needed her to be sure, because he'd fallen for her hard. The last thing he wanted to do was scare her away, because he knew in his heart that there was no going back for him.

He took a cold shower and fell asleep thinking about what could happen if she decided to let herself admit that she was his, and had been from the first time they laid eyes on each other.

Chapter 28

Grace forced herself to work on the trim, brushing a coat of stain onto the wood with a steady hand. It was amazing how much more settled she felt now that she'd opened her mind to the prospects of a relationship with Brady. They'd been texting all day--he was orchestrating deliveries of supplies for the party; and although she was incredibly tempted to go help him, she knew it would be a major distraction for both of them. Especially after the way they'd left things last night.

Brady had sent some pictures, and Grace couldn't believe the transformation of his large front yard--round tables with white tablecloths surrounded a long buffet table, a DJ stage sat on the north side of the house, and tiki bar with a thatched roof had been erected in the center of it all.

"I should've known better," Brady texted. *"Jared doesn't do anything small."*

"Obviously," Grace responded. *"It's going to be a great party. Can't wait."*

Her entire body tingled when she read his response. *"Would rather have a private party--just you and me. Really need to see you. Tonight, I'm initiating it."*

Anticipation tingled in her gut, and Grace savored the rush before responding, *"Now I really, really can't wait."*

Jeanie was noticeably worried at first when Grace called to tell her she'd be driving her own car to Brady's, and she'd had to promise at least a dozen times that she wasn't bailing out on the party. Twice Grace almost told her that she and Brady had decided to take things to the next level, but the anticipation of seeing the looks on their faces when they heard the news helped her keep it under wraps. They'd be happy for her, she knew, and it felt right to celebrate it all together.

Except for Jordan. The only downside to the evening was the distinct possibility that he'd be hurt because of her, and she still had no idea how to broach the subject with him. She didn't know if he'd be back for the party--he hadn't responded to her text--and she selfishly hoped he wouldn't be. Grace couldn't think of a worse time or place to drop that bomb on him. There was no good way to do it, but she at least hoped to be able to tell him in private, so she could tell him how amazing he was, and so he could come to terms with it in his own way before having to deal with her and Brady as a couple.

It was the only wild card in what would otherwise be a spectacular evening full of innumerable moments of joy; a bridge she'd have to cross when she came to it.

She wiped the stain off the trim, then closed up the shed. Tonight was a celebration, and she took her time getting ready, carefully applying a hint of jade over her eyes and some pink to her lips. She didn't bother with blush—Brady would take care of that as he always did. Slipping into frilly panties and a lacy bra, she appraised her image in the mirror; even to her it was impossible to miss the happy glow and genuine smile.

Pausing for a moment before walking out the door, Grace took a deep breath and closed her eyes, then walked out to start writing the next chapter of her new life.

∞ ∞ ∞

Brady was standing with the girls when she pulled in, and she felt almost dizzy when she saw him, especially when he locked onto her eyes and flashed her an electrified smile. There were so many birds flocking in her stomach that she feared she might actually take flight. He held up a finger to excuse himself, and headed in her direction while she fumbled with the seatbelt, anxious to get to him.

He reached her in a few long strides, folded her into his arms, and spun her in a slow circle. "God, I missed you," he said softly. He tangled his fingers into her hair; tilting her head and pressing his lips to hers in a kiss that went from smolder to inferno in an instant. "I *really* missed you," he whispered, meeting her eyes for a moment before claiming her mouth again.

"Me, too," Grace breathed, snuggling into the nest of his arms. Every doubt, every fear, melted away as she tumbled into the urgency of the kiss--the raw and honest feel of his embrace. There was just something coherent about them together; like pieces of a puzzle that were finally put together.

"No going back," he whispered against her lips.

"No way," Grace agreed. The flutter in her stomach became a storm, and for a moment, no one but the two of them existed.

"Shall we?" He held out his arm and Grace wound hers through it, then they walked, grinning, toward three very surprised and excited ladies.

"And here I was worried that I was going to have to go and collect you," Jeanie said, her eyes twinkling.

"When did this happen?" Veronica said. "Just yesterday you weren't sure you could even face the man." She threw her arms around them both. "Congratulations! We're so happy for you both."

Jeanie and Lara joined the group hug, extending their own well-wishes and congratulations. "I can't believe it," Jeanie said. "I mean, I knew it would happen eventually, but…"

"It just happened last night," Grace said. "I finally realized I couldn't fight it anymore."

"Thank God," Brady said, pressing another kiss to Grace's lips.

"Everyone else may think this is a housewarming party, but we'll be celebrating something else entirely," Jeanie said.

"Thanks, guys," Grace said. "Your support has meant so much to me, and your friendship has…" tears of joy filled her eyes, and she hugged each girl in turn before returning to

Brady's arms. "Thank you. You'll never know how much you all mean to me."

"Hey," Jeanie said, "this is a party. There will be no tears here. I mean, look at this place. It's going to be quite a night, and we have so much to celebrate."

"I couldn't agree more." Grace wiped her tears and took a minute to scan the front yard. "This really is unbelievable, Brady. I saw pictures, but I'm still blown away."

"This," he said, with a sweep of his arm, "is Jared Little's idea of 'keeping it simple.' And as my first official guests, I should probably apologize right away. I'm afraid this is going to end up being more of an LA soiree than a Kanab shindig. I never should have let him do this--his middle name is 'over-the-top.'"

"Oh, but it's going to be so fun!" Jeanie danced excitedly. "What can we do to help?"

There were at least a dozen people hustling about, arranging place settings and lighting Sternos under silver chafers. Brady shrugged. "Jared's other middle name is 'let someone else take care of the details,' so everything's covered. I haven't even had enough time to mess up the house yet, so we can just relax. Let's have a drink together before things get crazy," Brady said, heading for the tiki bar. "Because, believe me, when the LA clan get here, things will likely get a bit out of control. I'm asking you to swear an oath to me, right now, that you won't judge me by their behavior. I already feel so far away from that life, and truthfully, I'm a little apprehensive about them being here."

The girls flashed the Girl Scout salute. "We know you, Brady...probably better than they do," Jeanie said. "LA Brady isn't nearly as awesome as Best Friends Brady. Of that, I'm sure."

"Yeah, well, I hope so," Brady said, uncertainty in his voice. "They can be pretty...intense."

"We can handle, 'intense,'" Veronica smiled.

The bartender mixed them a frozen concoction she called Rock Lobsters, and Jeanie held up her glass. "I want to make a toast...to fresh starts, and budding romances."

Brady twined his fingers through Grace's, and brought her hand to his lips. "I'll definitely drink to that."

One sip of the icy drink, and the girls were in heaven. "Your friend knows how to throw a party," Veronica said, "I like him already."

"Jared Little is one of a kind, that's for sure," he agreed. He set down his glass, plopped into one of the chairs, and pulled Grace into his lap. "So are you," he whispered, nuzzling her neck.

A woman in a chef's coat called to Brady, and he went off to chat with her. "Has anyone heard from Jordan?" Grace asked after he left.

"I did," Lara said. "His grandma's going to be OK."

"I'm so glad to hear that," Grace said. "Does that mean he's coming tonight?"

The girls shared glances that said more than words ever could. "He'll be late, but he'll be here."

"Oh, Grace," Jeanie said, resting her hand on Grace's arm. "How are you going to tell him?"

"I have no idea," she said. "I've been dreading it all day. I was kind of hoping he wouldn't make it, so I could tell him in private."

"I don't envy you that," Veronica whispered. "We'll be here when y'all need us."

"I know. Thanks," Grace said.

Cars began rolling in, and Brady was suddenly pulled in a dozen directions. He greeted guests, took them on tours, and shared toasts. Every time he tried to sit with the Dogtown crew, someone else wanted his attention. "It's OK," Grace whispered when he rolled his eyes as another car pulled in. "Enjoy the party. I'll be the last guest to leave."

"I'm counting on it," he whispered, stealing a kiss as someone else called his name.

The girls settled at a table with heaping plates of food. They toasted to Grace and Brady, and chatted with other staff members as they arrived. It seemed like nearly everyone showed up; many whom Grace hadn't seen since the party on Angel's Landing; and they enjoyed, as they always did, swapping stories about the other areas of Best Friends. Theirs was a common mission, and they talked easily about horses, birds, cats, and pigs. Brady popped over when he could, but the crowd was growing quickly, and Grace soon settled for quick waves and apologetic shrugs. She enjoying watching Brady interact with his guests--he had such an easy way about him; a quick grin, a confident swagger, a dynamic personality--and people were naturally drawn to him. Women were especially drawn, Grace couldn't help but notice, and her heart soared knowing that she was the one he wanted to be with.

Then Jordan's battered Jeep pulled up, and Lara's eyes widened.

"We'll just play it cool, right?" Jeanie said. "It's going to come from Grace when she's ready."

The girls nodded grimly, then pasted on smiles as Jordan strolled over, arms outstretched. "How're my girls?" he asked, wrapping them up in a group hug.

Grace saw Brady approaching and shot him a warning glance, which he returned with a knowing look. "Glad you could make it," he said, shaking Jordan's hand. "How's your grandmother?"

"Feisty as ever," he grinned. "She's going to be fine, but my being there was only raising her blood pressure, so she gave me the boot. Besides, I couldn't miss this." His eyes roamed over the crowd. "Damn, Cash...did you invite the whole town?"

"Pretty much," Brady said, shaking his head. "It's a bit over the top...I know. How about a beer?"

"Best offer I've had all day."

"I'll get them," Lara volunteered, "I need a refill, anyway."

Brady took the seat next to Grace, and rested his hand on her leg under the table. He slid the hem of her dress up to mid-thigh and softly stroked the inside of her leg. The sensation was incredibly sensual, and Grace fought to keep her face from betraying her arousal as Brady talked casually to Jordan about his former partner's idea of a little get-together. Brady's fingers inched higher, and Grace gasped unconsciously.

Just then, horns started blaring, and all heads turned as two stretch Hummers rolled into the yard. "Looks like California just showed up," Brady smiled, "I'll be back." He gave Grace's leg a quick squeeze, then walked over to greet them. The Kanab crew watched with interest as they spilled out of the vehicles and rushed to greet Brady.

The first person to pull him into an affectionate embrace had to be Jared; he was nearly as tall as Brady, but darker, and without the solid build or careless good looks. 'Coifed,' was the word that came to Grace's mind--dark, wavy hair, not a strand out of place, and designer clothes that almost succeeded at looking casual. Jared held Brady at arm's length and looked him up and down, grinning sheepishly. Grace couldn't hear what they said, but Brady beamed, slapping him on the back fondly, in the way of old, good friends.

A woman stepped up next, and from the description Brady had given, was most likely Lindsey, his replacement at the firm.

The rest lined up to greet him with lots of hugs and kisses on cheeks. It was good, actually, to see how much they all admired Brady; how glad they were to see him after a relatively short absence. From the look on his face, it was obvious that Brady had missed them, too.

He led the group over to the table, stopping for introductions. "These are my new co-workers," he said proudly, "This is Lara, Jeanie, Veronica, Jordan..." He looked at Grace, a question in his eyes, and she subtly shook her head. "...and Grace."

They exchanged pleasantries, then Jared turned to Brady. "There's one more group coming," he said. "They got a flat, but should be here soon. So, do we get a tour?"

"First, a drink," Brady said, grinning. "It's your party, after all."

"Now you're talking," Jared said, leading Brady, Lindsey, and a small entourage toward the bar.

"Well, Brady did say they'd be interesting," Jeanie pointed out as they made eyes at each other. The Dogtown crew took in the designer dresses, pricey suits, and expensive jewelry as the group dispersed around the yard; some settling at tables and others wandering over to the buffet.

"Wow, am I glad I don't live in LA," Veronica sighed. "I *so* don't miss city life."

The final limo arrived, spilling more designer dresses and suits onto the lawn. The last person to climb out was a woman wobbling on sky-high stilettos that sank into the sand as she tried to keep up with the rest of her group.

"Ladies and gentlemen, I think we have a winner," Jeanie giggled as the woman pushed through the crowd.

"Holy crap," Lara breathed. "Is that enough material to qualify as a dress? I think her boobs are going to pop out."

Grace frowned as the woman threw her arms around a surprised Brady, kissing him full on the mouth and running her hands down his back to squeeze his butt.

Brady jumped back, obviously surprised to see her, and Grace looked away just as he turned to see if she'd witnessed the exchange.

"Finally, you'll get to see the real Brady Cash," Jordan mumbled.

Grace felt a knot in the pit of her stomach, but Jeanie immediately came to his defense. "She grabbed him…and he doesn't exactly look happy to see her."

Grace turned to see Brady holding her at arm's length, a frown on his face and his eyes narrowed in warning. She took a deep breath and relaxed, shooting Jordan a warning look of her own.

"We'll see," he shrugged.

Chapter 29

"Surprise!" Alli said. She studied Brady for a moment, then wiped lipstick off his face with her thumb.

"What are you doing here, Alli?" he asked, teeth clenched as he turned to see if Grace had seen the kiss she'd planted on him. He grabbed a napkin from the bar, and wiped a pink smear from his face.

As usual, Alli was overdone; too much makeup, too little clothing, balancing precariously on her signature high-heels. It was obvious she'd already started partying, and a sour coil of uncertainty curled in his stomach--Alli was usually trouble.

"I'm here to see you, obviously," she smiled lasciviously. "I couldn't wait to see your new place, and we have unfinished business. You look good, Brady," she said, running her manicured fingers down his arm.

He stepped away as Lindsey came up behind him. "How about that tour? The place looks fabulous--I'm dying to see the view from those windows."

"Absolutely," Brady smiled, turning his back on Alli and falling into step with Lindsey and Jared. "You know, Jared, this is really too much," he said with a sweep of his arm as they walked across the yard. "What happened to keeping it simple?"

"This is nothing." He waved his hand in dismissal, and Brady cocked his eyebrows. "What? I was going to have elephants and a roller coaster. Consider yourself lucky I decided to keep it simple."

"He's not lying," Lindsey laughed. "I tried to rope him in, I swear I did--but you know Jared."

"Yeah, I do," Brady laughed, tossing an arm around Jared's shoulder.

Alli latched onto Brady's other arm, holding on for dear life. He tried to pull away, but she held fast. "I can't walk in this sand," she said, "hold me, Brady."

"What did you think?" he snarled. "This is the desert, Alli, did you not expect there to be sand?" Brady picked up his pace, hoping to shake her off, but she didn't let go until they reached the door. She teetered after them on the tour, gushing over the views, the furnishings, and sliding Brady a suggestive glance when they got to the master bedroom.

"I told you Lacey was an awesome designer," Jared said as they stood on the deck, overlooking the mountains. "This view is spectacular."

"Thanks again for the recommendation. I really do love it."

"How about a shot?"

Brady nodded. "I'll meet you down there in a minute. I need to talk to Alli for a sec."

He caught a few winks and mischievous grins from some of the guys, and shook his head at them. They'd barely stepped out the door and Alli was on him, grinding against him and shoving her hands up the back of his shirt. "Let's christen that huge bed," she crooned.

Brady grabbed her wrists and held her at arm's length. "Cut it out, Alli," he said firmly. "Right now."

"What do you mean? I thought..."

"Listen, I'm sorry if I sent you mixed signals at the going-away party, but I'd had a few too many, and I wasn't thinking clearly. I told you it was a mistake..."

"You mean right after you had your hands down the front of my dress? You wanted me, Brady--don't try to deny it."

Brady looked her straight in the eyes. "It's never going to happen, Alli...you need to understand that."

"I know what I felt in that kiss, Brady. You come and find me when you figure it out." Alli turned on her heel and practically tripped through the door.

Brady sat on the bed and breathed deeply. Why hadn't he figured Alli into the equation? She'd been after him for years;

wouldn't miss an opportunity for a free trip; especially if it meant a chance for her to get her claws into him.

He knew why. After just a few short weeks, his life in LA already seemed like a distant memory; and with Grace in his life, he hadn't even passed Alli a fleeting thought. He looked out the window, and saw Alli perched at a table with people from Parrot Garden, on the opposite side of the yard from where Grace was sitting. She had a tall glass in her hand, and he hoped she'd drink herself the rest of the way to oblivion and leave him to enjoy the party. Jared caught his eye and held up a shot glass, and Brady went to join him.

It really was a fabulous get-together. The music was great, and people had turned a little patch of sand into a makeshift dance floor. Everyone was in a good mood, but although it was nice catching up with his old friends, Brady found himself wishing they'd all go home, so he could have some alone time with Grace.

He stopped off at the table a few times, but she always gave him that warning look--the one that told him she hadn't yet given Jordan the news. It was hard to be close to her without touching her, and he considered, more than once, showing Jordan that they were now a couple. He wouldn't do it, of course, but the thought made him ache for her even more.

Another car rolled in, and he pasted on a smile to greet the next guests.

∞ ∞ ∞

There were four people waiting for the main floor bathroom, so Grace decided to go up and use the master. Brady was talking with a small group from California, and she tossed him a wave as she headed up. By the time she reached the landing he was behind her, his hand on the small of her back. He swept her into the bathroom, slammed the door with his foot, spun her around, and took her mouth like a starving man.

Waves of desire flooded her body and her breath quickened when a low lustful moan vibrated from Brady's throat onto her lips. She wrapped her arms around his waist, and let herself be ravaged.

Brady tilted her head and grazed her throat with lips and teeth, playful nips that made her stomach turn flip-flops. Then he brought his mouth to her ear.

"You don't know what you do to me," he breathed, his throaty whisper weakening her knees, "Why is it that we're hiding out in the bathroom, when I should be able to steal a kiss whenever I want? I want to introduce you as my girlfriend, Grace...you need to tell him." He kissed her again without waiting for an answer, and she swooned.

"I know," she groaned. "I just don't want him to be hurt, and it's a party...I want to tell him in private, and this didn't seem like the right place..."

"Bring him up here. It's quiet."

Grace cocked her head. "I hardly think your bedroom qualifies as an ideal location."

"I suppose not," Brady smirked. "The garden, maybe. The whole back yard is dark and quiet...or do you want me to tell him?"

"No," Grace said quickly. "It needs to come from me, but I can't throw it in his face."

"I wouldn't do that either, but I'm also not going to avoid you for his benefit. You're mine, now, and that comes with certain privileges. This is one of my favorites." He bent and took her mouth again, his tongue sweeping in to dance with hers as his hands skimmed down her back. "He's going to have to get used to it, Grace. Besides, we have a deal."

"A deal?"

"That whichever one of us you picked, the other would be cool with it." He pressed his lips to hers for a long, smoldering minute.

Grace stepped back, hands on her hips. "What made you so sure I would pick either one of you?"

"Oh, sexy woman, I knew you were mine from the moment I met you." He took her hands, and pressed them to his lips. Grace melted.

"OK...I'll tell him."

"Good." He cupped her face in his hands, and slipped her one more kiss. "I guess I have to get back. Come find me as soon as you tell him. I want to show you off."

Her stomach flipped over. "I will."

Her heart was palpitating in a whole different way as she watched Jordan throw his head back and laugh at something one of the girls said, his easy smile lighting his face. The last thing she wanted to do was steal that sparkle from his eyes, but it was exactly what she was going to do. She took a deep breath and made her way back to the table, waiting for a break in the conversation.

"Jordan...take a walk with me?"

The girls looked down at the table, and Jordan regarded them with narrow eyes.

There was already less sparkle when he met her gaze. "Yeah, absolu..." the rest of the word came out as a *harrumph* as the Brady-grabbing bleach-blonde in the too-small dress stumbled, bouncing off Jordan's shoulder and collapsing into the seat beside him.

"Hi," she said excitedly. "I'm Alli." She held out her hand, then threw out her arms. "Oh, I'm just going to hug you." She wrapped her arms around Jordan's neck, then air-hugged the girls in turn as they made faces at each other. "The people over at that table," she said, with a general sweep of her arm," told me that you work with Brady over at the dog place."

"Uh huh..." Jeanie said, drawing out the words in more of a question than a statement. The girls stared for a moment until finally, Veronica spoke up, and introduced everyone.

"I'm really happy to meet you. Everyone says you guys are the ones Brady hangs out with the most."

"Yeah, we're really tight," Lara agreed. "You worked with him in California?"

"Oh," she said with a sly grin and a wink, "Brady and I did a lot more than work together."

An unpleasant sensation shot through Grace's gut. She stiffened, and Veronica grabbed her hand under the table, squeezing it tight.

"Really," Jordan said, his expression smug. "I'm not sure I'm following you."

"Oh…Brady and I have had a thing for years," Alli said. "We had to keep it on the down-low while he was my boss, but since he left the firm…" a waggle of her painted-on eyebrows answered the rest of the question.

"So you two are an item," Jordan smiled. "How interesting."

Grace squeezed Veronica's hand hard enough to make her wince, while Jeanie shot daggers at Jordan.

"Oh, yeah. We talked about it before he left LA. That's why I was so excited to meet you. I mean, I want his friends to be my friends too, so when I come to stay, I can hang out with you guys. I like dogs… but I'm not scooping poop," she added with a giggle.

Grace's mind whirled. Did she mean they talked about it last week, when he was there packing up his things?

The girls fell silent, but Jordan kept on. "That would be great," he said. "You could sign up to volunteer. Brady can hook you up."

Lara kicked him under the table.

"I'll definitely do that!" Alli sloshed the frothy remnants of her drink around the bottom of her glass. "Looks like I need a refill," she grinned. "I'll see you again soon. Take care of my Brady for me until then."

There was stunned silence for a moment, then Veronica spoke. "No way…not possible. Brady would never go for *that*."

"I completely agree," Lara said. "He's got better taste and higher standards."

"She's drunk out of her mind," Jeanie added.

Jordan shook his head. "I keep telling you--he's not the real deal, girls. The real Brady Cash doesn't have relationships...he has flings. Lots of them. He's just charming enough to keep some of the dumber ones coming back for more...and that one's obviously not the sharpest tool in the shed."

Grace's head was reeling. It didn't make sense--after the way Brady just kissed her; after what he told her--that he had something going on with Alli. He'd said that he wanted to introduce her as his girlfriend.

"I still don't believe it," Jeanie said, putting her arm around Grace's shoulder in a show of support.

"We'll see," Jordan said. "How about that walk, Grace?"

∞ ∞ ∞

"So, I met your girlfriend, Brady," Lori said as they finished the tour. "She's...interesting."

Brady's head jerked to look at her, alarm bells already going off in his head. "What did you say?"

"Alli. She seems nice. Definitely a California girl."

Brady stopped short, and looked hard at Lori. "Alli is not my girlfriend. What gave you that idea?"

"That's what she told us."

Brady's eyes widened in horror. "Shit." He left Lori and rushed outside, brushing off two more well-wishers to hopefully avert a disaster.

Chapter 30

"Yeah, sure," Grace said, her voice thin.

Jordan laced his fingers through hers and held her hand tightly as he led her toward the back yard. It was surprisingly dark and quiet--almost ethereal--cast in long shadows from the lights out front. They walked in silence down the winding trails to the garden, and took a seat on one of the benches. Jordan said nothing; just stroked the back of her hand and waited.

"I kissed him," Grace whispered, afraid to meet his eyes.

"I know."

"Last night we...decided we were going to give it a try. I didn't know how to tell you. I didn't want to do it here, but there wasn't another..."

"I knew I shouldn't have gone back to the reservation," Jordan said, smiling thinly. His expression said he was teasing, but his eyes said something else entirely.

Grace took his hands in hers, and squeezed. "Oh, Jordan," she breathed. "I'm so sorry. I really wasn't planning for this to happen--with anyone." He shook his head slowly, and Grace pressed a soft kiss against the back of his hand. When he met her gaze, she looked deep into his eyes. "I absolutely adore you--I need you to know that. You're beautiful, kind, good...you have the most amazing heart..." She took a slow breath, and let it out on a sigh. "It's just that with Brady, there's this...electricity, or something. It's hard to describe, but it's also impossible to ignore."

"And now?"

"I don't know. I have to talk to him. Maybe there's an explanation."

Jordan nodded. He untangled their hands, and pulled Grace against him, resting his lips on the top of her head. "I just want you to be happy, Grace. I wish it could be with me, but I'll support you in whatever you decide."

"Thank you, Jordan...so much."

He stood and took her hand, and they headed back down the trail.

∞ ∞ ∞

Grace was not at the table. The fiery looks he caught from the girls told him that Alli had already paid them a visit, and his heart sank like a stone. Still, it was all a complete misunderstanding, and once he cleared it up, everything would be fine.

He couldn't take the time to explain things to the girls right now, so he asked around until someone pointed toward the back yard. Brady darted back into the house, pushing his way through the group that mingled in the kitchen, and out the sliding glass door. It was surprisingly dark behind the house. He couldn't see much, but as his pupils opened, he saw the outline of a woman, sitting alone, head in her hands, at his patio set. Grace. Without thinking, he jumped cleanly over the rail of the deck to get to her.

"I am so sorry," he said, rushing to her. "I can explain..." But when the head turned, it wasn't Grace at all. Instead, Alli stood, stumbled toward him, and fell into his arms.

"I knew you'd come," she slurred. "I forgive you, Brady."

"Oh, hell," he snarled, peeling her arms from his neck and leading her back to the chair. "Damn it, Alli...no. I thought you were someone else. Just sit down. I've got to go."

Instead, Alli used the patio chair as a springboard, and jumped at him. Instinctively, he caught her, and before he could regain his balance, she'd wrapped her arms around his neck, and coiled her legs around his waist like an anaconda. "I've missed you so much, Brady...you don't have to explain anything. Just take me to bed...we've waited so long..."

It took him a moment to get his legs, and he moved toward the chair with the intention of dumping her into it. He could see nothing with her breasts mashed into his face, and nearly lost his center of gravity as he knocked the chair over. When he tilted his head to look over her shoulder, Alli pressed her mouth to his, wrapping her arms tighter and imprisoning him in her grasp. Brady opened his mouth to speak, but the second he did, her tongue was in it.

He grunted and wedged a hand between their bodies so he could push her off. Instead, the clasp of his watch caught on the material of her dress, and when he tried to tug it free, the front of her dress came with it. His hand fell solidly over one fake, perky breast.

"Oh, yes, Brady," Alli moaned into his mouth as she tried to drive the kiss deeper. She swiveled her hips, grinding against him as he struggled to pull free.

∞ ∞ ∞

Grace and Jordan emerged from the trail, and took in the scene. Grace's hand flew to her mouth as she gasped, her knees betraying her. What she saw could only be described as frantic and desperate, and she felt as if her heart broke in two. Alli's dress was hiked up around her waist, exposing bare buttocks, and when Brady spun, she could see his hand firmly planted on her breast. Jordan put his arm around Grace's shoulders and pulled her close, leading her back and away from the scene.

"Shit. I'm sorry you had to see that, Grace," he whispered. "I told you he was a heartbreaker. I hate with a passion that he broke yours."

Grace couldn't form words. More than her heart broke in that moment, and she felt a meltdown coming on. "I have to go," she managed. "Walk me to my car?"

"I'll come with you," he said.

"No, Jordan." He started to speak again, but she interrupted. "I mean it. Just say goodbye to the girls for me, will you? It's fine. I just need to…" but she could think of no words to finish the sentence. Her heart was crushed, and she didn't want to face anyone. Especially Brady.

"Grace, please just let me…"

"I said NO, Jordan. Honestly, I appreciate your support, but I need some time alone right now."

"Fine," he said hesitantly, pushing his fingers through his hair in frustration. "Will you call me?"

"Sure," she croaked. She climbed into her car and drove away.

∞ ∞ ∞

Finally, things were going his way. He'd seen the invitation taped up on the corkboard in one of the octagons, and knew Grace wouldn't miss her boyfriend's party. He knew he wouldn't be welcomed with the revelers, so he arrived after dark and sat in his car, hoping that when the party broke up, he'd be able to follow her home. It was better than a Vegas jackpot when he saw her car speeding down the drive, with no passengers inside.

Dusty followed her out and trailed her car to an unmarked road. He passed the turn, drove until he could no longer see her tail lights, then circled back. Turning off his headlights, he cruised slowly, passing one house, and then coming to a long driveway with a little cottage at the end. Her car was parked in front.

Adrenaline pumped into his veins and he drove on, contemplating the best way to get to her. He finally had her, all by her lonesome, without her boyfriends or any of the big dogs from the sanctuary to protect her. He could end it all right now, with all the potential witnesses partying at Brady's lavish new place.

There was a clump of bushes about fifty yards from the driveway, and he figured it best to park there, in case his car could be seen from the house down the road. It took a bit to find a place to turn around, but once he was parked beneath the bushes, he reached over, pulling the long, serrated knife from the glove box.

His heart was dancing in his chest--it was going to end here, tonight, and he couldn't wait to get it started.

∞ ∞ ∞

"Get the hell off me!" Brady said, finally disentangling Alli and dumping her unceremoniously into the sand.

"Ouch," she said, smiling seductively and tracing a finger around her exposed nipple.

Brady spat in the sand and wiped the back of his hand across his face to remove her stink and more pink lipstick. "What the hell?" he asked incredulously.

"I missed you Brady," she slurred. "And Jared said you were probably tired of girls who smelled like dog shit."

"Fuck." Had Alli told Grace, too, that she was his girlfriend? And how much had Grace already seen that would make her believe it?

"Yes, Brady, that's exactly what we should do."

He pointed a finger at her, and growled, "Don't ever touch me again, and don't you dare tell anyone you're my girlfriend. You mean nothing to me, Alli—you need to get that through your head." Then he left her there, and jogged off down the trail to find Grace.

She wasn't in the garden or on any of the trails. He ran back through the yard, ignoring Alli's choking sobs, and bumped into Jared by the DJ booth. "Alli's drunk in the backyard, and you get to babysit her. I don't want her anywhere near me, do you understand?"

"Yeah, sure, man," Jared stammered, a confused look on his face.

Jordan was back at the table with the Dogtown crew, but Grace wasn't with them. Lara had her phone to her ear, and Jeanie was tapping frantically at her screen. He rushed to the table, ignoring their scathing looks. "Where's Grace?" he asked breathlessly.

"She left," Jordan said coldly. "She got a real good glimpse of the real Brady Cash in a lip-lock with Miss California, and bee-lined it out of here. Nice work, Cash. I knew you'd show your true colors eventually."

"Son of a..." Brady pounded the table in frustration. "And you just let her go? Where was your head?"

Jordan glared at him. "She insisted she needed time alone. I respected her wishes."

"Unbelievable," Brady mumbled, his face red. "I can't believe you would think..."

"What do you expect, Brady?" Lara snarled. "You tell her you want a relationship with her, then you're practically having sex with your California girlfriend in the back yard?"

Brady put his hands on the table and leaned down, his face furious, and looked directly at each of them in turn. "That woman is NOT my girlfriend, and I did not invite her. She is less than nothing to me. She jumped me, and caught me unaware." He glared at Jordan. "That's what you saw. Go ask Alli if I told her the same thing...her drunk ass is probably still lying in the sand where I dumped her." He hung his head and took a long, slow breath. "I meant everything I said to Grace...but hey--thanks for showing me what you really think of me." The girls' eyes all turned to Jordan, who hung his head.

"So, there isn't anything between you and..."

"NO. Emphatically and absolutely...NO."

Now it was the girls' turn to hang their heads.

"I'm sorry, Brady. You're right, we should've trusted you," Jeanie said softly.

He pressed his lips into a firm line. "Whatever. Where'd she go?" Brady demanded.

"We don't know," Lara said. "We're trying to get her, but she's not answering. I assume she'd go home."

"Damn it." Brady strode away, pulling out his phone and jamming his fingers onto the keypad. He jumped in his car and screamed off, kicking sand onto some of the partyers.

"Grace," he said, when the call went to voicemail. "Holy shit, I'm so sorry you saw that. It is absolutely not what you think, and I need to talk to you right away. You're the only woman I want, and I'm coming over right now." He tossed the phone onto the seat, and sped off down the road.

∞ ∞ ∞

I'm an idiot, Grace thought as she tossed things into a suitcase. She'd told herself a million times that she wasn't ready for a relationship, that she didn't need the complication of a man in her life. Why hadn't she listened? She Brady get under her skin, and damn it, now she was hurt. Everything about this journey had been healing and wonderful, and now she felt crushed. "*You can trust me, Grace*," Brady had said. He'd begged her to trust him...he'd promised.

She swept the contents of the bathroom counter into the case, and then tossed the bag into her car. Someone would be here soon, she was sure of it, and she didn't want to talk about it, didn't want to hear excuses. She definitely didn't want the sympathy.

Bryce and Zion had been on her to-do list from the start of this journey, and she needed some time away. Alone. She backed out of the driveway, and hit the road.

∞ ∞ ∞

"Damn it" Dusty growled as he watched Grace jump into her car. He jogged back to his Chevy, dropped the knife on the seat, and followed. He was screwed for tonight if she was going back to the party; but at least he knew where she lived now. Either way, it wouldn't be much longer for Grace Burton.

He cheered out loud as she turned the opposite way from Brady's, heading north on 89. If he did the deed out of town, it might keep the cops from asking for volunteer records from the shelter. He hummed to himself as he fingered the sheath of the knife.

Chapter 31

Brady expected Jordan's Jeep to pull up behind him, but so far, he was the only one on the road. Hopefully, the girls convinced him that it was Brady, and him alone, who needed to deal with this mess, although there was little doubt that Jordan would be waiting in the wings, ready to pick up the pieces.

Seeing the group from LA was a mixed bag, and he found himself wondering if he had actually been like them once. Self-centered, egotistical, misguided...not that long ago, he realized sadly. He was embarrassed for the Best Friends people to have seen the person he once was.

Alli had been a mistake. Most of them had been. The women he'd dated before--in his old life--were all the same. They came from money, and they always wanted more.

He wasn't the same man. Jordan had been right about him being a heartbreaker, but maybe that was because he'd never actually involved his heart before. Now that he was all in, he understood what heartbreak really was.

With Grace, everything was different. She was fresh, pure, kind, and unpretentious, and now she was hurting because of him. He would fix this...he had to. He needed to tell her how important she'd become to him, tell her that he was falling for her. That he needed her in his life. He was prepared to beg on his knees, if necessary, but when he pulled into her driveway, her car wasn't there.

∞ ∞ ∞

"Someone's gonna die tonight, someone's gonna die tonight," Dusty sang as he followed the taillights. They were on the only road out of town, but he kept his distance--he'd been dreaming of this day for too long to fuck it up now. Out here, at least, he wouldn't have to worry about the Indian or Pretty Boy Brady interrupting their little reunion. He looked forward to taking his time with her.

His dick hardened as he fingered the knife, anticipating her agony when he told her how the little girl screamed, how the husband begged for her life like a little pussy. He'd tell her that if she'd been there, he would've taken her and let them live…it was complete bullshit, of course, but it'd make for a hellova good show.

The road was deserted and they were miles from anywhere--maybe he should bump her car, drag her out into the desert, and leave her body for the coyotes.

He was grinning at the mental image of Grace being torn apart by wild dogs when suddenly, his car bucked. Frowning, he checked the empty rear-view mirror and pushed the gas pedal--but the Chevy sputtered and died. His eyes jerked to the dashboard as he slowed, his stomach sinking like a rock. He pounded his hands on the steering wheel and let out a long string of loud curses; every word he knew. The gas gauge had dipped below the big red E…he was out of gas.

Dusty jumped out of the car and watched in anguish as Grace's taillights blinked out of sight. He was miles from civilization, and, as if to accentuate the fact, a chorus of coyotes took up howling in the near distance.

∞ ∞ ∞

Brady smacked the steering wheel in frustration. "Damn it!" he yelled. He pounded on her door anyway, but the house was dark. He pulled out his phone and called her again.

"Grace, please talk to me," he pleaded. "I can explain everything, I swear it. I'm at your house, and I really need to talk to you. Please…call me as soon as you get this."

Jeanie answered immediately. "Did you find her?"

"She's not at the cabin. You haven't heard from her?"

"No…where else would she go?"

"I have no idea. I'm going to wait here for a bit, in case she comes back. If you hear from her, I want to know immediately."

"OK--same goes for you."

"I have to talk to her first," he said firmly.

"Fair enough. What about the party, Brady? People are looking for you."

"Screw the party," he spat. "Make my apologies, and find Jared. Tell him I'm not coming back--he'll get the California people squared away. Make sure Alli is the first one out."

"OK. And Brady? Good luck."

∞ ∞ ∞

Grace grabbed her phone and checked the number. Brady, again. Her phone hadn't stopped ringing and pinging since she left--this was at least Brady's sixth call. She tossed it back on the seat--she was not at all ready for that conversation.

However, she didn't want her friends to worry. She pulled off at a gas station, texting Jeanie while she filled the tank:

Stop worrying. Going away for a few days…need some time alone. Text you tomorrow.

A reply came almost instantly.

Where are you? Brady's frantic.

"Let him be frantic," she said, turning off her phone.

∞ ∞ ∞

Brady sat, paced, sat, and paced some more. It felt as if the coyotes had him surrounded--the howls came from every direction. The porch light glowed, but barely illuminated the front steps--it was too dark here, and he hated the thought of Grace being so isolated. As he was considering how to change that, his phone chirped.

Jeanie had copied and pasted Grace's text, then sent a second message...

She hasn't responded.

Brady balled his hands into fists, growling in exasperation and silencing the coyotes. God, he wanted to hit something. A few days? How in the hell was he supposed to wait that long to explain things to her? It killed him that she was going to spend days believing that he'd betrayed her--that he'd told her in one breath that he belonged to her, then made out with Alli in the next. He'd practically begged her to trust him...he shuddered to think what she thought of him now.

She obviously wouldn't take his calls, but a text would pop up on her screen automatically. He sent her a message in small bits, so all the words would show up.

Pls call me, he sent.

She is nothing, he sent.

Huge misunderstanding, he sent.

U can still trust me, he sent.

I love you

He deleted the last line before sending it--that was definitely not something to say in a text. The realization that it was true, however, fell on him like a tank, and made him feel even worse.

His heart soared when the phone chirped, but quickly sank when he saw it was from Jeanie.

No response from Grace. Told everyone you had an emergency and had to go. Mostly cleared out over here, CA people left, Jared says he'll call u. Want us to wait?

Damn it, there was no sense in hanging around here. She wasn't coming back tonight. He texted Jeanie back.

No, I'd be horrible company. Thanks for clearing the place out. Let me know immediately if you hear anything.

Jordan's Jeep and the rental truck were the only vehicles left when Brady pulled up to the house; the tiki bar the only sign that the party even took place. His vision frosted when he saw Jordan stand and wave; Brady saw only the smug look he'd worn when he announced that Grace had seen him tangled up with Alli. He could only imagine what Jordan must have told Grace about his past with women; and then he'd let her leave, alone, when she was a mess. That was not OK with him.

Brady closed the distance between them in three big strides, took a swing, and connected solidly with Jordan's jaw. Caught completely unaware, Jordan fell backward over the chair, landing in a crumpled heap.

He spat blood on the sand and looked up at a fuming Brady. "I guess I sort of deserved that," he said, waiting for Brady to calm before attempting to stand up. "You didn't have to hit me so hard, though."

Brady unclenched his fists and took a deep breath. "Fuck, I'm sorry," he said, extending a hand to help him up. "You didn't deserve it--I just really wanted to hit something."

"So glad I waited around to help you out with that," Jordan said, flexing his jaw; his face twisting in pain.

Brady strode over to the tiki bar and poured two neat shots of Scotch, handing one to Jordan. They tossed them back, and Brady grabbed the bottle, dropping it onto a table between two lawn chairs. He sat, poured another, and tipped the bottle toward Jordan.

They sat without speaking for some time, watching the catering truck pull away and thrusting them into the silence of the night.

"Let me get you some ice for that jaw."

"Nah, it's OK. You don't really hit that hard." He tried for a wry smile, but cringed instead.

"Why did you say you deserved it?"

Jordan's eyes dropped. "Let's just say I wasn't exactly singing your praises, and I was with Grace when she saw you in that lip-lock. I could've told you that she was leaving, or told her to wait for an explanation; but I didn't. Sorry, man."

"It wasn't a lip-lock. She attacked me."

"I believe you; but that definitely wasn't what it looked like from where Grace was standing."

"It kills me that she saw that, and I can't even explain it to her." He poured another shot. "Alli's a very 'ex' ex. Apparently, Jared told her I might be missing home, hungry for some LA booty."

"And she was happy to oblige. Must be tough to be you, Cash."

"Some days are better than others. This one pretty much sucks."

"Yeah. Sorry about that."

"So, you planning out how to move in and pick up the pieces? This isn't over, you know." Brady pressed the heels of his hands against his temples.

"I didn't figure it would be." Jordan poured each of them another shot, held the glass of amber liquid up toward the porch light before tossing it down. "Tell me the truth, Cash."

"It is the truth--Alli..."

"Not about Alli. How do you really feel about Grace?"

Brady looked at him, then at the ground. "I can't tell you before I tell her."

"That's what I figured," Jordan sighed. He poured another shot, threw it back. "We said we'd support her decision, right?"

"I haven't forgotten."

"Well, I support her decision."

"What's that supposed to mean?"

"It's you, man," Jordan conceded. "She let me down easy tonight; told me about the chemistry she felt with you--but even before that...I know that look in a woman's eyes...and she wasn't looking at me."

"I'm not so sure. Not after what she saw tonight. She thinks I betrayed her."

"I'm sure. You'll get her back."

Brady put out his hand. "Thanks, man, I really hope you're right."

Jordan shook it, squeezing hard and making Brady wince. His hand was swollen from the punch and already turning purple. "I guess I kind of deserved that."

Jordan grinned. "Yeah, you definitely did."

Brady grabbed the bottle from the table and headed for the house. "Come on, we could both use some ice. You can crash in the spare room."

"Why's that?"

"Because I'm counting on you to help me polish off this bottle."

Chapter 32

Grace hiked to the bottom of Bryce Canyon and up again, pushing her muscles to the limit, hoping exhaustion would clear Brady Cash from her head. It didn't work. She meditated on a quiet little trail, hoping to settle her heart, but that didn't help, either. Finally, she tried to focus on snapping pictures of the incredible landscape, knowing she'd barely remember it, since all her thoughts were of him.

He had no idea how hard it was for her to trust again; to let someone in when the greatest loves of her life had left her behind--she didn't know if she had it in her to reinvent herself again.

Oh, hell...even she didn't believe that. Now she was having abandonment issues, too? Her family had been taken-- they hadn't left her. Somehow, though, the feelings in the aftermath were too much the same.

Apparently, Jordan had been right all along, but she'd been too mesmerized, like so many others before her, to see it. Brady made her feel so special, so...desired. Then a woman from his past shows up, and he couldn't even wait to get her somewhere private before tugging off her clothes. She tossed her head to try and shake loose the image--the urgent grunts from Brady, the passionate moans from Alli...his hand on her breast.

Maybe if she hadn't fallen under Brady's spell--if there hadn't been that intense electrical charge between them, she might have looked at Jordan differently; might have come to see him as more than a dear friend. It sounded good in her head, but her heart knew it wasn't true. Somehow, even though it led to another heartache, she was meant to fall for Brady Cash.

You can't escape fate...Maybe you can alter it a bit, make it your own. She'd obviously failed miserably at that.

So, what now? There was no way she could stay in Kanab without running into Brady constantly. He was part of their group of friends, too, and she wouldn't ask them to take sides. She thought back to her conversation with Mandy, right before she started this whole journey. It felt like a lifetime ago, and in many ways, it was. Had she lost her way again? Or did she just need to get her head on straight?

When she got back to her room, she turned on her phone. Her friends were probably freaking out, and she didn't want them to worry. The screen was full of texts--she didn't need to read them to know what they said, and she definitely didn't want to see any from Brady. Grace swiped her finger across the screen to clear them, and sent a group message to everyone but Brady. Quit worrying--just trying to get my head on straight. I'll call when I'm ready to talk...but not yet. Then she powered down and tucked the phone into her pocket.

Zion was majestic and beautiful in a whole different way than Bryce. Where Bryce was all hoodoos and red rock, Zion was greener, the rock more twisted, the mountains more dense. As she stood under the Weeping Rock, she couldn't help but think of the two men in her life; completely different, but incredible in their own ways. Now Jordan was hurt because of her, and she was hurt because of Brady.

As the ancient water fell on her shoulders, Grace couldn't help but admire the tenacity of nature. Twelve hundred years had passed since the water entered the mountain, clawing its way through solid rock before drizzling out to splash on her skin. Determination. Perseverance. Will. They were qualities she'd gained on this journey, and she would never let them go--she wouldn't sink again.

She'd worked hard to get back to a place where she felt stable, and would fight to keep it that way. Every fiber of her being wanted to stay...forever. This was her home now, and she loved everything about it...even Brady.

Damn it…especially Brady.

How had that happened? When she'd first arrived, so many people told her she'd fall in love here—they said it would be impossible not to. Not once, though, had she even considered the possibility of finding this kind of love again; in fact, she'd been determined not to. Chalk another one up to fate—no matter how hard she tried to keep control of her heart, it had given itself away, anyway. She'd believed Brady was her spark--but now…

Exactly, she thought. *What now?*

They'd have to figure it out…find a way to stay friends. She'd get over him eventually, right? It wasn't like she was a stranger to heartache.

For now, while the pain was fresh, she could avoid Dogtown; just until she found a way to resist the incredible pull he had on her. When they went out as a group, she'd make sure there was enough distance between them that their electricity couldn't span it. Maybe he didn't even know what he did to her.

Grace hopped the tram and rode it to the end, taking a cleansing dip in the frigid river--a baptism of sorts into her new life. One she would hold on to, no matter what fate threw at her.

∞ ∞ ∞

His friends had forgiven him— Jordan had seen to that. He'd explained everything, and the whole crew stopped over at Brady's in the early afternoon, apologizing with flowers and lunch.

"It'll be fine," Lara said, giving him a supportive squeeze. "Once she knows what really happened, you'll be OK."

"It's just eating me alive that I can't explain--I keep texting her, but I don't think she's reading them."

"We're not getting answers, either. I don't think she even has her phone turned on."

Brady sighed. "What if she doesn't come back? Remember when she said she'd traveled across the whole country by herself? Had she ever mentioned that to any of you?"

They all shook their heads.

"And how is it that she has nothing to go back to? God, there's so much I don't know about her. Did she tell any of you that she was an RN?"

They exchanged glances, then Lara answered for the group. "No. We never knew that."

"She told Doc Mary when she was interviewing for the job. When I mentioned it later, she got real quiet; told me it was in another lifetime. I let it go--said she could tell me about it when she was ready--but it makes me wonder. Is she running from something?"

"I wish we knew," Jeanie said softly. "I always wondered why she was so adamant about not getting involved in a relationship. We all knew she had a huge thing for Brady, but she tried so hard to avoid it...Sorry, Jordan."

Jordan shrugged. "She told me more than once that her life was complicated--that she had a lot to figure out."

"God knows she had a hard time trusting me," Brady said sadly, "and now she thinks I betrayed her. I hate that she's hurting because of me." He hung his head in his hands, and the girls rested their hands on his back, reassuring him.

Sometimes she seemed so fragile, he thought, like she was haunted by something that robbed her of the smile he loved to see in her eyes. Other times, though, she was incredibly strong. Her emotions ran deep, constantly shifting between peaks and valleys. She'd be with him, and then she wasn't...her eyes fading as she went somewhere else in her mind...somewhere no one else was allowed to go.

"She'll be back," Veronica said confidently. "There's no way she'd abandon PG, and even if she doesn't want to see Brady right now, she wouldn't run out on the rest of us. I'm sure of it."

"God, I hope you're right," Brady mumbled.

Whatever it took, he would fix it. He was in love with her, and he would make her believe it. He had to.

The house was too quiet when everyone left. Brady went for a walk, but it did little to clear his head--instead, when he emerged from one of the little trails, he could see the indentation in the sand where he'd dumped Alli, and it brought the whole scene rushing back. He immediately left another voicemail and sent a couple texts, but knew in his heart that he wasn't going to hear back from her. She was too hurt and disappointed.

There was only one person he could really talk to when his life tanked, and that was Lindsey. She was a great listener, gave solid advice, and never got pissed off when he didn't take it. It was only four o'clock, and he didn't think he could stand to sit in the house all night, waiting for a call that almost certainly wouldn't come. He picked up his phone and punched in her number.

"I was just about to call you," Lindsey said. "Are you OK? What was your emergency?"

He told her the abridged version, then let out a big sigh. "I wish you were closer, Linds. I could really use your shoulder right about now."

"Then it's your lucky day. Your place inspired me, and I decided to hang around for a bit. I'm in Mount Carmel, at Zion, and there's a great restaurant at the ranch where I'm staying. Join me for dinner?"

"I'll be there in thirty."

Chapter 33

Grace shoved another log into the burner and sat on the floor with PG, stroking her head and taking great pleasure in the wag of her tail. She hadn't told anyone she came back early--she needed one more night alone, in her own place, to build her strength before she saw Brady again.

Tomorrow she would ask him to meet her somewhere public, face him with all the courage she could muster, and lie to his face. She'd tell him that she understood; that she wasn't angry. Then she'd suck it up and continue building her new life. Eventually, she told herself for about the millionth time, she'd get over him.

PG rolled over for a belly scratch and Grace happily obliged. The scarred pittie was, perhaps, her best incentive to stay. She'd already decided that she'd adopt PG as soon as she was eligible, and just thinking about it made her smile. Like Payton had done years ago, working with Gracie had brought her to a place in her life where she was fully ready to make a real, fresh start. They'd embark on the next chapter of their lives together.

PG rolled back onto her side and let out a contented sigh before getting to her feet and nudging Grace's hand.

"Time for dinner, Princess?" she smiled. "There's some of your favorite wet meal left...I'll moosh it in for you." PG wagged her stump, and followed Grace into the kitchen, watching eagerly as her human pulled the can from the fridge. Just as she put the dish into the microwave, PG's ears perked and she rushed to the door, growling low in her throat.

"Are the coyotes here?" Grace asked. She didn't hear any howling yet, but PG always seemed to know when they were close. It was the only sound she ever made, that low growl when she determined a threat was near.

"Uh oh, your kibble container's empty," Grace said, giving it a shake. PG ignored her, continuing to stand guard at the door.

"Oh, my, PG…you must have missed them over the past couple days. It's not like you to ignore dinner preparation." Grace slipped into some shoes and grabbed a hoodie from the hook next to the door. "It's OK, Sweet Pea," she said, patting her head. "Sit tight…I have to get some kibble from the shed."

PG whined and fidgeted anxiously, swiping at Grace's leg with a paw. When Grace opened the door, PG tried to push her way out, and Grace had to scoot her back. "Goodness," Grace said, "are they that close?" PG whined again, and Grace sighed. "OK…I'll leave the door open, so you can watch me." She flicked the light switch, and pushed the screen door shut, clapping her hands sharply and yelling, "Go, coyote!" as she always did when she stepped out into the night.

Grace picked her way carefully over the rough stone walkway that led to the shed. Distant lightning illuminated her way for a brief second, then a rumble of thunder added an empty threat of rain. A shiver ran up her spine, and she decided she'd best bring in some more wood to last the night.

She swung open the large door and pulled the chain for the light, which flickered a few times before filling the shed with its harsh glow. Organizing the shed had been on her list of things to do; and now that she'd be avoiding run-ins with Brady, she'd have the time to do it. Maybe it would help to keep her mind off him. *Yeah, right.*

Skirting the huge sheet of plywood that held the trim, she weaved her way to the back workbench and hefted the bag of kibble, pouring some into the container. It was just over half full when the light suddenly blinked out, plunging her into near-total darkness.

Grace's stomach lurched; a primal fear instinct; and the bag dropped from her hands, sending tiny nuggets raining to the floor. She laughed at herself, first blaming the blackout on the impending storm and a possible lightning strike; but when she glanced out the dirty little window at her right, she could see the porch light burning brightly; the silhouette of Gracie scratching at the door. Just the bulb, then, she reasoned--she'd change it tomorrow. She grabbed the container with shaking hands, trying to make sense of the shadows. She'd only taken one tentative step toward the door when she heard the soft flick of a lighter, then the telltale crackle of a first inhale. Panic gripped her heart, adrenaline burst into her veins, and blood pounded in her ears. When she smelled the acrid scent of cigarette smoke, her heart thumped faster, her breath heaving in short gasps.

Survival instincts kicked in, and her senses heightened as she tried desperately to assess the threat. She felt around the top of the workbench for anything she could use as a weapon, sending another spray of kibble skittering to the floor. They sounded like gunshots as they bounced off cardboard, wood, and concrete, and Grace cringed. A shuffle of footsteps moved outside, seemingly in no hurry, and then the silhouette of a man filled the entrance of the shed, lit by the orange glow from the tip of a cigarette as he pulled in a drag. Grace held her breath, hoping to remain invisible in the darkness.

"Hello, Grace," he whispered. "Lovely evening, isn't it? For me anyway. For you...not so much."

Oh, God, she thought, *he knows my name.* That meant it wasn't a random incident, but a purposeful intrusion. Grace's blood ran cold. Every cop show she'd ever watched flicked across her brain in a series of flashes, and she realized that if he knew her name, she likely knew his, as well. Danger charged the air, and every one of her senses flipped to high alert. "Who's there?" she whispered hoarsely as she frantically searched for a weapon. Finally, her hand fell on cold metal, and she pulled a pry bar into her right hand, closing her fist around it.

"Deliverance, Grace," the familiar voice said, menace dripping from every syllable. He drew out her name in a hiss, and she knew who he was.

"Kevin?" she croaked, her stomach lurching. Why would he be here, and why did he sound so full of malice? Her fight or flight instinct kicked in, and because she was cornered, her body and mind prepared for fight.

"Name's Dusty, actually. But you can call me Nightmare." He raised the cigarette to his lips, the orange glow reflecting off something in his other hand. *Oh, God,* she thought. *Is that a knife?*

Grace inhaled on a gasp, trying to gain some composure as he took a step closer. She needed to distract him--keep him talking--until she could figure out what to do next. It occurred to her that no one knew she was home--she was completely on her own. "I don't understand. What are you doing here, Kev...Dusty?"

He sucked a long drag and blew the smoke into the shed. "Oh, Grace...you really don't know, do you?" The chuckle that rumbled from his throat turned her blood to ice, even as a sheen of sweat dampened her skin. "I wasn't entirely sure I could pull it off, but you really are clueless, aren't you? I thought you might've recognized me the first time we met, but it just went right over your head. Love really must be blind."

Oh, God. He'd watched her--he'd seen Jordan kiss her and spied her in Brady's arms--he'd asked questions about whether she was seeing someone, and she'd turned him down when he asked her out. Could he have been harboring jealousy all this time? Because he thought she was in love with either Jordan or Brady? "I'm not blinded by anything, Dusty," she said, trying to keep her voice soft and even. "I'm not involved with anyone."

"No? Brady finally have enough of your mood swings? Or maybe he caught you making out with the Indian behind his back, and gave you the boot. Is that why you went running off?"

Oh, God…how did he know this? "We just decided it wasn't the right time. I'm not interested in a relationship right now. With anyone."

"And why is that, I wonder?" he asked sarcastically. Before she could open her mouth to answer, to tell him that she'd lost her entire family in the hopes that sharing her personal tragedy might make him more sympathetic, he continued. "Could it be that you can't stop thinking about your poor, murdered family? Your husband, your little girl and your stupid fucking mutt?"

Another dose of adrenaline shot through her veins, and a bead of sweat broke out on her forehead even as her skin dimpled in gooseflesh. "How do you…"

"Let me tell you a little story…Grace," he spat. "You see, I know all about loss, too. I had a brother once."

"I'm so sorry," Grace whispered.

"Are you really?" His voice raised, both in pitch and volume, and the hand holding the knife--definitely a knife--shot toward her.

"I really am," she said, her butt pressed against the workbench. He was still a good distance away, but in the dim light, the blade looked long enough to reach her anyway. "It's horrible to lose someone you love."

"I don't want your sympathy, bitch…I just want you to hear my story." Grace swallowed, and he continued. "He was more like a father to me than a brother," Dusty continued. "My old man up and left us when I was just a kid; never said goodbye, never called. Dale was all I had, and I worshiped the ground he walked on."

Warning bells started going off in Grace's brain. Dale was the name of the killer at the bank--the one who'd murdered her unborn child. Her voice shook as she answered. "Dusty, I'm truly sorry for your loss, but it doesn't have anything to do with me. You're frightening me, and I really want you to leave. I won't tell anyone about this if you just go right now."

Instead of turning to go, he took another step into the shed and bumped into the rider. So little light filtered in that he was nearly lost in the shadows, and she opened her eyes wider to follow his movements.

"It has everything to do with you, bitch!" he hissed. "He's dead because of you!"

Sheer panic swamped every cell of Grace's body and her heart pounded furiously. She tried to keep her voice calm, but even to her it sounded crackly. "Your brother was at the bank. I didn't kill him, Dusty, it was another inmate…"

"You put him there! You testified against him, and they put him in that goddamn jail to rot! They killed him like a lamb at the slaughter!"

"He killed my baby!" Grace screamed back, surprised by the clarity in her voice. She saw him tense, and purposefully lowered her voice to try and calm him. "He went to that bank with a gun that he was prepared to use--and did use. He killed people, Dusty, including my unborn child. He deserved to go to jail."

"He went there to save his family. To save me."

"It was the wrong way to save you," she said with as much false sympathy as she could muster. "He put his family in danger the second he…" she stopped, another thought gaining clarity in her mind. He knew who she was because of the testimony in court, but how could he…

"Starting to sink in, is it?" Dusty smiled. He took one last pull and dropped the cigarette, crushing it under his boot.

"Oh, God."

"I'm the only god here tonight." In the dim light, she saw the evil grin spread across his face.

"You…"

He held his arms out to the side and cackled. "Finally!" he said, clapping his hands together, faint light reflecting off the jagged edges of the knife. "I wondered if you'd ever figure it out. Good for you, Gracie…you've got something going on upstairs after all." He took another step into the shed, and Grace bent her knees, ready to flee. "It was you I was after that night. You *owed* me, and I came to collect…only you weren't home."

"You killed my family." It was more of a statement than a question; Grace already knew the answer.

"And you killed mine. For a while, I thought it made us even."

White hot anger bubbled up, and Grace fought to stay calm. "The way I see it, the scales are tipped in your favor. You lost one person--and not by my hands. You and your brother killed four of mine." She fought the urge to charge him--to beat him with the pry bar until he was nothing but a pile of rubble--but she knew she needed to keep the situation under her control. It was obvious she was dealing with a madman.

"Not even close," he hissed. "You know, for a while, I got more pleasure out of your suffering than I would've seeing you dead. I watched you, Grace. You sat in the parking lot of that storage unit so many times. It was a long time before you finally went in."

Her thoughts went to her sister's family and the chilling realization that they could have been in danger because of her.

"It was a living hell," she said, hoping he'd find satisfaction in her pain.

"But you moved on, Grace, and that just doesn't sit right with me. I was kicking myself for not being more attentive...I couldn't believe you'd taken off...but I knew I'd find you. It was really nice of you to post that blog; it started me on my own journey of healing and retribution. It's been a damn frustrating one for me, though, since I could never catch up, but when I read your article about this place, I figured you'd stay for a while. I'm glad you did. I wanted to get to know you."

"Hopefully you realized that I'm a good person, Dusty. That I deserve a second chance at life after everything I loved was taken from me."

"You deserve nothing!" he bellowed, making Grace jump. She thought she heard a growl in the distance, or perhaps another rumble of thunder. "I was left with nothing when my brother was murdered!"

Grace couldn't keep her cool any longer. "I was left with nothing TWICE, thanks to you and your 'family.' I lost everything I ever cared about, too, but I found a way to heal, Dusty, and you can, too. I can help you…" She hated the pleading tone in her voice, but was powerless to keep it at bay.

"Oh, I know all about your little self-help pep talks, and your so-called, 'sparks.' And no, thank you very fucking much. I'll be healed once I've avenged my brother."

Grace could hear frantic whining and scratching in the distance, and let her eyes dart to the window just long enough to see the silhouette of Gracie pawing frantically at the closed screen door. "You won't be healed, Dusty, you'll be scarred for life. Having another murder on your conscience…"

"You want to see 'scarred for life?' I already am, thanks to your goddamn mutt."

"Gracie?" she asked automatically, but then she realized, and said, more softly, "Payton."

Dusty produced a flashlight, and Grace squinted at the sudden burst of light that filled the shed. "That cocksucker busted through the door. Mangled my arm and took chunks out of my leg and my face before I was able to get the fucker."

Grace then saw the glaring explanation for why "Kevin" was always covered, despite the heat of a desert summer. His entire right forearm was a twisted, gnarled mass of scar tissue--raw, pink vines over bleach-white skin.

She looked away, taking advantage of the sudden and temporary blast of light to visualize escape routes on either side of the makeshift staining table. At least she'd have that advantage, she thought, glad she hadn't had a chance to de-clutter the shed.

"I'm not sorry for that," she growled, no longer able to maintain her fragile grip on control. "I wish he'd gotten your jugular, you bastard."

PG was really barking now--a horrifically mean-sounding snarl that the pittie must have heard a thousand times in her previous life. Grace glanced out the window to see her pushing at the door, trying to get out.

Dusty laughed; a deep, rolling, threatening chuckle that sent shivers all the way to her toes. "He was the one that went down in the end, though, wasn't he Grace? You know why? Because I'm a survivor. Your husband tried to get me too...what a pussy he was. He cried like a baby and begged for the little girl's life."

Grace gasped, and pressed her lips together. She would not give him the satisfaction. No matter what he said, she would hold her ground, and she would have the last word. Blind rage and steadfast determination rose up in her, and she gripped the pry bar tighter.

"I killed her first--did you know that? Held her up by her hair and slit her pretty little throat while your husband pleaded and howled." He lifted the knife into the air, and held it up for her inspection. "This is the knife that ended them, Grace--the same one that's going to end you. I want you to know, though, that I told them it was your fault that they were going to die. I told the little girl that her mommy sent me to kill them both."

An involuntarily moan escaped Grace's throat, and hot tears streamed down her face.

"Hurts, doesn't it? You're going to experience a lot more pain tonight, Grace, before I send you to join them."

"Bring it on," Grace growled as her fury threatened to explode. "You will not take me, too. I'm going to send you straight to hell."

Dusty's shadow darted left, so Grace went to her own left, deftly jumping the boxes she knew were there and heading toward the door. His move was only a ploy, though, and after his quick fake he moved right, coming at her full on, knife swinging. Grace turned and tripped over the same boxes she'd just vaulted, dropping the pry bar as she thudded into the workbench. He was almost on her, but she managed to grab the heavy metal and swing around, connecting with a sickening crunch.

"Bitch!" he wailed, grabbing a handful of her hair as she darted around the rider and headed for the door. She screamed in pain but kept moving, feeling her scalp tear as the hair was ripped from it. Fear drove her legs and she darted out the door into the dark night. She ran for the cabin, but he was faster; he grabbed the hood of her jacket and yanked her back violently.

Grace felt the blade stab into her right side; felt the blood soak her jacket as it was jerked out, but she felt no pain whatsoever. She took another swing with the pry bar and connected with his left shin; heard the sharp snap of fragile bone. Dusty howled in pain and went down, but didn't loosen his grip. Grace went down with him; cracking her head on one of the cobblestones of the walkway. Dizziness and nausea gripped her immediately, and she lost her hold on the weapon as she fought to stay conscious.

PG was barking frantically now, a sound Grace had never heard before. It sounded savage and vicious, and Grace prayed that Don would hear her and send help.

"Shut up, bitch!" Dusty yelled. "Don't worry," he snarled at the intensely agitated pittie, "I'll get you next." Grace took that split second to look up at Dusty, her stomach curdling when she saw the maniacal look in his glazed eyes. He swung the knife downward and she rolled to the side, grabbing for his wrist, but instead got a good handful of sharp blade. It sliced across her palm, bringing a fast flow of blood and another wave of dizziness as he swung his bad leg around and straddled her, grinning down at her.

In that moment, Grace accepted death. Dusty had at least six inches and sixty pounds on her, and he was determined. She tried to scoot away and felt herself slipping in a pool of her own blood as colors exploded in her head and then, everything went black.

Chapter 34

"I'm sorry, Brady, really I am," Lindsey said as she swept another sushi roll onto her plate. "I had no idea about your past with Alli. I would've run interference if I had."

"I wouldn't even call it a past, but I still should've known better. I should've kicked her out the minute she walked in."

"You'll talk to her--you'll explain."

Brady sighed. "I just hope it's not too late."

"What's her name again? I met her at the party, right?"

"She was one of the first ones I introduced you to." He told her about the situation with Jordan; the reason he hadn't had been able to introduce her as his girlfriend. If not for that little snafu, none of this would have happened. He'd have made sure everyone at the party knew that he and Grace were together. "Grace Burton."

Lindsey squinted. "Why does that name sound familiar?"

"Maybe because you just met her a couple days ago?"

"I remember the introduction, but I'm sure you didn't use last names. It sounds familiar, though...I swear I've heard it before." She pulled out her phone. "Sorry, but you know it'll bug me if I don't check."

Brady smirked and let Lindsey do her thing. She ran a Google search on pretty much everyone she met, figuring it helped to keep her one step ahead of the game.

"This is her, isn't it?" Lindsey asked after a moment, holding up the phone.

Brady looked at a picture of a younger, smiling Grace, and his heart ached. "Yeah, that's her."

Lindsey scrolled her finger down the screen, her face becoming more pinched as she read.

"What is it?"

"Oh, Brady. What do you know about her past?"

"Pretty much nothing, actually." Wow, did he feel stupid saying that. "We were just talking about that earlier, as a matter of fact. She doesn't really talk about it much. I mean, I know she's a grief counselor, she used to be an RN, she's writing a book, she's from Chicago, and that she loves dogs." It was a pathetic amount to know about the woman he loved. "She has a sister," he added.

"Oh, honey…brace yourself." Lindsey handed over the phone and Brady skimmed the article, his heart getting heavier as he read. "Holy shit. Her whole family was murdered?"

"That's why her name sounded familiar--the story was all over the news in New York. I can definitely understand why it was so hard for her to let someone into her life again. No wonder she took off."

Brady tapped the back button and found the link for Grace's blog. He skimmed through the first post, then scrolled down, reading some of the more recent ones, where Grace talked about how she finally felt whole again; how she'd found new sparks that helped her to see life was worth living. She called one of the sparks, 'PG,' and the other, 'B.' He suddenly felt nauseous, and handed Lindsey her phone.

"Holy shit."

"Her life was destroyed, Brady, and she thought she was getting it back. Now she believes that the person she finally decided to trust betrayed her."

Brady hung his head. "Oh, God. I can't even imagine what she's been through."

"That has a tremendous impact on a person's psyche--I can see why it was so hard for her to let you in. Her husband didn't divorce her, he didn't cheat on her--they didn't even have a fight. He was murdered, and I can't even imagine how hard it would be to move on from that."

He couldn't either, and when he thought about how much she gave, how strong she was, he had a whole new respect for her. He closed his eyes, balled one hand into a fist, and pressed it hard to his forehead.

"You've got it bad for her," Lindsey whispered, laying her hand over his.

Brady took a deep breath, pushed it out through clenched teeth. "I'm in love with her."

Lindsey's eyes widened. "That's huge, especially coming from you. Does she know that?"

"No. She only agreed to give us a chance the night before the party."

"Wow. You need to be there when she gets back, Brady. You need to get the biggest bouquet of flowers known to man, fall on your knees, and tell her."

Brady grabbed his wallet from his pocket and threw down a hundred. "I have to go."

Lindsey laid her hand on his arm. "Yes, you do. Good luck."

He was just pulling out of the lot when he got a text from Lara.

She's back. Picked up Gracie for a sleepover--just found out.

He didn't bother to reply, just put pedal to the metal and screamed out of the parking lot.

∞ ∞ ∞

A strange sound pulled Grace from the dark place where she was resting. No, she thought-not resting--dying. She tried to shake the fog from her brain, but everything was so fuzzy, and she couldn't make anything connect. Then, in a rush, it all came back to her, and she moaned, rolling onto her side.

The sound was tearing, ripping, and suddenly PG was there; snarling ferociously and snapping her jaws. The shy pittie burst onto the scene as she must have seen so many attack dogs do in her previous life. She hit Dusty square in the chest, just as he was about to strike the fatal blow. "Gracie!" she wheezed.

"Fucking *bitch*!" She heard Dusty grunt as PG hit him full on, taking him down to roll on the ground and clamping onto his arm. She watched in horror as Dusty brought the knife around and buried it into the dog's hind quarter. Gracie's scream was horrific, but she pulled back only briefly and went in for another bite, catching the arm that held the knife, sending it flying. Grace tried to scramble for it, hoping to make what could very well be the last act of her life putting the bastard down for good. Dusty threw the dog off, his arm snapping out to backhand Grace hard across her cheek, throwing her back just as her fingers brushed the handle.

"This ends now!" he bellowed, closing his fist around the knife and rising up to his knees. But before he could turn, Gracie pounced again, her huge jaws wrapping around Dusty's neck, shaking him like a rag doll. He squealed in pain, trying desperately to swing the knife back around to connect with PG's muscular form. The dog threw him forward, and Grace heard the *whoosh!* of air as Dusty was pushed onto the knife, deftly puncturing his own lung. "Goddamn bitch, goddamn, *bitch*!" he hissed, struggling to a sitting position and staring incoherently at the shaft sticking out of his chest. His breath wheezed in his throat, each inhale a struggle, and Grace saw shock in his eyes for a brief moment before the dangerous intention set back in. He took a wild swing that connected with PG's head, knocking her to the ground where she lay horribly, silently still.

Grace spied the dull glint of the pry bar a few feet away and crawled toward it in slow motion, dizziness threatening to overtake her. Her stomach betrayed her and she heaved uncontrollably, the pain in her side blooming and stealing her breath in a bright shock of pain. She crawled through the sick and the blood, ignoring the pain and wrapping her hand around the cold metal. She turned to Dusty, who had his own hand wrapped around the hilt of the knife. He caught sight of the weapon in her hand, clenched his teeth, and in one painfully short motion, ripped it from his rib cage. His face was beaded with sweat; his skin flushed with fire as he struggled for breath.

He wasn't finished, though. He crawled slowly toward her as she struggled to right herself and get positioned for a good swing. Every movement seemed to rip at the hole in her side, gaping it open to spill more blood, but she clenched every muscle in her body against the pain and pushed herself to her knees. From behind Dusty's right shoulder, she saw Princess Gracie's leg twitch once, twice, and then watched as the pittie pulled herself up in a final attempt to protect her master. A vicious snarl escaped her throat and she threw herself at Dusty, clamping her jaws down on the wasted arm that Payton had mangled months earlier. Dusty swung the knife once more, planting it in PG's shoulder. The howl of pain nearly burst Grace's ears and her heart, and the dog once more fell to the ground, still. Dusty turned to grab the weapon again, but it was all the time Grace needed.

In a burst of what could only have been the most fundamental survival instinct, Grace rose to her feet. "You will not take me, too!" she yelled. Grace swung the pry bar with all her might, a war cry bursting from her throat. It slammed into her attacker's head with a sickening crack that sent waves of pain vibrating up her arm. Dusty's eyes met hers for just a moment--just a brief glimmer of knowing— then he fell to the ground, arms and legs twitching horrifically. She stood for a moment longer, watching the breath bubble haltingly from the pool of blood that puddled from the wound in his chest before spilling like a dark river to the ground; watched until the bubbles stopped coming. One look at his glazed and open eyes told her what she needed to know. Dusty was dead.

Tears streamed down her grimy, blood-smeared cheeks, and she fell to her knees beside PG, wrapping her arms around the limp body. "I'm so sorry, baby girl," she whispered into her fur. "Thank you for saving me." The dog whimpered weakly and placed her front paw over Grace's hand, then Grace welcomed the dark that enveloped them both.

∞ ∞ ∞

Brady almost hit Jordan's Jeep as they reached the driveway from two different directions. Instead of backing up, Jordan threw it in park, and jumped out.

"Don called me," he said frantically as Brady leaped out of his own vehicle. "He said he heard barking and screaming."

Panic flooded Brady's system as they both sprinted up the driveway. His heart nearly stopped when he saw the dark shapes lying motionless on the ground.

"Grace!" he screamed, reaching the shadowy masses and falling to his knees, laying his hand on her face.

PG whined, her tail flicking ever-so-slightly.

"Holy shit," Jordan stammered, yanking out his phone. "Is she alive?"

Brady pressed his lips to Grace's bloody cheeks, and felt a puff of breath. "She's breathing," he said. "Gracie's hurt, too. Bad."

Jordan frantically relayed the information to the police and hit the flashlight on his phone, shining it toward the other form. "Holy shit, I think that's Kevin. His face is all bashed in, but he's wearing long sleeves."

"Fence guy Kevin? Damn it--I knew there was something wrong with that dude. Why didn't I push the issue?"

"Shit. He's dead, man."

"What the hell is he doing here? Do you think he did this?" Brady didn't wait for an answer. "Grace," he said, cradling her in his arms. "Talk to me, baby."

"I don't know," Jordan said frantically, ripping off his shirt and pressing it to PG's bleeding shoulder.

Grace moaned softly, and Brady thought it was the most beautiful sound he'd ever heard. "That's it, baby. Listen to my voice. Don't you let go." He pulled her closer, felt warm blood spilling over his hand. "Oh shit, she's bleeding bad. I need to get her out of here."

Sirens screamed in the distance, getting closer. "They're coming," Jordan said. "I need to take Gracie."

"Call Doc Mary," Brady said. "Let her know you're coming."

Jordan punched his phone, breathlessly giving her the news.

Grace began to choke, struggling for breath, and Brady cradled her head. "Don't you leave me, Grace, you hear me? Stay with me, baby. I love you so much Grace…please don't go."

Jordan laid a hand on his shoulder, then scooped Princess Gracie into his arms. "Call me as soon as you know anything," he demanded.

"I will."

Jordan jogged back down the driveway and gently put Gracie in the back of the Jeep, then sped off as the ambulance arrived.

∞ ∞ ∞

Grace floated on a cloud, painlessly, and saw, in the distance, the Rainbow Bridge. She heard the joyful sounds of dogs playing, and watched as one dark figure broke away from the crowd.

She dropped to her knees as Payton ran to her, tongue dangling and tail in full wag as he flung himself against her body, his soft tongue licking her face.

"Payton," she said, holding his wriggling body as close as she could. "I've missed you so much, buddy."

His ears popped up and he ran toward the bridge, looking back at her. She was meant to follow, she knew, and as she approached, she saw Danny and Zoe standing in the center of the walkway; a bundle that she knew must be Briana in Danny's arms.

"Oh my God," she breathed, rushing to greet them. "My babies." She took the infant into her arms, the child that she never got a chance to hold. Zoe hugged her leg, and Danny put his arms around her. "Everything's perfect, now," she said, pressing her face against Danny's chest and putting her other arm around Zoe. "We're all together."

Danny shook his head. "It's not your time, yet, Grace. You have to go back."

"No...I don't want to go back," she insisted. "I want to stay with you. Please let me stay."

"Not yet," Danny said, pressing his lips to her forehead. "You still have things to do."

"It hurts to go back," she whispered.

"It'll hurt for a little while, but you'll get better. Don't be afraid. Trust Brady."

"But..."

"It's OK, Grace," Danny said. "He's the one for you now."

Her family looked at her and smiled, then they faded away.

Chapter 35

Grace felt as if she were trying to surface from the bottom of an ocean of syrup. She could hear sounds, but they were distant, muffled, and from no particular direction. She tried to speak, but her tongue wouldn't form words.

It would have been so much easier to give up; settle to the dark bottom and sleep, but instinctively she knew that she had to keep pulling for the surface; keep fighting against the forces that tried to hold her down.

"Come back to me Grace…open your eyes, baby." It was Brady's honey-voice--far away, but getting closer. "You can do it, Grace. Please open your eyes…please see me."

She knew the instant she regained consciousness--felt the searing pain in her face, her side, her hand. Her head throbbed, the pounding of blood like a drum, and the light blinded her, even from behind closed lids. Squinting, she opened her eyes slowly, and Brady was there, smiling down at her, his eyes full of relief, hope, and utter devotion.

"Hi," he said, gently brushing back a strand of her hair. He held her good hand in his, and brought it to his lips. His face was tired and strained; dark circles rimmed his eyes and hollows sank his cheeks. Still, he looked like an angel.

"Hi," she croaked, trying to smile past dry, swollen lips.

"I'm so glad you're back," he whispered, pressing a gentle kiss on her forehead. "I missed you."

"Hurts."

"I know, but you're so strong, Grace…so strong." A tear spilled from his eye, and fell onto the blanket that covered her. "You just keep fighting, you hear me?"

"You're crying."

Brady swiped at his eyes. "Happy tears, because now I know you're going to be OK."

It all started coming back to her--the struggle for her life, the admission of her would-be killer, the dog who ripped through the screen to save her. "Gracie..."

"She's going to be fine. Jordan's looking after her."

"He killed my family. I never told you...I'm so sorry."

"I know, Grace... it's OK. He'll never hurt you again."

"Gracie saved me."

"You saved each other, and now you just have to concentrate on getting better." He wiped away another tear, and looked into her eyes. "Don't ever leave me like that again, OK?"

"OK." She had no energy left, and every word was a struggle. "Tired," she managed, no longer able to keep her eyes open.

"Sleep now," he said, brushing the back of his hand over her cheek and pressing her hand to his lips. "I'll be right here when you wake up."

"Trust Brady," she whispered, already drifting off.

"Yes, Grace," he whispered, a sob in his throat. "You can always trust me."

The next time she opened her eyes, she felt much better. The throbbing in her head had subsided, and the pain in her side was down to a dull ache. Her right hand was bandaged, and her left rested in Brady's.

He was asleep in a chair next to her bed, lips slightly parted and his breath coming in long, even intervals. Still, the moment she stirred, his eyes fluttered open, and he smiled.

"There you are," he said softly.

"What day is it?"

"Tuesday," Brady answered. "You needed the rest," he said when he saw her pained look, "and you look so much better already. I should call the nurse."

"Wait," she whispered. He leaned toward her, eyebrows raised slightly. God, she loved his eyebrows. "I'm so sorry, Brady. For everything."

"Oh, Grace. I'm the one who's sorry. You didn't do anything wrong."

"You asked me to trust you, and I couldn't do it."

"She threw herself at me. She means nothing to me, Grace, I need you to know that. You are the only woman I want in my life."

"I know. Will you kiss me, Brady?"

She watched his eyes melt, saw in them that he was more than deserving of her trust. He bent down, brushed his lips feather-light over hers, and held them there for a moment; a soft kiss that held healing, promises, and a definite future. He rested his forehead against hers, and brushed another strand of hair from her face with a gentle finger. "I trust you," she whispered.

"I'm so glad to hear that. Now we need to get you better and get you out of this place. I'm going to call the nurse, and everyone else is dying to see you. Are you up for company?"

She smiled. "Definitely."

∞ ∞ ∞

The next day, Grace gave her statement to the police, with Brady at her side. It was only a matter of time until they matched Dusty's DNA to the murders in Chicago, and her family would have justice, after all, by her own hands. She would be released from the hospital the next day, with strict orders for plenty of rest and no strenuous activity for at least a week. The bruise on her face was already fading, and she was able to walk, slowly, without feeling like there was still a knife in her side.

The Dogtown crew walked in after the police left, and Grace looked around the room at the best friends she'd ever had in her life. They kissed her gently, in turn, and settled around the room.

"I don't think I can go back to the cabin," Grace whispered.

They exchanged glances, and Lara stood suddenly. "We're going to grab some lunch--what can we bring you, Grace? We're going to Nedra's."

"Oh, I'd love some fried chicken."

"We'll be back in a bit." They all stood and hustled out.

Grace frowned. "Is it me, or was that a really sudden departure?"

Brady pulled the chair up to the bed, and took her hand in his. "We've already talked about it, and we all agreed that there's no way you're going back there," he said. "Lara has your key, and with your permission, she and Jordan will get your things." He leaned over, pressing a kiss to her forehead. "Every single one of us offered to take you in, Grace, but I'm really hoping you'll come and stay with me."

"Oh," she said, then again, "oh."

"I've got the space, and I can do a lot of my work from home, and...we'll take everything at your pace. I want you there, Grace. I want to watch more sunsets with you. A lot more."

Her eyes closed, and she was filled with an inner peace, a bright light. She opened them, saw the hope in his eyes, and her heart melted.

"I won't be too much trouble..."

"You won't be any trouble. I'll take good care of you."

"...I should be back on my feet in a couple weeks. I can look for a new place in the meantime."

Brady took her face gently in his hands and brushed his lips over her bruised cheek, the end of her nose, her lips; then looked deep into her eyes. "The invitation's open-ended, Grace. Please come home with me."

She rested her hand on his arm, smiled up at him. "Yes, Brady. There's nothing I'd like more."

∞ ∞ ∞

"There's someone here who will be very glad to see you," Brady said as they pulled into the driveway. He opened the door and swept Grace into his arms.

She giggled. "I can walk, Brady...really...I'm feeling pretty good. I'm supposed to get some exercise."

"And you will," he said, fumbling with the lock. "But right now, I want to carry you. Indulge me." He swung the door open and carried her inside, setting her down gently in the foyer.

Grace heard the familiar whine, and PG limped around the corner, her stub of a tail thumping back and forth. "Princess Gracie," Grace smiled, leaning down to pet her. Brady let them have a little reunion, then led them both to the living room, tucking Grace onto the couch, and lifting PG to lie with her. Grace bent over and hugged the dog to her, accepting the enthusiastic licks and frantic cuddles. "How's my heroine?" she asked, running her fingers lightly along the new pink lines that scarred her body.

Princess Gracie responded with an excited growl and another lick.

The front door opened, and Jordan, Lara, Jeanie, and Veronica came in; Jordan toting her suitcases, and Lara carrying a box of the things she'd collected; the beaded coyote basket sitting on top. Jeanie and Veronica dropped cloth grocery bags on the table, and rushed over to welcome their friends home.

"We thought we'd have a little feast tonight," Veronica said, bringing over a plate of veggies with dip. "The boys are going to grill--Jeanie's already got chicken soaking in her famous tequila marinade."

"Sounds fabulous," Grace said. "I'm starved."

"Want to show me where you want these?" Jordan said to Brady.

"Follow me." He led Jordan up the stairs, and the girls surrounded Grace.

"You know," Veronica said, "he never left your side the whole time you were in the hospital."

"He was worried sick. I mean, we all were, but it really took a major toll on Brady," Lara added. "That girl at the party? She was an ex-girlfriend. Apparently, Jared told her that Brady might be missing California girls, and she wanted to find out. If you'd seen the way Brady sped out of here when he found out you were gone, you would know that she didn't mean anything to him."

Grace reached out and touched her arm. "I do know, but I appreciate you telling me."

"He really cares about you, Grace. I know it absolutely."

"Thank you," she smiled, "I'm so lucky to have all of you in my life."

Grace opened her eyes, unsure for a minute where she was. It was fully dark outside, but a nightlight illuminated the room with a soft glow, and she could see the beaded bowl sitting on the dresser alongside the bed, the coyote howling at the risen moon. She sank into the fluffy pillows, remembering her first evening home from the hospital. Brady had made a little spot for her on the back deck, on a hugely oversized lounge chair with pillows, blankets, and a dog bed alongside it for PG. She'd eaten like a horse, she recalled, then somewhere along the way, she must've fallen asleep--she vaguely remembered Brady carrying her upstairs and tucking her into bed. PG was curled on the dog bed in a corner by the window, her feet twitching as if she were chasing a rabbit in a dream.

She eased herself out of the bed and tiptoed to the door. Brady's door was open across the hall, and she crept over, poking her head in.

He slept on his back, his face illuminated by the waning moon that shone through the window. He looked so peaceful and beautiful in the muted light that it stole her breath. The soft rise and fall of his chest told her that he was sound asleep, so she resisted the urge to climb into his bed and lay her head upon it.

"You're the one for me now," she whispered, then she crept back to her room and slipped back into the bed.

She was awakened by PG's nose pushing against her hand, and scratched the pittie automatically behind the ears. "Good morning, Princess Gracie," she smiled. PG pressed against the bed, stretching over to give Grace a lick.

"I thought I heard you stirring." Brady stepped in, holding a large tray.

"Breakfast in bed?" she asked, taking a peek. "It looks amazing, and I'm starved. Thank you."

"You're more than welcome. I'll join you, after I take Gracie out."

"I'll wait for you."

She watched as he gently picked up PG and carried her out of the room. In a couple minutes he was back, with a tray of his own that he set on the desk.

"How're you feeling?" he asked.

"Better. Stronger. Pretty soon I'll be cooking for you and earning my keep."

"I can hold my own in the kitchen," he grinned. "You'll see."

"There's so much I don't know about you yet. So much I want to know."

"Same here. Let's have breakfast, then go sit outside. I want you to tell me about your family, Grace."

Chapter 36

The One Box was on the nightstand, and Grace asked Brady to bring it down. He propped Grace up with pillows on the oversized lounge chair, and settled PG on her dog bed. Then he sat close, his hand resting on her leg, as Grace set the box on her lap.

She pulled out the items one by one, sharing the precious memories each one held. Brady watched the video with her, wiping tears from her face as she shared the happiness her family had brought to her life. Every word was pure joy, until she told him about their final night, the night Dusty Pitts ended their lives.

She paused a moment, and her voice got soft. "I killed a man, Brady."

He dropped to his knees, and wrapped his arms around her; nestled her head on his shoulder. "A man who deserved to die...who would have killed you if you hadn't. You survived, Grace, and that's what matters."

"I know, but it's still hard."

"We'll get through it together. You're not alone anymore, baby--I'm here for you."

"God, I'm so lucky to have you," she murmured against his neck.

"I'm the lucky one," he whispered.

They spent the day outside, Grace enjoying the feel of the sun on her face, and PG stretching out on her dog bed. They took a slow walk together along the little trails that led to the garden, and Grace plucked some flowers to brighten her room. Brady grilled some filets, and they enjoyed an early dinner on the lower deck; Brady tucking more blankets around her to ward off the late-afternoon chill.

"I like having you here, Grace," Brady whispered, stroking her hair and brushing his lips over the healing bruise on her cheek.

"I like being here," she smiled. "I'm so glad you asked me to stay."

Damn it, she woke up in the bed again. Fresh air, cleansing conversation, and more good food knocked her out, and once again, Brady had had to carry her up. She looked out the window and saw the shadows deepening, puffy clouds darkened to purple by the setting sun.

Grace knew she'd find him on the balcony, watching the sunset. The door was open and she stepped out, wrapping her arms around him from behind and resting her head on his back. His hands came up to take hers, and he lifted the wounded one, pressing his lips to the jagged line that crossed her palm.

"Hey, sleepyhead," he said, turning to rest his hands on her waist.

"I need to quit doing that. You need to wake me when I fall asleep in the middle of the day."

"You were so peaceful, I couldn't disturb you. Feeling OK?"

"I feel good," she said, snuggling into him and resting her cheek on his chest. "Better now."

He wrapped his arms around her gently. "Should be a good sunset tonight," he said. "There are a few clouds in the sky."

Grace looked up at him. "I'm not going to break, you know."

"What do you mean?"

"You're being so sweet with me, so gentle...but I'm not that fragile."

"I just don't want to hurt you."

She backed up a step and looked into his eyes. "I'm initiating it."

He looked at her, puzzled. "What?"

"Kiss me, Brady."

It was all the invitation he needed. Hungrily, he took her mouth, and his breath quickened immediately. One hand slid up to cup the back of her neck, tilting her head to drive the kiss deeper, and the other slipped down to pull her in. The hum of being close to him went all the way to her marrow.

Grace's lips parted, and the taste of him, sweet and intoxicating, made her feel as if she was spinning, so she held on tighter. Her hands slid up his shirt, and she felt the tension in his muscles as he tried to hold back; to be gentle with her. Grace squeezed him tight, pressing her body to his as a low moan escaped his throat. She didn't want gentle.

"Oh, Grace," he murmured. He pushed her back slightly, trailed his fingers up her arm, down her shoulder, and over her breast. He cupped it in his hand, his thumb tracing circles in the center.

Grace gasped, and he stole the breath with his mouth. His lips moved to her neck, and she threw her head back as he nibbled his way down to her collarbone.

His hands slipped under her shirt, unhooking her bra with one quick flick of his finger. He slid both off in one quick motion, tossing them carelessly off the balcony. Then, he stopped, and stared.

"So beautiful." Brady dropped to his knees and ran a finger along the scar at her waist, pressing a soft kiss to the healing wound before standing. He cupped her breasts, one in each hand, and brought his mouth down to one, then the other, each flick of his tongue setting Grace on fire.

That slow and gentle could come with so much heat, she'd never imagined, and Grace didn't think she could stand it. She tugged his shirt up and he slipped out of it, letting it flutter to the ground.

He pulled her to him, her soft curves molding to his hard lines, his hands skimming her body.

Grace was gone. She wanted only to lose herself in him, to get lost in his eyes, his mouth, his hands. She was his--no guilt, no remorse, only the incredible feeling of being loved, of sharing everything with him. She realized then that she had been his from the start--from the moment she saw him standing in her spot at The Village, and had stopped to admire the view that was Brady Cash.

"Take me to bed, Brady," she whispered.

"Oh, God, Grace, yes," he moaned, scooping her up and laying her gently on the soft duvet.

He stared deep into her eyes before taking her mouth with a kiss that left her breathless. He slipped off her pants and then fumbled with his jeans, kicking them to the floor, and finally, there was nothing between them.

His hands were everywhere at once, leaving her nerve endings tingling. She allowed her own fingers to roam freely, tracing curves and sharp edges, hard and soft.

Such desire, such intense need; Grace thought she would die if it wasn't fulfilled.

Brady took her so thoughtfully, so carefully, that it nearly melted her heart. They took a long, slow ride to the top together, his muscles straining to keep the easy pace. Finally, breathlessly, they reached the summit together, tumbling over in a delicious spin through cotton clouds and fiery sky.

"No going back," he whispered, kissing her slow and sweet. He rolled to the side and pulled her in, making a pocket of his body and tucking her there, her legs resting over the top of his.

"No way," Grace murmured.

They lay there for a moment, breathing deeply, then Brady turned to her. He ran his index finger over her lips, slid it along the contour of her chin, and kissed her softly.

"I love you, Grace," he said, staring into her eyes, "more than anything--I was coming to tell you the night I found you and I was so scared I'd lose you that something broke inside of me. God, I love you so much."

"Oh, Brady," she smiled, taking his face in her hands. "I love you, too. I think I have since the minute I saw you."

He kissed her again just as the sun disappeared, and pulled her into his arms. "Best sunset of my life," he whispered.

Chapter 37

Christmas in Kanab was like no other place on Earth. Snow had dusted the vermillion cliffs just before nightfall, and the stark contrast of virgin white against ancient red rock made for an incredible backdrop. They'd spent the morning at the sanctuary, delivering stuffed animals, chew bones, and squeaky toys to their dogs, then gathered at Brady and Grace's to celebrate.

An enormous tree sat in front of the window, Zoe's baby booty gleaming in the twinkling lights, and dozens of glittery presents sat beneath it. Gracie and Gummi Bear were curled up by the fire and Leroy was outside, rolling in the fresh snow. Jordan sat on the love seat, and the girls were busy in the kitchen, arranging appetizers and making homemade egg nog.

Brady put his arm around Grace and pulled her close. "It doesn't get any better than this," he said, looking around the room at the people they both loved.

"I couldn't agree more," Grace smiled, resting her head on his chest.

When they sat down to the feast, Brady raised his glass for a toast. "Here's to Best Friends, and best friends," he said. "One brought us together, and the other keeps us together. I wouldn't have it any other way."

"Here, here!" they said in unison, as Brady leaned over to give Grace a soft kiss.

The dogs enjoyed a special Christmas dinner of turkey scraps, and were the first to open their presents. Leroy got a stuffed hedgehog; Gummi Bear, a chew bone as big as his head; and Gracie, a Chicago Bears collar and a small toy football, full of tooth holes. They raced off to hoard their treasures as the friends exchanged gifts; some funny, some meaningful, and some poignant.

After lingering goodbyes, Grace and Brady settled in front of the fire. "This has been the best Christmas of my life, Grace, because of you. I look forward to so many more."

"Me, too, Brady...I love you so much," she smiled.

He pulled down a blanket and they made love in front of the fire, the twinkling of the Christmas lights playing over their bodies.

Late in the night, Grace woke, Brady snoring softly at her side. She slipped out of bed and into her robe, tiptoeing into the spare room, which she'd taken over as her office. She powered up her laptop, thinking about how lucky she was.

Mandy, Matt, and Eva would be coming to visit on New Year's Eve, and Gummi Bear would greet them with a Best Friends 'Adopt Me' bandana tied around his neck. She knew Eva would fall in love instantly, and that Mandy would tumble soon after.

Life was good, and she felt complete peace as she took a few cleansing breaths before opening the file that held her book.

It was nearly finished now, but she had an idea, and went to the first page. Her fingers warmed up on the keyboard, and she rewrote the beginning.

It all starts with a spark. Every great symphony, every raging fire, every undying love, starts with one fiery note, one flaming ember, one burning look. Something seemingly small and insignificant on the surface can grow into something immeasurable, incomprehensible, all consuming.

Healing is that way, too. What seems insurmountable, can be overcome.

You may not know it when you see it--it may come on four legs, or two, or perhaps none at all, but when it starts to burn, your life will never be the same.

It all starts with a spark...

Author's Note

Dear Reader,

Thank you, so much, for reading this book. It means so much to me that you are willing to take a chance on a self-published author, and I am both grateful and humbled. If you have enjoyed the story, and are so inclined, an Amazon review is much appreciated.

Best Friends is a very real place, and I've had the privilege of volunteering there on several occasions. Each time I visit, I'm already planning my next trip. The first time I traveled there, I knew I'd write a story that was set at the Sanctuary, and that it would be a story about healing; because that's what they do there. Find out more about the amazing work they do at bestfriends.org.

About the Author

By day, Kim is a middle school math and language arts teacher. She holds a master's degree in education, and lives in the Chicago area with her husband and her rescued brindle Pit Bull mix, Princess Gracie, who came into her life after the initial drafts of this manuscript were written. Kim enjoys travel, the outdoors, reading and music; but spends much of her free time these days writing.

Other books by Kim DeSalvo

Incidental Happenstance

InHap*pily Ever After

Made in the USA
Lexington, KY
16 May 2017